The Legend of Pearl Cave

The Legend of Pearl Cave

DAVID AKSEIZER

ILLUSTRATIONS BY ROSEMARIA KALOGERAKIS

An imprint of Parables & Books
www.figlopress.com

Text copyright © 2014 David Akseizer
Illustrations copyright © 2014 Rosemaria Kalogerakis
All rights reserved.
Published by Figlo Press, an imprint of Parables & Books, LLC.

Printed in the United States of America

10 9 8 7 6 5 4 3 2 1

First Edition

Book typeset in Lunchbox and Minion Pro

Library of Congress Cataloging-in-Publication Data
is available upon request.

ISBN: 978-1-939682-10-9

Visit us on the web!
www.figlopress.com

Acknowledgements

I dedicate this book to all who have yet to unleash
the hero within. May you have the compassion to
always do the right thing and the courage to stand
up to injustice. Be brave, my friends.

I would like to thank my family, friends
and publishing team for all their hard
work, self-sacrifice and dedication.
I would also like to thank my wife for
her patience, support, and most of all, her
unconditional love and caring. This book never
would have come to fruition without her in my
life. She makes all of my dreams
a reality. Thank you, Sandy.

- David Akseizer

Contents

Contents

Contents

Contents

Chapter One

The Heartbeat
of Eternal Memories

The sweet aroma of breakfast permeates the lake house. Eggs, bacon and sausage sizzle on the skillet, creating an intoxicating scent that would lift the spirits of any hungry young boy, any hungry young boy but Samuel Waters, that is. The smell of breakfast does not distract him from remembering what he lost on this summer day nine years ago.

Samuel sits idly at the kitchen table on an old wooden chair. He waits patiently for his grandfather to mend what's left of his broken heart. Samuel slouches, his thoughts consumed by the anniversary of the death of his parents. Grandpa, Samuel's guardian and last living relative, tries his best to brighten his grandson's somber mood.

In the past, Grandpa lifted Samuel's spirits by cooking up a bountiful breakfast that included crisp bacon, sweet sausage, wholesome fried eggs and fluffy pancakes soaked in syrup and topped with fresh whipped cream. But this morning, his culinary efforts fail. Samuel is growing older and the memory of what his parents were like slowly fades away.

"You haven't touched your food," Grandpa says.

"I'm not very hungry," Samuel replies.

Grandpa peers over the bent corner of a crisp newspaper

that looks like it was freshly ironed, revealing his oversized black-rimmed glasses. They practically take up his entire face. Grandpa is in his mid-70s, but you would not know it from the way he keeps up with an energetic 13-year-old. The two are inseparable. They spend most of their time together when Samuel is not in school. They talk for hours, play board games and watch television while cozying up underneath some blankets.

Though a lot of time has passed, it still hurts Grandpa to talk about the tragedy in which Samuel's parents were unexpectedly taken away by angels. Not that it was anybody's fault. It was an accident. Still, he blames himself for no other reason than having no one else to blame. Every so often, while Samuel is still fast asleep, Grandpa lies in bed, staring at the ceiling, and thinks about his only child — his baby girl — and her husband. He then thinks of Samuel and finds purpose in taking his next breath, reminding himself that he must set a brave example for his grandson. Samuel motivates him to face each day with a positive attitude.

"Samuel, look at me," Grandpa commands. "How about we take a moment to discuss the elephant in the room? You're sulking. Tell me what's on your mind," he implores, even though he already knows the answer to the question.

Samuel looks up from his plate and tilts his head to one side. "Grandpa, can you tell me about my mom and dad?" he asks, continuing to scrape his fork over his fried eggs, sighing as the bright yellow yolk oozes all over his plate and onto his bacon and sausage.

"What do want to know?" Grandpa asks. His gray eyebrows are jagged, coarse and spread out in different directions like the bristles of an old broom. His sagging face looks as wrinkled as a sand dune during a windstorm.

Samuel lets out another lengthy sigh. He looks directly at Grandpa with wide, grief-filled eyes, examining his grandfather's aging face. Aside from a slightly receding hairline, he still has a full head of hair, though now, in his golden years, it has turned silver-gray from jet black. Grandpa grooms himself religiously, ironing his clothes before putting them on, shaving the stubble from his withered face and neatly parting his hair down the middle with a wet comb. He prides himself on maintaining healthy habits, like taking daily walks each night after sundown.

"I don't know," Samuel replies, looking down at his plate as he swirls the egg yolk with his fork. "Did they love me?"

"Loved as in past tense?" Grandpa quickly replies. "They've never stopped loving you. They're loving you as we speak."

The sound of rain just then grows heavy on the rooftop. Samuel usually spends his summer mornings exploring outside, but now he feels trapped inside the lake house and in his own thoughts. His eyes swell with tears.

Grandpa places his newspaper down on the kitchen table and reaches for Samuel's hand, which is half the size of his own. "There, there. Don't cry. It was an accident, Samuel, just an unfortunate accident. That doesn't change the fact that they still love you more than anything in this world."

Grandpa pauses to collect his thoughts. "When I lost *my* mom, your great-grandmother, I was about your age. At the time, all I did was cry. Then one morning, my father turned to me and said, 'There are no answers to be found in darkness, so face the daylight and live your life.' That is what your mom and dad would want for you."

Grandpa points toward the window above the kitchen sink. Samuel's teary eyes drift toward the window. The blinds are up, revealing the ancient oak tree in the back yard, its leaves dripping with water from the pouring rain.

"Look. Look out there," says Grandpa as a sunbeam pierces some parting clouds in the distance. "That, Samuel, is what your parents want for you. They want you to climb out of the darkness and face the daylight. Don't focus on the rain. Focus on the light. In light, you'll find joy."

Grandpa turns his attention away from the window and back toward Samuel. He melts every time he lays eyes on that skinny little face, his straight brown hair streaked with subtle blond highlights. He reaches for the cowlick toward the front of Samuel's part. Grandpa tries to pin it down by brushing it to the side with his fingertips, but it springs right back up to its original position.

"Every morning, when I wake up, I look outside and say to myself, 'It's time to face the daylight.' That's what you should do. Face the daylight, Samuel," says Grandpa.

"But how?" Samuel asks.

"It's tricky, but not impossible."

Grandpa scratches his temple. "Let me try to answer that question in a way you'll understand. You see, my boy, it's okay to remember your parents and grieve their loss, especially today. Hold on tight to their memory and don't let go." He pauses. "Still, no matter what hardships we encounter in our lives, we must all find ways to enjoy ourselves. The show must go on! Your parents love you and are with you always. That's why you need to go on living a normal healthy life.

That's what they would want."

Samuel looks up from the yolk-covered canvas he created with his fork. "Grandpa is right," he thinks to himself. He knows his parents are always watching over him. He even can feel their love shining down from Heaven from time to time, but he is afraid that he has forgotten them. He forgets what they look like, how they loved each other and how life was when they were around. It is a lot for a young boy to process, but Samuel misses them and needs to reminisce every now and then. That is how he copes with his loss. Grieving helps preserve the memory of his parents, but it is not working today.

"But I can't remember them, Grandpa," Samuel sobs, squeezing his guardian's leathery hand. "Help me remember them. Please!"

Grandpa takes a deep breath through his wrinkled lips. He exhales through his nose, ruffling the gray hairs that stick out from his nostrils, then places his hand on Samuel's oval chin and lifts it up from Samuel's chest. "Your mother was exceptional. She had golden blond hair like a field of tightly packed sunflowers and a smile that changed a rainy morning into a sun-filled afternoon. She truly was exceptional. She cared more about you than her own existence. From morning to night, she was always hugging you and kissing your cheeks. She just couldn't get enough of you. I can't remember any moment, aside from when she was sleeping, when she wasn't by your side, laughing with you, playing games with you, reading you a story." Grandpa pauses to hold back his tears. "Most important, loving you unconditionally."

Samuel begins to show signs of a smile. The corners of

his lips tighten. He listens intently, perching his chin on the open palms of his hands with his elbows on the kitchen table.

Grandpa continues. "Your father…your father was unique. No matter how tough times would get, that man never let you or your mother know it. Not for one second. Not when he was out of work for months at a time, not even when he struggled to put food on the table. He was always determined to take care of his family the way that a good father and husband should."

Grandpa shoots a serious look at Samuel. He raises his left jagged eyebrow. "Now it's true, your father and I got into arguments every now and again, but when it came to taking care of you and my baby girl, I never felt the need to give him a really hard time because I knew he would make the right decisions for you and your mom."

Grandpa's eyebrow relaxes back into place. "Looking back at all the challenges your family had to overcome, I have to give the man credit. He was the concrete that held the family together. There was nothing he wouldn't do for the two of you. Handsome, too. A good man he was, your father!" Grandpa says, shaking his index finger for emphasis.

Samuel's eyes perk up. "They both sound great," he says. "I only wish I had been old enough to know them a little better. I wish we had more time together before…" He lowers his head again, gently resting his chin back down on his chest. "I guess I'm just worried."

"About what?" asks Grandpa, taking a sip of freshly squeezed orange juice.

"About forgetting them. Every day, I feel a little piece of them slipping away. At this rate, I'll wake up one morning and not remember them at all."

"That's a heavy weight to carry on these narrow shoulders of yours," Grandpa says as he grabs his grandson's shoulders and shakes them gently. Grandpa wants Samuel to enjoy his childhood. He feels that Samuel is maturing quicker than he should because of his parents' tragedy. "No boy should have to endure this amount of pain," Grandpa thinks to himself.

"You know, you and I aren't so different," he continues. "I tend to carry a lot of weight on my shoulders, too. But that's a story for another time."

Grandpa takes another sip of his juice and places the glass back down on the red-and-white checkered tablecloth. "This is a time in your life when you should play and explore all of the wonders that the world has to offer. Enjoy your youth. Seek adventure. You have plenty of time to worry about such things when you get to be my age and become forgetful." Grandpa laughs. His talk calms Samuel. There is just one more layer of gloom to peel away.

"For now, it's simple. When you're feeling sad, as if they're fading away, all you need to do is look to the sky and remember them in your heart. It's your heart that keeps their memory alive. They're a part of you, Samuel, and the beating of your heart strengthens their memory, making it live on every passing day." Grandpa gets up from his chair, wraps his arms around Samuel and squeezes him tightly.

"Stop, Grandpa! I can't breathe!" Samuel cries as he tries to escape his grandfather's bear hug.

Grandpa loosens his grip.

The rain begins to let up outside. As fewer drops echo off the rooftop, Samuel realizes he might be able to salvage the day after all.

Chapter One

Grandpa gets up from the kitchen table and walks over to the window. "Looks like it's finally drying up out there. Any chance you feel like going outside and finding that adventure I mentioned before?"

Samuel looks toward the kitchen ceiling and presses his right hand hard against the left side of his chest. He can feel his heartbeat like the vibrations of a passing train. He gets up from the kitchen table, leaving behind a half-eaten breakfast, and says, "You know what? You're right. I think I'll face the daylight."

Before heading upstairs to fetch his backpack, Samuel pauses at the kitchen entrance. Grandpa begins clearing dirty dishes from the table.

"Grandpa?" asks Samuel.

"Yes?" he mumbles as he scrapes food off Samuel's plate and into the garbage.

"Thank you," Samuel says warmly.

Grandpa places the dish into the sink. A crinkled smile forms on the corners of his withered lips.

"I love you, Samuel. Now go outside and have fun."

Grandpa knows he cannot change the fact that Samuel's parents are gone, but he will do whatever he can to help him cope with his loss. In a way, their chat reminded Grandpa of how important it is to talk about lost loved ones and reflect.

Samuel leaves the kitchen smiling and heads upstairs to his bedroom. After their uplifting talk, he feels reborn. Having just arrived at the lake house yesterday, he has not had much time to unwind and explore. He is revved up and cannot wait to go outside and stir up some action.

Samuel likes the lake house more than their home in the

suburbs, where they live so he can attend a good school. To Samuel, the suburbs are loud, boring and claustrophobic, but the lake house and its sprawling rustic surroundings enchant him. Back home, they share a two-bedroom ranch with a small backyard that is just large enough for a barbecue grill and two lawn chairs. Their house is identical to all the other houses on the block except for the cobalt-blue paint job. This house, on the other hand, sits on a wildflower-covered hill in front of a vast dense forest full of tall pine and oak trees. The complete opposite of claustrophobic.

When Grandpa and Samuel reach the lake house, they drive up a stone driveway that forms a lazy S curve as it winds toward the house from a narrow two-lane road. At the beginning of the driveway, Samuel's father had built a wooden mailbox that looks like a miniature replica of the house. On its side, a red flag is raised or lowered depending on if mail has been delivered. They do not get much mail here, so the flag is usually down.

The cozy two-story colonial overlooks what seems like a never-ending lake. It is painted bright white with moss-green shingles on the roof. Two wicker rocking chairs sit lazily on the expansive wrap-around porch to the right of the red front door. Grandpa and Samuel spend many nights on the porch, rocking back and forth while watching the bright red-orange sunset over the lake. A red brick chimney rises from the ground on the right side of the house, poking through the top right corner of the roof. The windows are trimmed with wood shutters that match the moss-green shingles. Grandpa keeps the shutters open, allowing plenty of sunlight to stream in through the windows.

Inside, a living room off to the right of the front door is filled with antique furniture and knickknacks. A fireplace helps keep Grandpa and Samuel warm during the chilly winters when they visit on weekends and holidays. Whenever they use the fireplace, Grandpa lets Samuel roast marshmallows, one of his favorite foods. He enjoys watching marshmallows turn black, melt and drip off the end of his roasting stick.

Samuel spends a considerable amount of time in the large study where the family has collected hundreds of books, family photographs and old paintings. He actually never has read a book from the study himself, but he still enjoys running his fingers across the titles, even when dust rubs off on his fingertips. He has fond memories of sitting with Grandpa in a large brown leather chair while reading a book of Samuel's choice. He enjoyed listening to long stories and would spend hours laughing at the voices that Grandpa used to distinguish one character from the other.

Samuel's favorite spot is the wooded backyard. Much like the horizon and the lake, it seems infinite. Last year, when he turned 12, Samuel was allowed for the first time to roam the woods unsupervised. One day that summer, Samuel disappeared into its vastness and found an abandoned tree house where he began hiding memorabilia that he had collected throughout his childhood. This is where Samuel plans on heading first after finishing his talk with Grandpa.

As Samuel basks in the serene view of the lake from his bedroom window, he thinks about what he will need for his trip to the tree house. He grabs a few items and tucks them securely in his backpack. Samuel looks around his room one last time and makes sure he does not forget anything.

He likes his room simple and clean. There is a bed, a mirror and an antique dresser with a turtle tank resting on top. He heads straight for the tank. It contains a few large rocks and just enough water for his turtle Lennox to swim and take baths. Next to Grandpa, Lennox is Samuel's best friend. He often takes him wherever he goes.

"Hey there, Lennox. Did you miss me?" Samuel asks, removing the tank's cover. He reaches in and gently caresses the turtle with both hands, raising him close to his eyes.

"Guess what? You and I are going on a little adventure."

Lennox stares blankly in response.

Samuel tugs on the chest pocket of his blue hooded sweatshirt. "For you," he says, gently tucking Lennox inside the pocket. He pokes his head out from inside Samuel's pocket, takes a deep breath and then retreats back into his shell.

"I guess it's time we get going," Samuel says to Lennox as he races down the stairs with his backpack draped over one shoulder.

"I'll be back later, Grandpa!" Samuel yells as he runs through the front door, slamming it behind him. While running into the woods, Samuel can hear Grandpa yelling something about being home before dark.

Though Samuel does not know it, today's outing will mark the beginning of the greatest adventure that he will ever know. Secrets lurk in and around the lake house, and soon will begin to reveal themselves.

The Mysterious Voice
from Beyond the Forest

Samuel reaches inside his backpack and pulls out a shiny brass compass that his grandfather gave him when he was only seven years old. It is just one of the many useful tools that he grabbed before leaving the lake house. The compass' black needle spins out of control until it finally rests on "N," pointing in the direction of the abandoned tree house that Samuel discovered last year. He searches for a clear passage into the woods.

"Over there, Lennox! That's where the trail begins!" Samuel exclaims, pointing toward a lush, verdant path covered by a thick grass carpet and partially hidden by bushes and long vines hanging listlessly from the trees.

Lennox ignores Samuel's comment. For the moment, the turtle keeps his head tucked deep inside his shell within the chest pocket of his owner's sweatshirt.

Samuel walks briskly toward the path, certain of a new adventure and sure he will arrive in a reasonable amount of time if he keeps a steady pace. "I think we'll reach the tree house in an hour," he says to Lennox with a smile.

Samuel often speaks aloud when he is by himself or, in this case, with someone other than a human being. It helps calm his nerves. Besides Lennox and Grandpa, Samuel does not have anyone to talk to. He does not choose to be an introvert; he is withdrawn because other kids his age tease and bully him, shaking his self-confidence.

Back home, Samuel is reclusive. During school, he hides from the other kids, frightened by the abundance of eighth-grade bullies who surround him during recess and in the hallways. Before and after school, when Grandpa drops him off and picks him up, Samuel peeks around every corner to make sure no ruffians have spotted him. Thankful for Grandpa's safe rides, he can only imagine what mean kids he would encounter if he had to walk to and from school by himself.

Samuel is easy prey being short and thin. In fact, he fits easily inside his cramped school locker, which not many other kids his age do. He spends most of his lunch period inside his locker to avoid the dangers lurking in the hallways and playgrounds of middle school. Inside, he eats the lunch that Grandpa packs for him and shines a flashlight on the crisp white pages of exciting adventure novels. He enjoys living vicariously through the lead characters of each book. Samuel hides during lunch whenever he can.

Except for one time.

One day, Samuel veered from his normal routine and decided to spend recess on the playground with the other kids. He sat down on a black tire swing attached to three chains that met at an overhead wooden post. As soon as he started swinging back and forth, four bigger kids approached him with malicious intent. They taunted him and made fun of his skinny physique. They stood around him chanting, "Sam the loser so tiny and weak. He's all by himself 'cause he's such a geek." Then one of the boys grabbed one of the swing's three chains and began to spin Samuel faster and faster against his will. His face turned as green as Lennox's skin. He could feel his stomach erupt, forcing his lunch up through his esophagus and out of his mouth. He had eaten a tuna sandwich and a chocolate-covered almond bar for dessert. He vomited in every direction as he spun around, spraying thick streams of puke and soaking his four tormenters from head to toe. By the time the bullies realized what was going on, Samuel started a chain reaction. Each of them began vomiting on one another until they were all covered in additional layers of puke. At least the bullies got what they deserved, but from that day forward, Samuel vowed never to go outside during recess again.

Samuel basks in the near silence as he walks through the thick forest. His feet kick up layers of moist, decomposing brown leaves lining the forest floor. A light wind rustles the leaves of the tall oak trees. He hears the pitter patter of pine cones occasionally dropping from branches high up in the triangular pine trees. One by one, the pine cones hit the carpet of leaves. Samuel takes a deep breath of fresh air and soaks in the serenity of a place where he does not have to look constantly over his shoulder or tread cautiously to evade bullies.

The forest offers freedom, silence, comfort and lots of space. It is a stomping ground bigger than any school locker. Samuel embraces all of nature's offerings with a welcoming smile: the friendly curious animals, the sweet smell of tree sap, even the bugs that buzz around his ears.

He stops to watch a squirrel scurry up a tall old pine tree with dark-gray bark and thinning branches with wilting needles. "I bet that tree is at least 100 years old," Samuel says to Lennox.

The tree reminds Samuel of something he learned at a museum. He was told that you can tell a tree's age by counting the rings that form inside its trunk. Each ring counts the passing of one year.

Samuel shakes his head back and forth and realizes he and Lennox are wasting valuable daylight hours on their way to the tree house. "Let's keep it moving, Lennox," he says. "You're supposed to let me know when we're running behind," he jokes.

The two press on, being mindful to limit the number of stops they make to admire Mother Nature. Samuel wants to get to the abandoned tree house and return home before it gets dark. He is not scared of the dark, but he respects Grandpa's request that he return home before nightfall. But just in case he runs late, Samuel remembered to pack a trusty flashlight. If it does become too dark, all he has to do is point the flashlight at the compass, and he and Lennox will eventually bump into the lake house.

Samuel's compass leads them right where he expected it to. He spots the tree house from afar through a gap in the densely packed trees. It is a castle protected by a wall of branches, perched high up in a large oak tree overlooking the entire forest in all of its splendor.

"We're almost there, Lennox. It's just up ahead," he says softly, patting his chest pocket.

Samuel speeds up, hurtling forward with a burst of energy as if he were heading for a finish line, which just so happens to be the base of the beautiful tree house.

From underneath, he looks up at the entrance, a small square hole cut into its floor. The tree house is nestled in strong branches about 15 feet from the ground. A series of crooked wooden steps nailed into its trunk leads up from the ground to the entrance in the floor.

As old as the tree house is, it has held together nicely through the years. Only a few cedar shingles are missing from the roof. Windows on all four sides let Samuel gaze out at the vast forest. They are portals to the outer world, put in place for Samuel to spot enemies trying to invade his castle. The walls are made of pinewood planks, stacked and nailed securely together, not one missing. They are as sturdy as the day the tree house was built. To an adult, it is a one-room shack, but to a 13-year-old boy with an active imagination, it is a palace.

Hanging near the opening in the floor is a long rope with a knot tied at the end. Samuel puts the compass in his backpack and throws the bag over his shoulder. He grabs the rope, ties it around his waist for safety and carefully climbs up the wooden steps nailed into the tree trunk. Climbing is Samuel's best skill in gym class, one of the few athletic talents for which he is praised for by his gym teacher.

He squeezes through the floor opening, removes the rope from around his waist and takes a moment to catch his breath. The light inside the tree house begins to dwindle as the sun begins to lower in the sky. Samuel and Lennox must have taken longer than they thought to arrive, and evening will soon approach. Soon they will have to embark on their journey home.

Gray clouds now begin to form overhead, darkening the forest even more. The temperature slowly drops, creating a slight chill.

Samuel removes his flashlight from his backpack and turns it on. He carefully removes Lennox from his sweatshirt pocket. The turtle spent most of the trip trying to claw his way out, only to tire himself out to the point of exhaustion.

"Sorry, pal," says Samuel, patting his pet's shell. "I know you've been in there for awhile." Lennox looks relieved to leave the confines of his owner's pocket.

Samuel holds Lennox with his left hand. With his right hand, he holds his flashlight and scans every nook and cranny of the tree house. "So, what do you think?" asks Samuel. "This place hasn't changed one bit. It looks just as awesome as it did last summer."

Lennox looks at Samuel and blinks twice.

A small table sits forlornly in one corner. Samuel brushes off the dust that settled over it and places the turtle down on the table. "Need I remind you, Lennox, that no one knows about our castle. We must uphold its secrecy," instructs Samuel. "Do you think you can handle that?"

Lennox remains still, his head slightly protruding from his shell. His tiny legs poke out from the sides of his hard green shell. Lennox starts walking in circles at a leisurely pace, searching for food.

Samuel points the flashlight toward a lunch box that he tucked away during last year's visit. It has not moved an inch. The lunch box rests in the shadows underneath the table. Samuel approaches it eagerly, excited to view the treasures within. The funny thing is, he already knows what is inside the lunch box, but is excited to pretend otherwise.

Last year, Samuel discovered the tree house and began adding "sacred" items to the lunch box. He uses it as a time capsule, and when it is full of trinkets and knickknacks, he plans to bury it. When he is older, he plans to return, dig it up and sift through the by then long-forgotten memorabilia of his youth.

Samuel picks up the lunch box and opens it with care. Inside are toy soldiers, bubble gum, baseball cards and a comic book. At the bottom is a wrinkled photograph of his parents. In the picture, his father is standing next to his mother, who is holding baby Samuel in her arms. He runs the tips of his fingers over his mother's face, longing for her to hold him once more. Consumed by sadness, he wishes for some kind of distraction.

And then he gets it.

He feels a sudden chill from the wind. The swishing of leaves and branches sounds like a soft and steady drum roll on a snare. Samuel zips up his sweatshirt, pulls the hood over his head and continues looking at the picture of him and his parents. The shingles that seemed securely fastened to the roof begin to rattle like playing cards wedged in the spokes of a bicycle wheel, slowly clacking louder as the wind grows stronger. The tree house begins to sway, causing the wooden planks to creak and shift like tectonic plates. Some of the planks loosen as they shift, and pushed by the wind, they begin smacking the house. Clack, clack, clack, clack.

Samuel panics. He holds onto a windowsill with both hands to maintain his balance. The wind is so strong that it rips the roof right off.

"Lennox! What's going on?" Samuel shouts as he crouches down on the floor in fear. He looks up toward the sky where the roof used to be and watches the clouds speed by as if someone pressed fast forward on a DVD player.

Lennox retreats into his shell and falls off the table onto the floor during what seems like the start of a tornado. Samuel picks him up from the floor and holds him close to his heart. The walls shake some more. Wooden planks thump harder and harder against the tree house, as branches slap it over and over. The table moves from one side of the room to the other, its legs etching the dust on the floor as it changes locations. The sliding table makes a noise like fingernails dragging across a chalkboard.

Samuel is now past the point of panic; he begins to hyper-ventilate. "What's happening? Someone, anyone, help me!" he shouts, but no one comes to his rescue. His heart races. "It will pass," he says to himself over and over again to help slow his heart rate. His breath grows heavier and heavier.

Samuel closes his eyes. He curls up on the floor in a fetal position with Lennox cradled in his arms. And just like that, the wind stops in an odd manner. It does not taper off like a normal gust of wind. It stops abruptly, as if someone waved a hand and ordered it to cease.

Samuel opens his eyes, first one, then the other. He stands up cautiously, unsure of what to expect. Then he hears a voice. The soft sound of a woman's voice calls out Samuel's name. It is not a scary voice; rather it is sweet and soothing. At first Samuel thinks it might be his mother calling him.

"Mom? Is that you?" he asks softly.

The voice says his name again. It sounds as if it is coming

directly from the skies above. He looks up toward the top of the tree.

"Mom, I can hear you!" he shouts back as he searches for the source of the voice. It does not answer and the surrounding forest grows silent again.

"Great! I'm hearing things, Lennox," says Samuel, doubting his sanity. Still holding his pet in one hand, Samuel drops to his knees and crawls toward the tree house's tiny entrance on the pinewood floor. He pokes his head out of the opening and shines his flashlight on the ground, hoping to find someone down below. But there is no one in sight.

Then the voice unexpectedly returns from above. "Samuel. We need your help."

The sudden break in the silence catches Samuel off guard. He bumps his head on the edge of the opening. Then he stands up and looks up.

"Who…who needs my help? Who are you?" he asks, slightly dizzy from the bonk to his head. Samuel wonders if he is losing his mind.

"The lake. Go to the lake," the voice says, echoing off the sides of the tree house. "There you'll find Pearl Cave. Go inside. From there you must trust your instincts."

"Pearl Cave? What's that? Why must I find Pearl Cave?"

"The legends are true," says the voice as it gradually fades.

"What legends? What are you talking about?"

Samuel waits a few minutes for a reply, but there is none. He puts Lennox back in his front pocket and decides it is time to split. If there is something or someone else in the woods, Samuel does not plan to stick around to find out who or what it is.

The Mysterious Voice from Beyond the Forest

It does not take long for Samuel to shimmy down the rope and head for home. He notices the sun setting in the distance and realizes that time had mysteriously passed much faster than it should have. Nightfall is now right around the corner.

Samuel runs quickly for 30 minutes with Lennox tucked securely in his chest pocket until he feels they are safe. He then goes from a sprint to a brisk walk. He walks a little while longer before he sees the lake house through a break in the trees. He approaches it and enters through the back door. Grandpa is making dinner on the kitchen stove and hears the door creak open.

"There you are. I was just about to send out a search party," says Grandpa, slightly joking as he hunches over the stove. "You're right on time for dinner. Are you hungry?" he asks.

Samuel is distracted and still somewhat in shock. He wants to tell his grandfather what has happened but is not sure he will understand.

Grandpa turns around to see why Samuel has not answered. "Are you okay? You look like you saw a ghost," he says, staring at Samuel's frightened face.

"Who me? A ghost?" Samuel replies with a gulp. "Of course not. That would be just plain nuts," he says as he lets out an awkward laugh.

"All right." Grandpa rolls his eyes. "If you say so."

Grandpa cannot quite put his finger on it, but he knows something is bothering Samuel. He decides it will be best to leave whatever is irking his grandson alone. If there is one thing he has learned from all his years of living, it is that people will let you know when something is bothering them when they are good and ready, but not a minute sooner.

"Come," Grandpa gestures with his hand. "Sit and eat. I made spaghetti and meatballs."

"Sounds perfect. I'm starving!" Samuel replies. He gently places his backpack beside the table and sits in his usual white chair. Samuel leaves Lennox tucked inside his front pocket while he stuffs his face with spaghetti and meatballs. He paints his lips bright red with pasta sauce.

Samuel remains suspiciously quiet during dinner. By the third meatball, his mind begins to obsess over the mysterious voice in the forest. What does it all mean? How will he find a cave he never heard of before? If there is one thing Samuel knows for sure, it is that he is happy to be back sitting safely next to his grandfather. Grandpa has a natural gift for making him feel safe.

After dinner, Samuel brushes his teeth, puts his pajamas on and gets into bed. His body heat warms the sheets and comforter as Grandpa tucks him in and tells him to get a good night's sleep.

"Get your rest, Samuel. Tomorrow you and I will wake up early and go fishing. I'll show you all of my secrets — as long as you promise to keep them secret. As you well know, I'm champion of the lake when it comes to fishing, but that's a story for another time. Just remember this. I won't have that rotten neighbor of ours stealing the fishing techniques that I honed over the years, techniques that made me the winner of the annual fishing contest year after year. Anything I teach you stays between us, always and forever."

Samuel agrees to complete secrecy. He has never gone fishing before and cannot wait for his first lesson. Up until now, he had been too young. Grandpa gives him a kiss on the forehead and turns off the light before closing the door behind him.

Samuel tosses and turns in his sleep. His mind is working overtime. Between today's events and tomorrow's excitement, it is hard to sleep. His thoughts finally settle down, and soon his mind empties and he fully drifts off into a deep dream-filled sleep.

Dreams of Things to Come

Shortly after Samuel has fallen asleep, he opens his eyes and discovers that he is submerged in water, floating in an upper corner of a dimly lit underwater cavern. Samuel cannot tell if he is dreaming or awake.

He flails his arms in every direction and gasps for air. "This has to be a nightmare," he says to himself as his lungs fill with freezing water. "Can a person drown in a dream?" he wonders. It feels as if someone is forcing him to drink an icy cold bottle of spring water. Soon, however, Samuel realizes he can breathe underwater. He inhales and exhales the cold water, and his panic gradually subsides.

Samuel then pushes his body away from the cavern's upper corner, but no matter how hard he tries, he keeps floating back up toward the sharp rocks bulging from the ceiling. He uses his hands and legs several times to push away from the ceiling, but he rapidly floats back up like a bubble trapped in the cabin of a sunken ship. He smacks his head against sharp rocks with each failed attempt. A magnetic force has a hold on him, and he cannot pull away. He gives up after a small bump rises on the top of his head.

Samuel looks down at his hands and notices that his

body appears ghost-like. He is semi-transparent, not completely invisible, but blending in like a chameleon with his surroundings. Anyone not paying close attention would not notice him.

Still nervous, he closes his eyes and counts to three, hoping he will wake from what does not feel entirely like a dream anymore. But no such luck. As Samuel opens his eyes, he is right where he was before, floating in the cavern stuck up against a rocky ceiling.

Just then, Samuel looks below and sees 11 creatures sitting directly beneath him. They seem preoccupied, focused on an important discussion of some sort, as they sit around a large table carved from an enormous boulder. 12 seats made from smaller rocks surround the table, but one is empty.

Samuel sees three glass bottles spread out evenly across the table. Each bottle is turned upside down and contains tiny glowing fish to help light the cavern. He looks around the room and sees, hanging from the ceiling by strands of kelp, several corked bottles housing more glowing fish, all swimming in circles and contributing to the cavern's comforting dim glow.

Samuel now turns his full attention to the creatures' faces. He is scared yet relieved that none of them notices that he is floating above. Samuel remains motionless and watches in silence, hoping to remain undiscovered. He slows his breathing to become less conspicuous.

The unusual beings are much smaller than Samuel. They are wearing tiny outfits made from what looks like strands of kelp woven together into cable-knit tops and pants. Some are young, some middle-aged and some older. The young ones are boisterous; they cannot sit still and are more outspoken than their elders. The middle-aged creatures are much more reserved. They calmly add their two cents to the discussion without seeming pushy. The older ones do not appear to converse much at all. Instead, they periodically spout out agreeable phrases like "hear, hear" when someone sitting at the stone table says something noteworthy.

Samuel observes in silence. He studies their appearance with great interest. He wants to get a better understanding of what he is dealing with and what dangers he might be up against.

The sentient life-forms vary slightly from one another in their physical features, but they all share basic traits. Each has deep-blue scaly skin, large oval eyes that are completely black and tails with spear-like tips. Tiny midnight-blue fins line their spines, poking out through their cable-knit clothes. Their facial features — eye lids, button noses and wide mouths — are similar but not identical to those of humans. Thick strands of dark hair cover their heads, some black, some brown and some gray, all braided in different ways. Their lips are shiny black and their hands and feet are webbed like a duck's to help them swim through the water.

Samuel spots bubbles floating from what he thinks are their ears, making it seem as if they breathe through them. But his initial assessment is wrong. The aquatic beings inhale through gills on their necks and exhale through tubes shaped like piccolo trumpets that look somewhat like ears. Below the tubes are two tiny slits through which they hear. Samuel finally realizes that the tiny slits are ears because whenever one of them speaks at the table, the elder gray-haired versions cup their webbed hands around the slits and turn their necks in the direction of whomever is speaking.

Samuel quickly covers his nose. An unpleasant odor rises up from beneath his dangling feet. One of the younger ones inadvertently releases bubbles out of a different opening, and the others quickly cover their gills with their webbed hands. Samuel hears the child giggle and excuse himself. He hopes the smell will quickly dissipate.

Now the creatures seem anxious. At first Samuel attributes their anxiety to the obnoxious smell overwhelming the cavern, but as he listens closely, he overhears them discussing the imminent arrival of a guest with some kind of news.

Samuel turns his attention to someone whose regal appearance secures him a seat at the head of the table. Everyone is participating in the discussion except for him. It is not hard to figure out that the quiet creature is in charge.

Samuel examines the leader from his head to his webbed toes. His features are slightly different. He has a long pearly white beard and a crown made from a shiny candy bar wrapper that he proudly wears on his head. In his right webbed hand is a royal staff, which he uses to quiet down the other creatures when they grow too boisterous. The staff is carved from an old wooden oar salvaged from a shipwreck, and the top is shaped like a crown.

Samuel initially thinks the leader looks silly wearing a candy wrapper crown, but he does not want to make assumptions. He learned from his grandfather that prejudging often warps perceptions, leads to false conclusions and prevents someone from truly understanding people for whom they really are.

"Silence, everyone!" commands the leader as he strikes the bottom tip of his royal staff against the hard cave floor.

Chapter Three

The clamoring comes to an abrupt halt. Everyone sits at full attention. "I believe it's just about time. He'll arrive at any moment with the news we've all been waiting for." His voice is deep and slightly raspy, much like that of an older gentleman in his late 60s.

Just then, Samuel hears a strange knock coming from the other side of a massive boulder wedged in an opening near the front of the room. "The boulder must be some kind of door," Samuel thinks to himself.

Thump…thump…thump thump. The sounds repeats. Thump…thump…thump thump. Unbeknownst to Samuel, the rhythmic knock is a secret known only to those allowed inside the cavern. Strangers who do not know the secret cannot get inside the hideout.

The knocking causes the rock door to open automatically. The boulder slides to the right, slowly scraping against the lake floor, pushing aside small rocks and silt to create a small cloud of debris.

Samuel watches in awe as a large beast, towering over the rest, glides in from the shadows outside the doorway. Two oversized fins extend out from each side of its torso, flapping slowly back and forth to help him maintain his balance as he floats into the cavernous room.

If Samuel is dreaming, he wants to wake up immediately. He is frightened by the newcomer's appearance. He looks fierce yet strangely beautiful.

His body is covered with flowing strands of whitish gray hair. A snake-like bony white tail protrudes from his backside. His head is shaped like that of a vicious wolf with a long snout and face covered with sparkling silver scales.

Two shark-like fins, one larger than the other, protrude from the top of its head. His eyes are fiery orange and yellow with black oval pupils. Sharp pointy fangs stick out from his upper and lower lips.

When Samuel catches sight of the strange being's paws, his mouth drops in amazement. Five long claws at the end of each of the four paws are shaped like swords. If that were not intimidating enough, icicle-like spikes run along the length of his spine and line the sides of his arms and legs.

"That thing looks fearsome," Samuel thinks to himself as he wonders why no one is fleeing in fright. He cannot help but be scared of the mystery guest, because he is focusing on his menacing looks, and in his rush to judgment, fails to see the good inside of him.

"Figlo, so good to see you," says the crowned leader with a welcoming smile and open arms. "I'm so glad you arrived safely, old friend."

As far back as the council can remember, Figlo has been a faithful ally and humble servant to the king. He is not of the same species as the others, but he has always been treated as if he were one of their own. Figlo has an extremely close relationship with the crowned leader, also known as King Zedorious.

"Yes, sire. It wasn't a difficult journey. In fact, it was quite a rewarding one," replies Figlo in a respectful tone.

Figlo receives a friendly pat on his back from the king and then fills the empty seat at the stone table. His backside and tail are much larger than the stone chair, which practically disappears when he sits down on it. The council members remain silent, patiently waiting for Figlo to share his report with them.

"What news do you bring from the Oracle?" asks the king.

"The Oracle sends her regards. She foretells that the boy will arrive soon. She took it upon herself to personally deliver the message to him and assures me that he'll comply."

The others at the table rejoice at the glorious news. They all stand up to cheer.

Samuel listens to Figlo's gentle, soothing voice as he delivers the good news. He concludes that Figlo has a good heart and is a close friend of the creatures below. A sudden calm replaces his inner fears. Despite Figlo's threatening looks, Samuel no longer feels uneasy.

"Soon we'll all be free again to live in peace!" yells one of the youngsters as he exhales a stream of bubbles in excitement from the tubes on top of his head.

It has been a long time since the council has had a reason to celebrate, but knowing that help is on the way is all they need to lift their spirits and instill a sense of hope.

"Please, we must remain calm and level-headed. We're not in the clear yet, my friends," reminds King Zedorious. "We have a long road ahead of us, but one day soon, everything will return to the way it was. Life as we know it will return to the days before our skies were filled with an abundance of darkness."

The other members of the council embrace their leader's words with cautious enthusiasm. "We will do whatever you think is best, sire," says one of them.

"I agree with King Zedorious," adds Figlo. "Be patient my friends. Our fates are entwined with that of the boy's."

Samuel wonders if he is the boy that Figlo speaks of. And

could the voice that he heard in the abandoned tree house have been the Oracle's?

Samuel laughs. He tries to remind himself that he must be dreaming and that none of what he sees is actually real. Soon he will awaken, and like with most dreams, he will forget everything he had seen.

"This is some crazy dream! I'll give it that," says Samuel as he laughs out loud.

"Sssshhh!" says King Zedorious. He commands everyone to quiet down again. He cups his webbed hand and places it by the two slits on the left side of his neck.

"Did anyone hear that?"

"Hear what?" asks one of the council members, scratching his head.

"It sounded like laughter," says the king. The king scans the cave looking for intruders. He fixes both eyes on Samuel and gives him a quick subtle nod, being careful not to tip off the others to Samuel's presence.

"How could he have heard me?" Samuel thinks to himself. He panics and wonders whether he is in danger. He begins to think that what he originally thought was a dream might actually be happening.

"I guess it wasn't anything after all," the king says, quickly drawing everyone's focus back to the discussion.

Samuel swims away from the ceiling in a clumsy attempt to flee, but whatever force is holding him against the ceiling snaps him back into place like a rubber band on a slingshot. He bumps his head on a nearby hanging rock, knocking him out cold this time.

Next thing he knows, Samuel finds himself awake in bed

at the lake house, remembering every detail of the dream. He runs his hand through his brown hair and stumbles upon a throbbing bump on top of his head.

"Nah, it couldn't be. I must have hit myself on the headboard," he says, gently rubbing the bump to soothe the pain.

Utterly confused, Samuel tries to make sense of his dream, but he cannot. He decides to ignore it and hopes to forget the details by the time he sits down for breakfast.

"Out of sight, out of mind," he says out loud, trying to comfort himself. As far as Samuel is concerned, he is not about to let his imagination get the better of him. There are more important things to focus on, like his first fishing trip with Grandpa.

Samuel reaches for the backpack next to his bed. He pulls out a bottle filled with turtle-food pellets. He gets out of bed and walks over to Lennox, who is resting in his tank on the antique wooden dresser across from the bed.

"Good morning, friend," greets Samuel. He drops a few pellets into the tank. "Boy! Did I just have the craziest dream, Lennox. I'll tell you all about it after my fishing trip with Grandpa."

Lennox seems completely uninterested in the pellets.

"Enjoy your turtle food, buddy." Little does Samuel know that the words "turtle food" and "enjoy" do not, in Lennox's estimation, belong in the same sentence.

Samuel throws his clothes on and races down the hallway to his grandfather's room. "Grandpa!" Samuel yells as if the house were on fire. "Let's go, let's go, let's go!"

Samuel jumps on Grandpa's bed only to discover that he is not there. Grandpa is already downstairs preparing breakfast. Samuel untangles himself from the blanket and takes a deep breath. He inhales the sweet scents of breakfast cooking. From the wonderful smells, he can tell that Grandpa is making his specialty: fluffy waffles with sweet powdered sugar and thick maple syrup.

Samuel exits his grandfather's room and stops at the top of the long sturdy stairs that lead down to the foyer. Today he will once again try to work up the nerve to slide down backwards on the oak banister. He had thought about doing it numerous times in the past, but when it came down to the moment of truth, Samuel always chickened out.

"Okay, I can do this," Samuel says out loud, trying to muster up the courage to perform the stunt. Samuel raises his hands above his head to acknowledge a crowd that exists only in his imagination. He turns around and carefully mounts the banister at the top of the stairs. Just as he is about to push off and begin his daring descent, Samuel looks over his shoulder with apprehension. The height is too overwhelming. He imagines himself accidently falling off and plumeting head first into the hard wooden floor that is seemingly miles below the top of the banister. In a nervous panic, Samuel decides to take the boring route and use the stairs. But before he reaches the last few steps he mounts the banister and slides down the last three feet. In a flash, it is over. He jumps off at the bottom, catching his step to make a perfect landing. With a final wave to the crowd, he makes cheering noises as if he had won an Olympic banister-sliding competition watched by millions.

"It's probably for the best that I didn't perform the stunt from all the way up there," he says out loud as he looks up toward the top of the banister. "If I had hurt myself or if Grandpa had seen me, he would've canceled the fishing trip for sure." Grandpa can be protective at times and hates it when Samuel risks injury. But Grandpa is busy in the kitchen cooking up a storm, and would not have seen a thing. Clearly, Samuel is making excuses to justify his cowardice.

Samuel walks into the kitchen with a bright morning smile plastered across his face. He looks at his grandfather, who is wearing an apron that reads, "If you don't like my cooking, call 1-800-M-A-K-E-I-T-Y-O-U-R-S-E-L-F." In his hand, a plate of waffles seems to be stacked as high as a sky-scraper. They are smothered in whipped cream, maple syrup and powdered sugar, making them look like a mountainous ski slope. Samuel sits down with a fork in hand and the appetite of a lion. He eats most of the waffles before badgering Grandpa about the fishing trip. Grandpa does not need reminding, but he sympathizes with Samuel's excitement and responds with laughter.

"Hurry up, Grandpa! Eat faster! I've been waiting to go fishing with you since I was in diapers," whines Samuel. Actually, it has only been two years since Samuel had begun to take any interest in fishing.

"Then you won't mind waiting a few more minutes. There are a few things I'd like to go over with you before we go fishing," he adds, taking a sip of his coffee. "First, we'll discuss some ground rules and the importance of safety."

"Yeah, yeah, yeah," says Samuel sarcastically as he stuffs his mouth with a fork full of waffles.

"Now listen up, you," warns Grandpa. "Fishing is a serious sport. It can be dangerous, and it's up to you to pay attention. You must listen carefully to everything I tell you so no one gets hurt."

Samuel nods. He will say yes to anything that his grandfather says just so he can start fishing. Besides, he wants to do something, anything, to take his mind off his dream from the night before.

The Legend of Pearl Cave

Samuel sits in the rocking chair on the front porch waiting for his grandfather and listening closely to cicadas chirp like an orchestra of maracas. The warmth of the rising sun lifts the chill left from the night before and evaporates the morning dew that formed on the blades of emerald-green grass. He turns his attention to the sounds of nearby birds as they sing sweet symphonies to one another.

Samuel gets up from the rocking chair. He walks down the front steps of the porch and glances at the wildflowers that blanket the hilltop. Colorful flower petals open up wide to greet the morning sun and soak up their first rays of the day. "Mother Nature is in high spirits," Samuel thinks to himself.

He sprints through the flowers toward the crystal-clear lake, carrying a bait-and-tackle box in one hand and sandwiches in the other.

He arrives at the fishing boat, which is tied to a post at the end of a short wooden dock. Samuel tosses everything into the boat and bends down and grabs a large flat stone resting on the dock. He side-arms the stone toward the lake surface. The stone skips three times, creating the first ripples of the day on the water's undisturbed mirror-like surface. Determined to outdo his first throw, Samuel picks up another stone. This time, he throws it with a little extra oomph. The stone skips six times across the top of the water's surface like a sprinter clearing a row of hurdles.

"Yes!" Samuel cheers, celebrating his performance.

Meanwhile, Grandpa sneaks up behind Samuel to catch him by surprise. He reaches out and lightly pinches Samuel's waist with both hands. Samuel jumps.

"Grandpa! You scared me!" Samuel's heartbeat accelerates and slowly returns to its normal rhythm.

Grandpa laughs. "You know, when I was your age, I used to be pretty good at skipping stones, but that's a story for another time."

He asks Samuel to hand him a stone. Samuel gives him what looks like the perfect skipping stone: shiny, polished and flat. He watches in awe as his grandfather pitches the stone into the water. Samuel loses count after the stone skips 15 times. Grandpa still has quite a pitching arm, and considering that he is in his 70s, Samuel is impressed by his strength.

"Wow! Nice throw, Grandpa!" Samuel exclaims. He now has a new record to beat, a new goal to strive for.

Inside the boat are two wooden oars that Grandpa uses to row forward and backward and steer left and right. Next to the oars are two fishing rods and the rusty bait-and-tackle box that Samuel tossed in. Grandpa pulls a brown bag filled with nightcrawlers from his pocket and places it between the two rods.

"Are they alive?" Samuel asks as he sticks his tongue

out in disgust. Nothing grosses him out more than a slimy, squirmy worm, at least nothing that he has encountered in life thus far.

"Of course they are. You know, the most effective approach is not always the most obvious choice," Grandpa replies with a playfully mysterious tone in his voice.

Grandpa begins the fishing lesson by showing Samuel how to cast the boat off from the dock. "See this?" he asks, pointing to a long piece of braided rope that ties the boat to a wooden post on the dock. "This rope is the only thing preventing the boat from floating away. If you untie it while you're on the dock, make sure you keep one hand on the boat, or it will surely float away." Grandpa points toward the center of the lake. "If that happens, you'll have a heck of time swimming after it. It happened to me twice before, and it's not exactly fun."

Grandpa bends down and grabs the end of the rope. Samuel watches as Grandpa teaches him how to tie a figure-eight, which is a special knot used by sailors to securely fasten a boat to a dock.

Samuel then learns the proper way to board a boat and how to use the oars to move and steer it. He enjoys steering the boat, even if he is only pretending so far.

Grandpa continues the lesson by teaching Samuel the art of baiting a hook. This is Samuel's least favorite part of the lesson.

"Do I have to, Grandpa?" Samuel asks, moaning and groaning.

"Yes, you do! Grab the worm by the head and tie its body in a knot around the hook like so."

"Like this?" Samuel asks as he gets nauseous. He can feel the worm's slimy residue sticking to his fingertips.

"Precisely. Good job!" Grandpa says in an encouraging manner.

Grandpa's method of baiting the hook seems curious. It looks as if it will be easy for a fish to pull the nightcrawler right off the end of the hook. It is almost as if he wants the bait to fall off into the water. But because it is Samuel's first time fishing, he does not question Grandpa's method.

"Enough with the nightcrawlers. Let's get going," directs Grandpa.

Grandpa instructs Samuel to grab both oars from the boat's floor. After his grandfather casts off, Samuel rows away from the dock. He rows for about 30 minutes when Grandpa decides they have reached a good spot to cast their lines into the water and give fishing a go.

Grandpa repositions the beige hat on his head, which is covered with colorful lures. He looks toward the distant shore and takes a deep breath of fresh air.

"This looks like the perfect spot," Grandpa says, instructing Samuel to place the oars carefully on the floor. Soon, the boat settles and stops drifting forward. He hands Samuel a fishing rod and picks up another for himself.

"All right. Watch closely," Grandpa says as he demonstrates the art of casting. He shows Samuel the importance of keeping your thumb on the reel as the line soars into the water. "If you don't keep your thumb on the wheel as the line unspools, it'll tangle up on you, and you'll spend more time untangling the line than actually fishing. Got it?" asks Grandpa as he casts his line into the water.

Samuel nods and lifts the rod up high and brings the end of it back behind his right shoulder. He snaps it forward with a flick of his wrist. The end of his fishing hook catches Grandpa's hat, pulling it off his head. Grandpa reaches for the hat but does not catch it in time. The reel whirs, and the end of the line with the worm, hook and hat sail through the air. The hat and nightcrawler break away from the hook in mid-air. The hat lands near the boat and gradually floats toward them, but the nightcrawler ends up somewhere at the bottom of the lake. Grandpa grabs an oar to retrieve his hat from the water. He places it next to him on the seat to dry and puts the oar back on the floor.

Grandpa looks at Samuel with only slight annoyance. He ties a fresh nightcrawler to the end of Samuel's fishing hook and says, "Try again. This time, be careful!"

Once again, Samuel lifts the rod up high and brings the end of the rod back behind his right shoulder. He snaps the rod forward with a more precise flick of his wrist. The reel whirs, and the hook sails effortlessly through the air. Kerplunk. Ripples of water grow larger and larger from the point where the hook and nightcrawler plunge into the water. The hook, worm and line descend farther and farther into the dark depths of the lake. When the hook hits bottom, the waters grow still again.

Samuel and Grandpa chat on and off while patiently waiting for their first bite. A few hours pass, and neither of them has any luck catching anything. Cast, reel in the line, re-bait, cast again. Soon the lake consumes almost all of their nightcrawlers. Samuel remains patient, which he quickly learns is an important trait for fishermen. All Samuel wants is to catch his very first fish, just one. If he catches one fish the whole day, he will be proud. He wants something to excel at, other than rope climbing in gym class.

They wait patiently for a few more hours. Then suddenly, Samuel feels a tug on his line. "I got one, Grandpa!" screams Samuel, jumping from his seat. The reel begins to spin wildly, giving off a high-pitched whir. The end of the rod almost bends in half.

Samuel fears soon he will run out of fishing line. He holds on tightly to the rod with both hands and braces his feet against the front of the boat. Whatever he has caught is strong enough to pull the boat forward.

Grandpa shoots up from his seat as fast as he can and stands behind Samuel. He wraps his hands around Samuel's fishing rod. Together they try to reel in what seems to be a massive fish. Whatever is at the other end of the line is pulling so hard that the boat begins to pick up speed. Their little rowboat moves faster and faster like a speedboat on jet fuel.

"Pull and reel, pull and reel!" Grandpa shouts. A powerful wind forms behind the boat, making it go faster than before, and then the line snaps. The mystery fish makes a great escape.

"NOOO! You've got to be kidding me!" Samuel cries, overcome with disappointment. He throws his fishing rod down into the boat in anger.

"I've had it!" he shouts. "This is stupid. We've been at this for hours, and something tells me that was my only chance. I can't believe I let it slip through my fingers!" Samuel pouts, crossing his arms and turning his back toward Grandpa.

"It's not your fault. Don't be so hard on yourself.

Sometimes they just get away from us. That's the nature of the game."

Samuel does not care what Grandpa says. His words will not heal the pain of failure. He refuses to try again.

"In any sport, there are winners and there are losers, but you're always a winner if you try," Grandpa continues, placing his hand on Samuel's shoulder.

Samuel forcefully pushes Grandpa's hand off his shoulder and continues to pout. He refuses to pick up his rod.

Grandpa gives Samuel some space. He does not quit as easily as Samuel and continues to fish.

While Grandpa keeps fishing, Samuel looks back toward the lake house and takes note of how far they have drifted. As he looks in the opposite direction of the lake house, he notices a far-off cave cutting into the side of a rocky outcropping at the edge of the lake.

"Grandpa, what's that over there?" Samuel asks, pointing toward the cave. He has never ventured this far out on the lake before, mostly having swum by the dock near the house.

"Oh that," Grandpa replies. He had hoped Samuel would not notice the cave during their fishing trip. He tries to stall by cleaning up the bait-and-tackle box whose contents spilled all over the floor when the boat abruptly accelerated. Grandpa wonders if Samuel is ready to handle the truth about what lies inside the cave.

"I suppose there's no way you'd agree to forget about the cave, is there?" he asks, stumbling over his words.

"No way, Grandpa! If anything, I'm even more curious now than before." Samuel refuses to give in. Is this the Pearl Cave mentioned by the mysterious voice yesterday at the tree house? "Maybe the woman's voice is real," he thinks to himself. Samuel has to find out.

Grandpa lets out a deep sigh. "Okay," he says as he leans his fishing rod against the side of the boat. "I suppose you're old enough to handle it." He sits next to Samuel and places his arm around his grandson's shoulder. "That over there is what the locals call Pearl Cave."

He tries to end the story right there, but Samuel demands to hear more.

"Grandpa," Samuel whines. "Why do I get the feeling you're not telling me everything. It's as if there's more to this story, and you're holding back." He puffs out his lower lip and looks at his guardian with puppy eyes, hoping he will give in and divulge more details.

Grandpa eventually caves in. "Fine. Just quit your whining!" he insists. "Pearl Cave. Hmmm. Where do I begin?" he asks himself, stroking his chin. "Legend has it that a magical oyster lives in the dark depths of the cave. Inside the oyster's mouth is a magical glowing red pearl."

"A pearl. Wow!" Samuel interjects. Annoyed by Samuel's outburst, Grandpa clears his throat. "Sorry. Go ahead."

"As I was saying before I was rudely interrupted," Grandpa scolds, "legend has it that when you touch the glowing red pearl, something special happens. Something magical. Some say you gain special abilities."

"Like what?" asks Samuel.

"Like the ability to breathe underwater. Some even say that you actually become a fish. No one knows for sure. These stories can get a bit distorted as they're told and retold from generation to generation."

Grandpa is obviously trying to downplay the legend. He tries to convince Samuel that it is a silly old story created to entertain the young folks who visit the lake in the summertime.

But Samuel believes the Legend of Pearl Cave is not just a silly story. Samuel knows there is some truth to the legend. He can feel it in his bones.

Pearl Cave is where the voice instructed him to go, and Samuel does not believe that finding the cave today is an accident. The only thing that Grandpa has managed to do is make him more curious about what is inside the cave. After reading so many adventure stories, Samuel might finally get his chance to become someone as special as the heroes in his books, someone whom others do not push around.

Grandpa reaches for his fishing rod and reels in his line. He notices that Samuel is deep in thought and knows what he has to say next. "Listen carefully. Pearl Cave is a dangerous place. It's not a playground for little boys."

"I know, I know," Samuel replies. He will say whatever is necessary to mollify Grandpa.

In the past, Samuel always obeyed his grandfather's wishes; that is what made him such a good boy. But this time, he does not intend to obey. In fact, he has already begun to concoct a plan. Tomorrow at first light, he will sneak off while Grandpa is fast asleep and return to the lake in search of Pearl Cave.

"That's exactly what I'm going to do," mutters Samuel under his breath.

"What was that?" asks Grandpa.

"Oh nothing, Grandpa. You must have heard the wind," Samuel replies.

At sunset, they decide to head home for supper. Before they venture home, Samuel looks around and makes a mental note of his location so he can easily find his way to Pearl Cave.

The Nightmare Trap

Shortly after getting into bed, Samuel falls into a deep sleep, where he finds himself floating underwater again. "This can't be happening," Samuel says, looking at his semi-transparent hands. "Not again!"

This time, the dream seems different from the previous one; it feels much more sinister.

Samuel floats along a cold dark deserted corridor made of rough gray stones. He realizes he is inside what looks like an old castle, but the castle is underwater. He freaks out as his body is dragged through the icy water, scraping along the coarse ceiling, by what seems like a powerful magnetic force. He struggles to fight the force, scraping his fingernails against the stone ceiling to keep from being sucked farther in, but the force is too strong. He surrenders and releases his chipped fingernails from the ceiling.

Samuel floats farther and farther into the corridor, passing hanging corked bottles filled with the same type of glowing fish that he saw in the cavern from his previous dream. He cannot quite figure out what it is, but he knows something is very wrong this time.

Chills run down the back of Samuel's neck, slowly through

his spine and all the way down to his toes. He is aware that he can blend in with the background, but he knows he is not entirely invisible to the naked eye. He keeps silent and hopes he goes unnoticed by anyone who happens by below.

Samuel's body turns a corner. Ahead, he sees two terrifying creatures standing in front of a large chiseled-stone door. He is relieved that they have not spotted his semi-transparent body floating toward them. He does not recognize either of them from his last dream.

When Samuel is above the door, the magnetic force releases him. He kicks his feet slowly to remain high above the door so no one notices him. He looks below and sees the two guards are sleeping, leaning on long spears to prop themselves up. Samuel can see the tops of their helmets, which are made from bottle caps. He can see their slimy muscular green arms, husky bodies and wrinkled green hands.

The monsters are snoring. Bubbles flow from their oblong mouths and rise steadily toward the ceiling, enveloping Samuel. Pop. Pop. Pop. The bubbles burst on contact, tickling him. But he manages to hold back his laughter. He tries to figure out why he is floating above the stone door and wonders who or what the guards are protecting.

A small window above the door opens up to a room on the other side. Samuel carefully unlatches the lock and begins to open the window. As he opens it, the window's hinges squeak, and one of the guards opens his eyes. Samuel clenches his teeth as he sees one of the guards move his head from side to side. He tries to remain calm and completely still. The guard looks straight down the corridor but sees nothing, then closes his eyes, leans against his spear and quickly drifts back to sleep. Samuel escapes detection, at least for now.

Samuel slowly opens the window, careful this time not to make the hinges squeak. He is unsure of what is on the other side but knows in his gut that he must have been drawn to it for a good reason. Maybe there are answers that will lead him to the magical glowing red pearl inside Pearl Cave.

Samuel holds his breath, squeezes through the small opening and braces himself for whatever he might find. He sees a bedroom, but it is not an ordinary bedroom. There is a throne made from branches, and in the far corner, a large entity is fast asleep in bed, its head sticking out from under the covers. Samuel stealthily swims toward the figure to get a better look. Whatever it is, it is large. "Something very ugly is fast asleep," he thinks to himself.

As Samuel swims closer, the water grows colder. The only warmth he can feel comes from the hot breath of the leviathan as it exhales. He stares at the monster below, trying to figure out what it is. It is much larger than Figlo, and its head and facial features look even more menacing than Figlo's. Its skin is bumpy and blood-red. Its face is covered in warts all the way to the tip of its nose, which resembles a respirator mask. Both of its eye sockets recede inward from its oval face, and its chin comes to a point like the tip of a crescent moon. A third eye is attached to the end of a long red tube that hangs like a limp hose from the top of its head. The monster is sleeping with its mouth open, revealing razor-sharp blade-like teeth, the kind that shreds the toughest food with ease.

Those are the only features that Samuel can see because the rest of the beast's massive body is hidden beneath a blanket. And that is all that Samuel cares to see for now.

It breathes heavily, sending streams of water and heat toward Samuel each time it exhales, tickling his nose. Samuel does everything in his power to hold back a booming sneeze. The tingling sensation is too much to bear. He cannot control himself.

"Haachoo!" Samuel sneezes loudly.

The monster immediately sits up, throwing the bed covers onto the floor as its three eyes dart about looking for the source of the noise. Each eyeball is the color of an egg yolk, with a fiery-red iris and pupil blending together in the middle.

Now that the creature is sitting upright, Samuel spots a key attached to a string that dangles from its neck. Luckily, it is still half-asleep, and the room is dark, making it difficult for it to see Samuel hovering above.

Long muscular tentacles attached to the behemoth's ribs reach out furiously, grabbing blindly for anything that might be nearby. Samuel slips through the tentacles' grasp multiple times, but as he begins to swim away, one of the tentacles grabs his leg. The monster wraps another tentacle around Samuel's neck, choking him. The brute pulls him closer and closer until they are face-to-face. Samuel stares into its fiery red pupils, wondering if he will ever wake up from this nightmare. The more he struggles to break free, the tighter the tentacle grips his neck. It seems as if there is no escape.

"Please. I can't breathe!" Samuel begs, pleading for his life. He begins to wheeze, using one hand to pull like crazy on the slippery tentacle wrapped around his neck while desperately reaching with his other hand for something to hold onto.

Chapter Five

"I can't breathe…can't breathe…I can't…"

In a matter of seconds, Samuel loses consciousness.

Grandpa hears an awful scream coming from Samuel's bedroom and dashes down the hallway. He enters and finds his daughter's son twisting violently, his body convulsing, sheets wrapped tightly around his neck. Without hesitation, Grandpa untangles Samuel and begins waking him.

"Samuel! Wake up!" he shouts. In a frenzy, Grandpa grabs a glass of water from the night table and throws the water on Samuel's face. Samuel shoots straight up out of bed, gasping for air. He is soaked from the waist up by a mixture of water and his own perspiration.

"Breathe, Samuel, breathe," Grandpa says while rubbing his back. Samuel gasps, fighting to refill his lungs with air. "You're safe, my boy. Take some deep breaths, son. You're safe now."

Samuel begins to regain his breath. As soon as he can speak, he recounts his nightmare. "Oh Grandpa, it was awful," he says, struggling to calm his nerves. "There was a hallway…and this bedroom. A scary monster was choking me. I thought I was going to die!" He is jumbling his words in his distressed state, and Grandpa is having a difficult time understanding what Samuel is trying to say.

Grandpa wraps his arms around Samuel and gives him a light hug. "Ssshhh. It's okay. It was only a nightmare. Try and relax now." He releases Samuel and gets up from the edge of the bed. "I'll go make us some tea."

"No, wait!" begs Samuel. "Please don't leave me here alone." His body is still shaking with fear, his heart pounding violently against his chest.

"Okay. I'll stay." Grandpa sits back down on the edge of the bed. "I'm not going anywhere."

"Promise?" asks Samuel.

"I promise," he says.

"Thank you, Grandpa. I don't know what would have happened to me if you didn't wake me up when you did."

"I'm sure you would've been okay. You're a lot braver than you give yourself credit for. Nightmares are tough, but so are you," Grandpa says, patting Samuel's back with the palm of his hand.

"I've had many a nightmare in my day," Grandpa continues.

"I'm sure you have," Samuel says.

Grandpa continues to talk to soothe Samuel's nerves. "Eventually, I learned how to stand up to my nightmares, but that's a story for another time. Just remember not to let nightmares get the best of you. Remember to be brave and stay in control. If you can stand up to your nightmares like you can stand up to bullies, they'll eventually back down. I promise, Samuel."

Too bad Samuel never stands up to bullies. Instead, he always runs away from them.

This will not be the last time that Samuel comes face to face with the evil monster from his nightmare. Only next time, he will listen to his grandfather's advice and be more prepared. Next time, Samuel will be in control.

❧ Chapter Six ☙

The Transformation Begins

Radiant streams of sunlight pour through the window, seeping through the cracks of Samuel's still-shut eyes. He releases a big yawn and stretches his arms out wide. With each stretch, joints crack loudly. He clenches both hands in tight fists to rub the morning gook from the corners of his eyes. Slowly but surely, Samuel awakens. Despite the horrific nightmare, he feels refreshed. He remembers how the monster almost choked him to death and how his grandfather saved him from suffocating. But Samuel starts his day anew without letting last night's dream traumatize him any further.

Samuel whips off his covers and jumps out of bed. He smiles as he gets ready to face the daylight. He knows Grandpa will wake up soon, so he dresses quickly and fills his backpack with the supplies that he will need for his secret expedition to Pearl Cave.

"Last night was rough, Lennox," Samuel says as he lifts his turtle from its tank. "But it doesn't matter. It was only a nightmare." Samuel tucks Lennox in the front chest pocket of his blue hooded sweatshirt.

"Still, if it's all the same, I hope we never have to see that monstrous creature again," he adds, cringing at the thought.

Lennox shifts around in Samuel's chest pocket until he finds a comfortable position. Samuel checks one last time to make sure he packed all essential gear, including a water-proof flashlight and compass.

"Okay, Lennox. We're ready to go. All we have to do is sneak out of the house without waking Grandpa," Samuel whispers as he walks toward the bedroom door with his backpack draped over his right shoulder.

From the bedroom, Samuel and Lennox enter a long hallway with an old oak floor. Lennox remains very still in the pocket as if he knows he has to keep quiet. Samuel tiptoes down the hallway toward the staircase, cringing every time a loose floorboard creaks under his feet.

They stop in front of Grandpa's bedroom door. Samuel listens carefully and can tell by the thunderous snores that Grandpa is fast asleep.

"Good. He's still asleep," Samuel whispers. "Still, we have to move quickly, or he'll keep us from finding out for our-selves whether the legend is true."

They continue toward the stairs. Samuel tiptoes as lightly as he possibly can. Grandpa's snores reverberate throughout the hallway, stopping temporarily whenever a floorboard creaks.

Samuel is relieved when they reach the bottom of the staircase and make it to the kitchen without being discov-ered. He decides to reward himself by making a peanut butter and jelly sandwich for breakfast. When he finishes preparing the sandwich, he rips off a tiny piece of crust and stuffs it into his chest pocket for Lennox to nibble on. Instead, Lennox devours the piece in one bite. Samuel swallows the rest of his sandwich in four big bites. His tongue, covered in peanut butter, smacks against the roof of his mouth. It is mouth suicide, but he manages to force the sticky peanut butter down his esophagus without the aid of any liquid but his own saliva. He then peels a ripe banana and shoves it whole into his mouth sideways, stretching his mouth into a smile. After gulping down the banana, Samuel thinks about packing some food in his backpack but figures they will be back before dinner.

Samuel and Lennox head toward the front porch. It is still very early and the morning chill has not yet dissipated, nor has the dew evaporated from the emerald-green grass. The cicadas and birds that made loud sounds yesterday are unusually silent, and the petals of the wildflowers carpeting the hilltop are closed tighter than a jar of jam, not open like on other mornings.

The fishing boat floats undisturbed on the lake's still waters, but not for long. Samuel runs down the hill as Lennox's body bounces wildly inside his pocket. They reach the dock, and Samuel slows from a sprint to a saunter. The sound of creaking planks is the only thing breaking the morning silence. He walks to the end of the dock and goes over Grandpa's instructions in his mind.

"First, untie the figure-eight knot," he says to himself as if Grandpa were beside him telling him what to do. "Let's see. Then I get inside the boat...no wait...first untie the rope from the dock, then get inside the boat," he says, smacking his forehead.

"Don't laugh, Lennox," scolds Samuel. "I've never done

this on my own before. It's easy to get confused."

Lennox wiggles from side to side inside Samuel's chest pocket, almost as if he were mocking his owner.

Samuel unties the boat with one hand while holding it with the other to keep it from floating away. Before boarding, he notes how his grandfather left everything after yesterday's outing.

"I have to remember to put everything back in the exact places where Grandpa left them. I don't want him figuring out that I used the boat, Lennox."

Samuel places his backpack on the seat and hops in, making the boat rock from side to side. He stretches his arms out wide to keep his balance. The rocking subsides and he sits down. Slightly nervous, he releases a long deep breath.

When he casts off, Samuel rows gently, only lightly grazing the water's surface with the tips of the oars to minimize splashing sounds. But he knows he will eventually have to row faster if he wants to reach his destination before his grandfather notices that he is gone.

"Finally, Lennox! It looks as though we're at a safe distance from the lake house. There's no way Grandpa can hear us all the way out here."

Samuel begins rowing faster and harder. He imagines that he is a fine-tuned racing car. "VROOOOOMMM…," he hums loudly as he rows with all of his might.

Samuel believes sound effects will help him row faster, but he quickly finds himself out of breath. He works up quite a sweat and decides to take a short break so he can dry off.

"Gosh, Lennox. Pearl Cave seemed a heck of lot closer yesterday. I know that something snagged my fishing line and pulled the boat halfway across the lake, but I never thought it would take us this long to retrace our steps," Samuel says, huffing and puffing.

After an hour of strenuous rowing, Samuel spots Pearl Cave in the distance. The sight of it reinvigorates him. He catches his second wind, rowing faster until they reach the dark semicircular entrance to Pearl Cave.

At first, Samuel is reluctant to enter. He peers carefully inside to check for anything strange or scary, like bats or the monster from last night's nightmare. The cave's interior is as dark as a cloudy, moonless night sky in the middle of a thick forest. Samuel cannot see anything at all, certainly not a dangerous monster with tentacles and three eyes.

"Flashlight…where is it?" he asks, fumbling through his backpack. "Ah…here it is," he says, pulling the waterproof flashlight out of his backpack. He points it at the cave's entrance, searching for magical oysters and potential dangers. But he sees nothing but rocks, dirt and stalactites up to two-feet-long clinging to the ceiling. Water drips from the tips of the stalactites into the water inside the cave. Plink. Plink. Plunk. The only sounds that Samuel hears are the sounds of dripping water. When he resumes rowing to enter the cave, the plinks and plunks are joined by the sounds of the boat's oars slapping the water and echoing off the rock walls.

Samuel eases the boat farther into the cave's interior, rowing forward cautiously at a snail-like pace. Each plink and plunk cause him to jerk and bite his lip. Every few feet, Samuel stops rowing so he can scan the cave with his flashlight. He then uses it like a headlight, wedging it between his shoulder and ear to hold it in place while he rows with both hands.

Despite the cave's tranquility, Samuel's imagination runs wild. He wonders whether the beast from his nightmare is hiding in the shadows of Pearl Cave. Even worse, what if it is hungry? The farther he travels into the cave, the faster his heart and imagination race.

Samuel turns around to look back. He no longer sees the entrance and now relies solely on the light that shines from his trusty flashlight to guide him forward.

Samuel feels alone with nothing but a pet turtle to keep him company and a flashlight and oars to protect him against anything that tries to devour him. So far, there are no signs of life, but the emptiness of the cave keeps him on edge. He expects something to pop out of the shadows at any moment. He hates not knowing what that something could be.

"Hello!" Samuel shouts.

"Hello…Hello…," the cave echoes back.

"Is anybody out there?"

"There…There…"

Samuel's echoing voice makes the cave seem eerier.

"At least no one answered my call," he says out loud.

"Call…Call…"

Samuel then spots some average-looking oysters perched along some ledges lining the cave's walls. None of the oysters glow, and none look magical. If a magical gem exists, it is nowhere to be found – at least not yet.

Samuel stops rowing. He lifts Lennox from his pocket and holds him close to his chest. It makes Samuel feel safe, as if nothing can harm him. Of course, how could a little turtle protect Samuel from the creature he saw in his nightmare?

"Look," Samuel says, pointing toward the boat's bow.

"The cave is narrowing. That must mean we're getting closer to the end of the cave, Lennox. Help me look for the magical glowing red pearl." Samuel's intuition is correct. Quickly, he reaches the end of the cave, and soon he will uncover a mystery.

Samuel is so preoccupied with looking at oysters to his left and right that he does not notice a large bed of rocks directly in front of him. The boat hits the rocks, abruptly stopping the boat and throwing Samuel off balance. Lennox flies out of his hands like a water balloon covered with grease.

"Lennox!" Samuel yelps in horror.

Samuel jumps out of the boat and immediately ties it to a nearby jagged rock. Using his flashlight, Samuel searches for his best friend among the rocks on the ground. Then he feels a sudden warmth hit the back of his neck. He looks at the ceiling and spies a crack from which three thin beams of light pierce the darkness. One beam is shining on Samuel, one beam illuminates an oyster with a glowing red pearl, and the third beam lights an oyster with a glowing blue pearl.

"I've found it! I can't believe it! It really does exist!" Samuel exclaims. "The legend of Pearl Cave isn't a myth at all. Funny, though. Grandpa never mentioned anything about a magical blue pearl."

Distracted by his discoveries, Samuel forgets all about searching for his best friend. Luckily, Lennox landed in the water, which cushioned his fall. His heavy shell dragged him down to the lake bed inside Pearl Cave, where he waits safe and sound for Samuel to eventually remember to rescue him.

But right now, Samuel is inching his way toward the glowing pearls. He creeps slowly toward them as if to expect the unexpected. He is torn over which pearl to touch first.

"I know what the red one does, but what about the blue one?" he asks himself. Blue happens to be Samuel's favorite color, though both pearls are magnificent sights.

After quick deliberation, Samuel decides to touch the magical glowing red pearl that his grandfather described on their fishing trip. This is it, the moment of truth. Samuel braces himself and reaches for the red pearl.

And nothing happens.

Samuel is surprised. He was so sure that Grandpa's story was true. "Go figure. It really was all just some silly myth," Samuel mutters with major disappointment in his voice.

Samuel begins to put the red pearl back in its oyster when a strong wind suddenly whips around his body. Similar to the mysterious wind that pummeled him inside the tree house, but this is even stronger. The red pearl begins to give off sparks, and the gust grows stronger yet, forcing Samuel to drop to his knees so he will not be blown over. A powerful burst of wind knocks loose some stalactites from the cave's ceiling, which narrowly miss Samuel's head as they fall into the water. The wind then lifts buckets of water from the lake, drenching Samuel from head to toe.

"I don't like the look of this!" shouts Samuel, fighting to be heard over the howl of the wind.

The wind turns into a tornado, scooping Samuel off the ground and into the air. He spins round and round, his face turning green from dizziness. Samuel, small of stature to begin with, begins to become smaller until finally, he is only one-foot-tall. His flashlight, backpack, shoes and even the clothes on his back shrink in the same proportion as he does.

"Help!" he cries in vain. But it is no use. No one else is around for miles. And now he is so small that his screams are almost inaudible squeaks. No one would hear his cries even if they were nearby, and he is way too small to be found easily in the darkness.

Samuel faints as the wind knocks him off the ledge and into the lake. He sinks like an anchor through the waters of Pearl Cave. Then the cyclone above the water stops as abruptly as it had started.

When Samuel reaches bottom, no one but Lennox is around to come to his rescue. He tries waking Samuel by slapping his face with one of his feet, which is used like a human hand.

"Wake up, Samuel!" Lennox begs. "Please be okay. What should I do? What should I do?" he asks himself as he shakes his friends shoulders.

Samuel opens his eyes. He sees a blurry green form that is an emotional wreck, crying and praying that Samuel is not hurt.

"Samuel! Are you okay?" Lennox pleads.

"What? I think so," Samuel replies as he lifts himself up from the lake floor. He is still dazed and disoriented as he picks himself up, unaware that he is underwater.

"Wait a sec…What happened to me? Where am I? And who, or should I ask, what are you?"

"All I can say is that one second you were holding me, and the next you were tossing me in the lake. Thanks a lot, by the way," Lennox says with a smart-alecky snicker in his voice.

"Lennox, is that you?" Samuel asks hesitantly as his vision comes into focus. He realizes that he is talking to his pet turtle, who is now nearly the same size as he is. Or perhaps it is the other way around.

"Who else could it be?" Lennox replies.

"How is this possible? You can talk! What's going on here?" asks Samuel, still dazed and confused.

"I've always been able to talk. You just never took the time to listen," Lennox retorts. He approaches Samuel with his green arms extended wide to give him a big hug.

"Stay back!" Samuel barks as he raises his fists.

Lennox springs backward and raises his front feet, palms facing out. "Samuel, it's me, Lennox. I'm your best friend, remember? Trust me. I want only to make sure you're okay, especially after what just happened."

Lennox gives Samuel some time to gather his thoughts. Standing upright, he places his right front foot on his temple, begins scratching, and rests his left front foot on the exterior of his forest-green shell. "Did you ever think that this might be just as weird for me as it is for you?"

Samuel raises his eyebrows as he ponders Lennox's question. "I guess I didn't give it much thought. But how do I know you're real and that I'm not dreaming? And how do I know you're not going to hurt me?"

"Me? Hurt you? Now why would I do something like that?" Lennox asks. He calmly approaches Samuel, walking upright on his hind legs and holding up both of his front feet like hands. As soon as Lennox gets close enough, he kicks Samuel in the shin.

"Ow! What did you do that for?" asks Samuel, rubbing his shin.

"Well, now you know two things. One, that I'm real. And

two, this is definitely not a dream," Lennox says, laughing.

Samuel continues rubbing the red mark that formed on his shin. His mind becomes less foggy. He recalls everything that happened on the lake's surface with clarity.

"Oh. I remember," says Samuel. "I fainted and fell in the water. Oh my God…I'm underwater!" Samuel's chest constricts. He grabs at his throat and gasps for air. All of a sudden, he remembers that in his first dream, he could breathe underwater.

"Relax. Just breathe," Lennox says, rubbing Samuel's back.

"Deep breaths, buddy. Inhale…exhale," says Lennox, demonstrating his own breathing technique. Shortly after his panic attack, Samuel calms down and realizes he is okay.

"That was some fall you took," says Lennox. "I was really worried. I thought I'd lost you there for a moment. I thought…" His eyes swell with tears.

"Are you crying?" Samuel interjects with a mocking smile.

"No. You kicked up a lot of dirt from the lake floor when you landed. Some of it must have gotten in my eyes," Lennox replies, hiding his face with his forearm. He blows his nose into the crease of his elbow.

"Of course it was the dirt. That must have been it," says Samuel, chuckling under his breath. He changes the subject to spare Lennox any more embarrassment. Do you realize how incredible this is? Do you know what this means?" He waits for a response.

"Does it mean you're finally going to listen to how much I hate the food pellets that you feed me every day?" Lennox asks in a sarcastic tone.

"No. It means the legend is true. There really is a magical glowing red pearl. I can't wait to tell Grandpa!" But how will Samuel tell Grandpa if he is only a fraction of his normal size? Samuel should be contemplating how he will return to normal. Instead, he is focusing on how totally awesome his transformation is.

Lennox clears his throat. "While I have your attention, I'd like to address this food situation," he says, still fixated on his dietary needs.

"Food? How can you think about food at a time like this?"

"There's always time to think about food. FYI, I think you've been trying to poison me," Lennox snaps.

"I'm not trying to poison you. The man at the pet store told me those pellets are the best on the market," Samuel replies.

"Oh, are they now? I didn't know he ate them himself... for every meal. Something tells me the man at the pet store either has no taste buds or has never tried eating the nasty pellets that you call food. Would it be too much to feed me something a little more appetizing?" asks Lennox, licking his lips.

"I'll take your request into consideration at a later date. If you haven't noticed, I have a more pressing issue to deal with right now," says Samuel while cleaning the mud off his pants.

Lennox continues his rant. He is relentless.

"What could be more important than a juicy piece of steak? A filet mignon cooked to perfection. Oh, what I wouldn't give for just one bite of a hot pastrami sandwich with a little bit of mustard." Lennox rambles on and on while Samuel examines the changes that his body has undergone.

Samuel feels strange, and understandably so. He runs both hands over his neck to discover slits on each side. He figures the slits are gills that make it possible for him to breathe underwater. His feet feel cramped inside his sneakers, so Samuel kicks them off and discovers that his toes are webbed. It is a lot to process. He wonders if there will be any more surprises.

"Look at these," Samuel says, pointing to his gills and webbed toes.

"Are you kidding? You're focused on your smelly feet, and I haven't had a decent meal my entire reptilian life," Lennox moans. He sulks, his head drooping halfway back into his shell.

Samuel ignores Lennox's snarky comment, then notices a small silver oyster shell with an unusual pattern of red and blue sparkles embedded in its surface. He picks it up and places it in his backpack as a keepsake. He then focuses again on his transformation.

"Watch this," Samuel says to Lennox. Samuel demonstrates the power of his webbed feet by kicking them rapidly, propelling him straight up and out of the water like a dolphin. He completes an impressive set of flips in the air before diving back into the water, head first, without making the slightest splash.

"Great. You can do tricks. Should I give you a treat?" Lennox asks rhetorically, unimpressed by Samuel's antics. "You know what would impress me? If you could make a pot roast appear before my very eyes. Go ahead, impress me."

"I'm afraid we're going to have to deal with your gastronomic obsession some other time. Right now, we've got some exploring to do," Samuel replies. He retrieves his waterproof flashlight from the lake floor. "Follow me, Lennox, and stay close. We don't know what's down here." Pointing his flashlight back in the direction of the cave's entrance, Samuel begins to paddle and kick.

Lennox, however, is not so keen on the idea of exploring an unfamiliar environment. "Wouldn't it be better if we just hung out where we are for a little while longer?" he suggests, trying to postpone the inevitable. The thought that his last meal consisted of a hard green pellet and a crusty piece of bread is too much to bear.

"It wouldn't be called exploring if we stayed in one place. Now quit dragging your feet and follow me." Samuel continues swimming in the direction of where he thinks the cave meets the open lake.

Though it feels a bit strange at first, Samuel quickly grows accustomed to filling his lungs with water. He practices swimming by using his built-in foot paddles. Lennox follows closely behind, keeping a look out for anything unusual.

"This is absolutely amazing!" says Samuel as he tests out his new abilities. He swims swiftly through the waters of the cave, twisting and turning his body in different directions. Sometimes he swims facing up and sometimes facing down. Before they know it, both Lennox and Samuel stray pretty far from the waters inside Pearl Cave and swim out into the open lake.

Samuel's new abilities fill him with a sense of empowerment. He never felt so alive, so sure of himself. Lennox is beginning to get the impression that Samuel might never want to change back into a real boy and return home, which would mean no filet mignon in his foreseeable future.

Encounters of Fate

Samuel and Lennox swim pretty far from Pearl Cave into the lake's open waters. Samuel continues to explore the lake bottom and practices using his new talents while an apprehensive Lennox follows closely behind.

"Look, Lennox. Over there!" Samuel says excitedly, pointing to a sunken sailboat resting on the lake floor. The decaying boat is tilted ever so slightly on its side.

"What do you say we take a closer look?" asks Samuel.

"Do I have a choice?" Lennox fires back, his fear increasing as they swim farther from Pearl Cave.

"No, silly. Of course you don't," answers Samuel with a laugh.

"I was afraid you'd say that," Lennox retorts. He continues to follow his friend swimming closely behind as they move toward the sunken sailboat.

It is a decent-size, about 30 feet in length and large enough to accommodate a spacious cabin and rooms for cooking and sleeping. At some point, it must have been magnificent, but now, most of the paint has peeled off the exterior of the sad vessel, and the long wooden mast that once stood proud is broken in half. The main sail is torn and tattered, a useless rag swaying slowly in the current. The deck is thickly carpeted with underwater plant life.

Schools of tiny fish, all shiny gray, swim in a circle around the sailboat as if they were inside a snow globe, nibbling at the algae that formed on the boat's keel. Samuel and Lennox join the fish, swimming around until they find a hole in the hull where a wooden plank is missing. Samuel is just about to squeeze through the hole when Lennox warns him of the dangers that might lurk inside.

"I don't know, Samuel. It doesn't look safe," a trembling Lennox says in a shaky voice.

"Don't act like a hatchling," Samuel replies.

"A hatchling?" Lennox shouts angrily. "I'm not acting like a hatchling! I'm being smart. It might be wise to think twice about entering a scary abandoned boat that we know nothing about."

"So you admit it. You're scared," Samuel says, taunting Lennox.

"Oh, never mind," Lennox responds in frustration. He folds his arms and turns his back toward Samuel.

"Don't be sore, Lennox. I was only joking." Samuel slaps the back of his shell. "Tell you what. How about you stay out here and keep watch?"

To Lennox, standing guard sounds much safer than going inside. "Well, if you insist," He replies, unfolding his arms but keeping his back to Samuel. Lennox is too proud to admit he is scared. "Don't be long. Okay?" But Samuel does not hear him. Lennox turns around to see Samuel has already entered the boat.

Chapter Seven

"Great. Now I'm alone. I'm starting to believe I'd be happier inside the pocket of that smelly sweatshirt." Lennox whistles nervously to calm himself and break the uncomfortable silence.

Inside the abandoned wreck, glowing fish swim about, shining just enough gloomy light for Samuel to see the boat's abandoned contents. Everything is covered in algae, including the tarnished pots and pans that rest forlornly inside the kitchen sink. The partial remains of mud-covered oven mitts float lifelessly around the cabin. It is like visiting a place that time forgot.

Samuel looks up toward the ceiling and notices a life preserver. He then swims deeper inside the boat, leaving the galley to discover what must have been the captain's bedroom. Samuel examines a withered queen-size bed whose mattress is still securely fastened by rope to the bed frame. The mattress has deteriorated over time, exposing rusty springs.

Above the headboard, Samuel spots a picture secured to the wall. It is a family portrait. He assumes that someone in the photograph once owned the ill-fated boat. He carefully runs his hand over the picture frame's broken glass to wipe away the mud and algae. The picture is faded, but Samuel can just about make out a man and a woman, holding an infant. They are smiling widely as if someone had just said cheese. The photograph is distorted and warped from water damage, so the features of the people are not clear.

Suddenly, an unnerving groan from under the bed shatters the calm.

"Who's there?" Samuel asks in a fearful, weak voice, his eyebrows raised. He looks all around. "Hello," Samuel says, waiting for a reply. "Is someone there?" The continued silence unnerves him.

Samuel cautiously swims toward the floor to get a closer look. Two enormous yellow eyes light up beneath the bed. He almost gets close enough to make out what it is when the bed suddenly flips over. Samuel freezes in fear. There he is, floating face to face with an angry fish at least seven times his size.

"Another scary monster! Not again!" Samuel exclaims, slowly backing away as the colossus snarls.

The fish salivates. Bubbly white foam appears from the corners of its mouth. Its teeth are like freshly sharpened swords. Two stick out from its upper lip and two others shoot up from its lower lip. Spikes line its long muscular tail. Warts cover its slimy dark-purple body. The mammoth's mouth is so big that it could eat Samuel in just one bite.

"Here we go again," says Samuel as he recalls his near-death encounter with the monster from his recent nightmare.

The creature curls up like a venomous snake and lunges at Samuel, who panics and swims away furiously, leaving behind a trail of bubbles that temporarily blind the beast. But not for long. The enormous fish chases the boy with a fierce, hungry look in its eyes. Samuel paddles frantically for his life, kicking his webbed feet as hard as he can. The beast follows him out of the bedroom and through the galley, all the while nipping at Samuel's legs. Thinking fast, Samuel grabs a pan from the kitchen sink on his way to the hole on the side of the hull.

As Samuel approaches the hole, he yells ahead to warn Lennox. "Swim for your life, Lennox! Swim as fast as you can! Go!"

Chapter Seven

Lennox hears fear in Samuel's voice.

"Swim back to the cave! I'll meet you there."

Lennox is not sure what is wrong, but he heeds the instructions and speeds off toward Pearl Cave as if his life depended on it.

The fish comes close to biting off Samuel's feet, but he turns around and uses the pan to smack the monster on the side of the head. Samuel delivers a powerful blow to its temple, then lets go of the vibrating pan. The fish, barely fazed by the blow, shakes its head for a second, then returns to attack.

By then, Samuel reaches the opening in the side of the boat. As he squeezes through the tiny hole, Samuel gives the creature a swift kick to the nose. Startled, it falls back but quickly recovers again. It shoots forward but is too big to fit through the hole. The angry beast stops abruptly right before reaching the hole, then turns around and backs up, determined to smash through. The monster builds momentum. Its oversized fins flap furiously like the wings of a hawk chasing a mouse in an open field. It swims straight toward the opening, crashing into the hull and knocking itself unconscious.

Unaware that the fish has subdued itself, Samuel swims as fast as he can to meet up with Lennox in Pearl Cave. He is so petrified of becoming the monster's dinner that he never looks back to see if he is being followed. The first time he stops to rest is when he runs out of breath. His gills burn. Huffing and puffing, Samuel leans against some coral while he catches his breath and regains his composure.

As his breathing slows to a normal pace, Samuel hears someone whimper from the other side of the coral. His first instinct is to swim away, but he decides to check it out. Cautiously, he peeks around to the other side of the coral. He moves with the stealth-like grace of a ninja to make sure he is not heard. As he turns the final corner, he comes upon a beautiful blue female with long flowing strands of black hair. She is very upset. Samuel watches quietly as she cries. He feels an odd connection with her as if he can feel her sadness.

She looks familiar. She has the same scaly blue skin, black oval eyes, trumpet-like ears and spiky tail as the creatures in Samuel's first dream.

Samuel has not been as quiet as he had hoped. While he admires the girl, another creature from his dream creeps up from behind. He wraps one arm around Samuel's torso and places his free paw over the boy's mouth. He struggles to break free. The noise and bubbles startle the weeping girl, who flees and hides behind a nearby rock.

"State your business," demands Figlo. "What is it you want from the princess?" Samuel's heart pounds against his chest. He quickly runs out of breath as he tries futilely to escape Figlo's powerful grasp. Samuel tries to reply, but with a large paw covering his mouth, he cannot say anything.

"Are you deaf?" Figlo repeats impatiently. "I said, 'State your business!'"

The princess peeks from behind the rock and notices that Samuel is trying to answer.

"Figlo! You'll have to remove your paw from his mouth if you expect an answer!" the princess yells from a safe distance.

Samuel recognizes Figlo's name from his dream. He stops resisting and tries to calm down. Figlo warns him not to try anything funny, slowly loosens his grip and removes his paw from Samuel's mouth.

"Figlo?" Samuel asks. "I know that name." He brushes Figlo's other paw off his chest and turns around to face his captor. Samuel's suspicion is correct. It is the beast from his dream, the strange being who delivered news from the Oracle to a table full of creatures who resembled the scaly blue-skinned girl hiding behind the rock.

"It's you!" says Samuel, as if he knows Figlo personally. "I've seen you before. You're the beast from my dream."

"Beast. That's a bit harsh, don't you think?" Figlo responds, his sharp claws shooting out from his paws. He is clearly offended by Samuel's description.

"Sorry. Where I come from, we're not used to seeing beasts…I mean creatures like you." Samuel cannot help but stare in amazement. He has never seen any being as fascinating as Figlo, not even at the zoo.

"Wait here," Figlo says, retracting his claws and swimming toward the princess.

The minute Figlo swims away, Samuel remembers that Lennox is waiting for him back at Pearl Cave. There is a good chance he already has had two heart attacks worrying about Samuel.

Figlo continues to swim toward the princess, who is no longer hiding behind the rock. They huddle and begin discussing what to do with Samuel. Samuel is not dim; he knows they are talking about whether they should trust him. He swims closer to put in a word for himself.

"A-hem." Samuel clears his throat to get their attention. "I hate to break up your little powwow, but my friend and I have been separated. He's probably worried sick about me." Samuel bows to the princess and sharply nods his head at Figlo to bid them farewell. "I'm terribly sorry, but I really must go. Even though we didn't have much time to talk, it was a pleasure meeting both of you."

Samuel turns in the direction of Pearl Cave. But before he has a chance to swim away, the princess cries out.

"Wait. Before you go, I think there's something you should know."

Samuel pauses for a moment but resumes swimming.

"It involves you and your future," the princess says.

"Future? What could she possibly know about my future?" Samuel mumbles. Intrigued, he stops dead in his tracks and turns around to give her a chance to explain. Figlo and the princess swim closer to Samuel.

"Thank you for stopping. First, a proper introduction is in order. I am Izadora, Princess of Aquatania. It appears you already know Figlo."

Figlo bows his head following his official introduction.

"I'm Samuel, Samuel Waters. Pleased to meet you," he responds, holding his hand out to greet her. She is not sure why Samuel extends his hand. She slaps it with her webbed fin-like hand and giggles.

"What are you?" she asks. "You're so different from the other inhabitants of the lake." She swims around Samuel in circles, her pointy blue tail tickling him each time she circles him.

"Stop that! You're tickling me," he says, shaking with laughter. "I'm a human boy, or at least…I was," he replies, unsure of what he has become.

"A human boy. How delightful!" says the princess.

"Princess, we must tell the king of the boy's arrival, immediately," Figlo interjects joyfully, trying unsuccessfully to contain his emotions.

"That's a fantastic idea," adds Izadora.

Samuel does not display as much excitement as Figlo and Izadora. It makes him uneasy to think someone or something is expecting him.

"Slow down. The king? My future?" Samuel is beginning to freak out. "Listen, I already told you, my friend is waiting for me. I have to get back to him. I'm not sure what you think you know about me, but whatever it is, you'll have to wait until I find Lennox to tell me."

"Lennox? Who's that?" asks Izadora.

"He's my pet turtle."

"Pet turtle?" she asks with a perplexed look on her face. "What exactly is a pet turtle?" She seems intrigued by the sound of the words "pet turtle."

"Would you like to meet him?" asks Samuel, inviting Izadora to return with him to Pearl Cave.

"Sure. Why not? There's something I think you should see, and it just so happens to be in Pearl Cave. Our encounter with each other is no coincidence, Samuel. It's fate."

"Yeah, right. I'm sure our meeting was predestined," he responds, looking at her as if she is crazy.

"Don't you believe me?" she asks, her eyebrows fluttering.

Samuel begins to feel warm and funny inside. Her beauty is affecting his judgment. "Honestly, I don't know what to believe anymore," he responds.

"Don't worry. Soon enough you'll understand why all this is happening to you. Try to be patient and trust me," says the princess.

Trust is a funny thing. It seems as if someone is always asking for Samuel's trust as if he is supposed to comply without question. Still, she seems harmless enough. She hid timidly behind a rock when Figlo captured him. How much of a threat could the princess really be?

Izadora instructs Figlo to return to a secret hideout and tell the council of their discovery while she and Samuel venture off to Pearl Cave.

Figlo objects. "But princess, your father gave me specific instructions not to let you out of my sight. If something were to happen to you, I couldn't bear it, and I would be punished severely." Figlo knows that King Zedorious might exile him from Lake Aqueous if anything bad were to happen to his daughter.

"Well, I'm giving you new instructions," she commands. "Go. I'll be safe. After all, I have the boy to protect me."

Samuel looks surprised. Figlo hesitates.

Izadora yells one more time. "I won't ask again, Figlo. Now go!"

He caves in, his tail drooping between his legs.

Samuel is not sure that he can protect himself, let alone a princess, but he tells Figlo not to worry.

"It's okay, Figlo. Pearl Cave isn't that far from here," says Samuel. "I'm sure we'll be fine."

Figlo swims off toward the secret hideout, mulling over the consequences that he faces if Izadora is harmed. But he realizes there is not much he can do when she makes up her mind. She might look sweet and innocent, but the steely resolve that Figlo sees in her eyes makes it difficult to challenge her. As Figlo swims off into the distance, the princess suggests that she and Samuel head toward Pearl Cave.

"Shall we, Samuel?" she asks, pointing her webbed hand in the direction of Pearl Cave.

"We shall," he says, poking fun at her regal manner.

For some reason, they trust each other. Of course, Izadora has an explanation for trusting Samuel, which he will soon learn for himself.

The Writing on the Wall

Samuel and the princess arrive at the entrance to Pearl Cave, where the lake's bright blue waters meet the cave's darker waters. Izadora trails closely behind Samuel as he swims ahead anxiously in search of his best friend.

"Lennox, I'm home!" shouts Samuel, his voice echoing off the cave's walls. His eyes dart about in a frenzy when Lennox does not respond.

Samuel wonders if Lennox ever returned to Pearl Cave. His mind begins to drift toward the unthinkable. He begins to worry that the enormous fish that attacked him inside the sunken sail boat somehow got out and went after Lennox. Maybe he is hurt, or worse, dead.

"This is bad, very bad," Samuel says to Izadora. He cannot bear the thought of losing his one and only pet turtle.

"Don't give up hope, Samuel. Keep looking. I'm sure we'll find him," Izadora responds.

Princess Izadora helps Samuel search high and low, diving below the water's surface and returning above from time to time, all while shouting Lennox's name. But Lennox does not reply. They continue moving forward in the waters inside Pearl Cave.

Lennox, however, is far inside the cave, deep below the water's surface, leaning against the cave's wall and sobbing loudly. He does not hear Samuel or Izadora calling out his name over his own weeping voice. He is under the impression that Samuel is gone, consumed by whatever dangers that lurk within the deep dark depths of the lake. He sits down hunched over as he continues to weep for his best friend.

"Lennox? Is that you?" asks Samuel from afar, overhearing the crying. He is overcome with joy when he sees his friend sitting on the floor, alive and well. "Lennox! It *is* you!" Samuel exclaims as he swims toward him with open arms.

When Lennox hears Samuel's voice, he lifts his head from his chest to see Samuel and his unknown guest approaching. Lennox quickly clears the tears from his eyes, hurriedly lifts himself off the floor and charges at Samuel at full speed, slamming him against the wall.

"Do you know what you've put me through?" Lennox shouts at the top of his lungs. Lennox pins Samuel's wrists above his head against the rocky wall.

"What has gotten into you, Lennox?" Samuel yells, his back throbbing in pain from the impact. "Let me go this instant!" He fights to break free from Lennox's powerful hold.

"How could you? While you were out doing...doing God knows what, I was left here alone consumed by thoughts of horrible things that might have happened to you." The angry turtle ignores the princess as she watches the two tussle from a safe distance.

"Lennox, I'm fine," says Samuel, trying to calm him down and escape his grip.

"You don't understand. I thought you were de...dea...I

can't say it." Lennox releases Samuel's wrists and places one of his hands on his forehead. He has a flair for theatrics.

Samuel gently pushes Lennox out of the way and begins rubbing his lower back. "Look, all I can do is apologize for what you went through, though saying I'm sorry doesn't change the past," Samuel says as he tries to catch his breath. "Besides, I was dealing with my own issues. The good news is that I'm okay. See for yourself." He then swims in a full circle around Lennox, spinning around as he goes, to show that he has not been harmed.

"See, all this worry for nothing. There's not a scratch on me, aside from the bruise that you just gave me," says Samuel with a smirk.

"I wouldn't say it was all for nothing. At least I care," Lennox replies.

"Don't you think you're being a tad overdramatic?"

"Overdramatic! You think I'm being overdramatic?" Lennox asks, visibly annoyed. He crosses his arms and turns his back to Samuel.

"Come on now. Don't be like that. Who's my pet turtle?" Samuel places his hand on Lennox's shell and gives it a vigorous scratch.

"Don't think you can ju…jus…man, that feels good. A little to the left. Ahhh. That's the spot." Lennox's hind leg quivers like a dog's when scratched behind the ear.

"There you go, Lennox. Now isn't that better?" Samuel asks.

It does not take long for Lennox to forgive Samuel for abandoning him.

Izadora, meanwhile, has been observing from afar, finding their behavior peculiar. Unsure of what to make of it all, she impatiently taps her foot against the ground until she finds an opportunity to interrupt.

"I'm sorry to break up your reunion, boys, but we have more pressing matters to attend to," Izadora says as she flips back her black hair.

Samuel and Lennox turn to look at the princess. Lennox catches an intoxicating whiff of the sweet and salty scent of her hair.

"And who, might I ask, is this?" asks Lennox, repeatedly raising both eyebrows as he admires her beauty. Green or blue, turtle or mystical underwater creature, Lennox doesn't care.

"Lennox, allow me to introduce you to Izadora, Princess of Aquatania." Samuel announces her name in the royal tone that it deserves. He then places his arm around Lennox. "And this, princess, is my not-so-brave friend Lennox."

Lennox slaps Samuel's arm off his shell. "Not so brave? How dare you!" He turns to the princess. "Please disregard everything my so-called friend has just said about me. He's human and flawed. It's both an honor and a pleasure to meet you, princess."

He reaches for Izadora's webbed hand. "Or should I call you Princess Izadorable. Enchanté, mademoiselle" says Lennox in a thick French accent as he delivers a soft kiss to the webbing on the back of her hand.

Samuel rolls his eyes. Izadora yanks her hand away in disgust from Lennox's pale green lips. "Please, just call me Izadora," she insists, wiping the slobber on her hand off on her leafy clothes.

Izadora acts much more informally than Lennox thought

a princess would act. You would think a princess would like to be pampered and worshiped, but not Izadora. She prefers to blend in with average people rather than treat her subjects like inferiors.

"Isn't there something important you want to show me, princess?" asks Samuel, rescuing Izadora from her awkward romantic encounter.

"Yes, of course. Please, follow me." She begins swimming deeper into the waters beneath Pearl Cave with Samuel and Lennox close behind.

The light from the cave's entrance pierces through the water's surface but grows dim as the trio swims farther into the cave. Samuel pulls out his trusty waterproof flashlight from his backpack and switches it on.

"That's fantastic! Why didn't you tell me you've studied sorcery," Izadora says, mistaking Samuel's flashlight for a shiny magical wand.

"Yeah, princess. He's a regular magician," says Lennox in a snarky tone.

"Not exactly," Samuel laughs. "It's a flashlight." Samuel thought that naming the object would explain the reason behind its ability to produce light, but she continues to stare in amazement at the flashlight, which to her seems to be a miniature sun.

"It's basic science. Watch. It creates light." He demonstrates by turning it on and off and on again.

"I'm not sure I understand, but it's very impressive," she says. "Now, if you wouldn't mind, point your flaaashliiiight on this wall here." She stretches out the syllables to mimic Samuel.

Chapter Eight

Samuel lights the wall in front of them. He looks at Lennox, confused about what he is supposed to see. All he sees are lines scratched on the surface of the rock.

"Isn't it incredible?" Izadora asks, admiring the markings on the wall.

Izadora waits eagerly for a response but is disappointed by the puzzled looks on the faces of Samuel and Lennox. The strange linear markings, worn down by years of erosion, do not make any sense to the untrained eye, but to a native Aquatanian, the markings convey a compelling story.

"What's the problem?" she asks. "Can't you see it? It's right in front of you." She cannot understand why they do not grasp the significance of what they are seeing.

"All I can see are a bunch of scratch marks," says Lennox.

"I'm sorry, Izadora. I have to agree with Lennox. It looks like someone ran their claws across the wall," Samuel says as he takes a second look. "Oh. I get it now. Is this Figlo's work?" asks Samuel. But his interpretation is wrong.

Izadora, slightly frustrated, is determined to find a way to open their eyes. And then it hits her like a tidal wave. She remembers an ancient technique, designed by her ancestors, to help those who are not of Aquatanian blood see the writing on the wall.

"Okay, gentlemen. I think I've figured out our problem, only you'll both have to trust me," says the princess.

Samuel and Lennox look at each other, shrug their shoulders in unison, turn their attention back toward the princess and agree to do her bidding.

"Great. Now I want both of you to close your eyes," she says as she gently brushes her webbed hands over Samuel's eyes. His eyes flutter rapidly, and his breathing grows heavy. "Relax. Trust me, Samuel," she insists. He yields to her touch, tightly closing both eyes. Lennox follows Samuel's lead and closes his eyes.

Izadora continues. "I want you to listen to my every word. First, take a deep breath." She demonstrates by inhaling and exhaling deeply.

They comply, and the cave's cool water pours through Samuel's gills, filling his lungs and calming his nerves. Since he was transformed, Samuel has not had a chance to relax.

"Now, take another deep breath." The sweet sound of her voice soothes Samuel's nerves even more.

She begins to tell an ancient tale, one you might hear when sitting around a campfire. "A long time ago, my ancestors formed a specially selected group of Aquatanians who called themselves The Secret Council of Aquatania. Among them was a prophet who brought the council to the very spot that we're standing on. The prophet predicted that one day a young boy would come along to save my people from a great evil. As the prophet spoke, the members etched his words on the wall before us in the form of pictures. I could describe the pictures to you, but I'd rather you see them for yourself."

Izadora gently caresses Samuel's hand. "Don't be afraid, Samuel. And don't open your eyes until I tell you," Izadora says, her pointy tail floating back and forth in the current.

"As you wish, princess," replies Samuel, bewitched by her every word.

Izadora closes her eyes and concentrates deeply. In a matter of seconds, a tiny blue spark appears in the middle of her palm. She gently places the glowing spark onto Samuel's hand.

She opens her eyes and watches as the blue spark travels up the length of Samuel's arm, through his shoulder and neck, and explodes in a tiny flash of fiery blue light when it reaches his eyes. He remains calm as the painless burst of light creates a warm, comforting feeling inside him.

Samuel keeps his eyes closed as he was told, but Lennox does not. He has been peeking through one of his eyelids to witness the entire light show.

"What's going on here?" he asks, alarmed by the event. "What are you doing to my friend?"

"Shush!" commands the princess. "Everything's fine. Now shut your eyes! We're almost done."

Lennox sighs, crosses his arms, and shuts both eyes. He wonders if Samuel will be okay.

"And now for the final touch. On the count of three, I want you to open your eyes slowly," the princess says as she begins the countdown. "One, believe and the truth will unfold. Two, unleash the Wall of Prophecies. Three, open your eyes."

Samuel lifts his eyelids slowly. Tiny glittering stars pass from left to right over the etchings. The story behind the etchings is revealed to him, telling of Samuel's past, present and future.

"I can't believe it. I can see it!" Samuel exclaims.

"See what?" asks Lennox as he opens his eyes.

"You're right! It's incredible, princess," says Samuel, ignoring Lennox.

Feverish with excitement, Samuel runs his hand along the drawings on the wall. "There I am, touching a glowing red pearl. And look. Here we are at the Wall of Prophecies."

Lennox does not share Samuel's enlightenment. Because he did not follow the princess' instructions, he still can not see the pictures. "Um? Am I the only one who's sane around here?" he asks.

Samuel continues to ignore Lennox and looks farther down the wall. Dragging his fingertips gently across the etchings, Samuel traces his entire life as told by the prophet.

"Who is this supposed to be?" Samuel asks, pointing to a sketch of a young boy leading troops into a great battle against hordes of ghastly looking creatures. The horrid beasts are led by an ugly one that looks like the monster that tried to strangle Samuel in his nightmare.

"Why, that's you, Samuel," Izadora answers.

The color drains from Samuel's face. His mouth opens slightly.

"Don't you get it? That's why you're here." She reaches out, grabs his hand and presses his open palm against her heart. The color slowly returns to his face as she begins to explain the story.

"For as far back as I can remember, my people have been enslaved by Clatheron, the most ruthless, heartless being ever to reside in the lake," she says, filled with anger. Izadora points to the monster on the wall and places Samuel's hand in hers. "Clatheron has shown no mercy toward my people. With his loyal and ruthless army of Malquars, he stole our kingdom from us. That's why you found me crying when we first met. I get emotional every time I think about how they stole our way of life and left us with nothing. The only thing he can't take from us is our hope, the hope that one day you would come to save us. We can all rest easy now that you're here."

"Now that I'm here? Who exactly do you think I am?" Samuel asks, his mouth agape.

"You still don't get it, do you? You were brought here to conquer the beast and restore things to the way they were before his reign of terror." She speaks with resolve, which heightens Samuel's anxiety.

He panics. "But princess, it can't be me. There must be some mistake." Samuel isn't ready for such a huge responsibility. "I'm just a boy. I'm no hero."

"Wrong, Samuel. You *are* a hero. Our hero. You just don't know it yet." Izadora points again at the wall, tracing the timeline with her tail. "This is your destiny. And you can't run away from your destiny. It always finds you in the end."

Lennox has been quiet during Izadora's speech, but he cannot keep his mouth shut any longer. "If I might interject for a brief moment, princess." He turns to speak to Samuel. "Tell me you're not seriously buying into all this? Destiny, hero, monsters...seriously? Come on!" he shouts, flailing his hands above his head.

"It's true, Lennox. This is Samuel's destiny," she says, annoyed by Lennox's disparaging comments. "Go on, tell him, Samuel. It's all right there etched on the wall in front of us."

Samuel is still doubtful. He needs more proof. He cannot let himself believe everything that he is told by someone he has just met. His mind is spinning, and the shock of everything that has happened since he touched the magical glowing red pearl is really piling up.

"I'm not sure what I believe anymore, princess," Samuel says wearily. He backs away from the wall. "I need a moment." Just then, the batteries in his flashlight die, leaving him to contemplate his fate in the dark.

Samuel feels he cannot live up to the expectations of Izadora and her people. He spent years living vicariously through the heroes he read about in adventure novels. He never once thought that one day he would be called upon to be a hero himself. Even if Izadora is telling the truth and the pictures on the wall are truly prophecies, he has no idea how to defeat an army.

The princess convinces Samuel and Lennox to come with her and speak directly with the Secret Council of Aquatania. Izadora trusts the council will dispel any doubts or concerns.

And so they swim to the secret hideout, the Aquatanians' only safe haven during the reign of Clatheron and the terror unleashed by his army of Malquars.

Glimmers of Hope

Hidden far outside the kingdom's walls, within the vast waters of Lake Aqueous, is an underwater cave. Its location is known only to a council of 12 Aquatanians, their most trusted guards and their closest friends and allies. Here, safely hidden, the Secret Council of Aquatania struggles to plot an end to the rule of Clatheron and his army of Malquars.

Other Aquatanians and friends of the kingdom, who managed to escape Clatheron's clutches during the Great Invasion, scattered throughout Lake Aqueous to their own hideouts. There they wait patiently for the council's word on when, and how, they will return to a kingdom no longer ruthlessly ruled by Clatheron.

Outside of the hideout, Izadora, Samuel and Lennox stand before a large boulder. It looks familiar to Samuel, but he cannot recall where he has seen it before.

Thump…thump…thump thump. Izadora knocks on the boulder. The pattern reminds Samuel of the knock he heard in his dream two nights ago.

"Aha. That's where I've seen this place before," he says softly. The memories come rushing back.

"What's that, Samuel? What are you mumbling?" asks Lennox.

"Nothing," he replies.

Izadora repeats the secret knock. Thump…thump…thump thump. The boulder slides to the left, revealing a hallway, and past it, a hidden room. Izadora instructs Samuel and Lennox to follow her. They enter cautiously, both expecting the worst. Samuel wonders why the princess would ask them so nonchalantly to follow her into a place they have never been before. Until now, they have done whatever Izadora commanded. But what if she is leading them into a trap? Maybe he and Lennox are a little too trusting of the princess. Samuel raises his guard.

The council members remain silent as their guests enter the hideout. Figlo, ten other council members and the king sit at a table in the center of the room. Although Figlo is not of the same species as the Aquatanians, he has earned his spot on the council because he is considered their most loyal protector and friend.

Samuel immediately recognizes the corked bottles hanging from the ceiling from his dream. Each is filled with bioluminescent fish, as are bottles resting on the council's meeting table, which is carved from a large boulder. The glowing fish swim in circles inside each bottle, faintly lighting the cavernous hall. Except for the table and some seats made from rocks, the room is somewhat barren. In two far corners, doorways are covered by hanging vines. Samuel examines the room carefully, taking note of potential escape exits just in case he and Lennox have to flee in a hurry.

"Whoa. What is this place?" asks Lennox, amazed by

the mystical appearance of the room and its inhabitants. He looks around and spots tiny schools of colorful fish hiding in small nooks along the cavern's walls, their beady eyes focused on Samuel and Lennox.

"It's a secret meeting place," Samuel whispers to Lennox. "Now stay close to me and don't touch anything," he says nervously.

"Should I be worried?" asks Lennox.

Samuel does not answer. Instead, he continues to follow Izadora cautiously toward the large table at the center of the room.

"This is him, sire," Figlo eagerly reveals to the king. With a flick of his tail, he signals Samuel to approach the council. Lennox latches onto Samuel's back, using him as a human shield. As they approach, the council members begin to whisper among themselves, putting the two guests on edge.

The king gets up slowly from the head of the table, swimming closer to Samuel to get a thorough look at the boy. The council continues to speak softly among themselves as the king swims toward Samuel.

He stands still, bracing himself as he lets the crowned creature poke and prod him. The king examines him as if he were the product of some kind of weird science experiment. First, the king lifts Samuel's arms and watches as they float back down to his waist. Next, he holds the back of Samuel's head with one hand and with the other pulls up his eyelids, one after the other. Finally, he grabs Samuel's upper and lower lips and pulls them apart to look inside his mouth.

"Say ahh," the king demands. Samuel opens wide, humoring the king. "Uh huh…I see." The king acts as if he is taking mental notes that he will later enter into a medical journal. The king then swims repeatedly around Samuel to explore every inch of his body.

"What's he doing to Samuel," Lennox asks Izadora.

"Izadora cannot contain herself any longer and begins laughing hysterically. "Very funny, father."

The king himself bursts into laughter, and the other members of the council chime in quickly. The room fills with cackling and snorts. Even the tiny fish hiding in the nooks of the cave's walls chuckle.

Baffled, Samuel and Lennox remain silent. But it is all a big joke at Samuel's expense, just a little humor intended to lighten the mood.

"I think he has had enough," Izadora says, putting an immediate stop to the teasing.

"Aw, come on, my sweet daughter. I'm just having a little fun with the boy," the king replies with a chuckle. Then the king's grin fades as he formally greets Samuel. "Welcome, Samuel. I am the King of Aquatania, Zedorious. It's a pleasure to have you in our home...well, temporary home," he says with a faint glint of hope in his eyes.

Samuel is at a loss for words. He's in shock when he realizes he is speaking to a real-life king. He never dreamed he would go from being a below-average boy to the full-blown guest of a king and his royal advisers.

"This can't really be happening to me. Can it?" Samuel thinks to himself. "Just stay cool. Hear them out. Hear whatever it is they have to say and then leave gracefully. I mean, it's not like they can hold me here against my will. Can they?"

Lennox is not in as much shock as Samuel. He seems to accept the fact that he is underwater listening to a bunch of unusual blue creatures chatter on about fate and hope. He is more focused on his stomach, which is grumbling from hunger.

"Now that we have finished with all these wonderful official introductions...I don't suppose you have something to eat?" Lennox asks as he rubs his tummy. Only he would think about food at a time like this.

"Of course. Please, sit." King Zedorious welcomes his guests to the long stone table. He snaps his fingers, and two council members rise quickly to offer their seats. Samuel and Lennox happily accept. Samuel sits down and places his backpack on the floor beside his seat. Lennox clumsily plops down in the seat next to him. Each member sitting at the table greets them with a welcoming nod while King Zedorious returns to his seat at the head of the table.

"Food for our guests," commands King Zedorious as he claps his hands. The two members who gave up their seats swim through one of the cave's vine-covered doorways to fetch something to eat. Within seconds, they return with two plates piled high with food, placing one plate directly in front of Samuel and the other in front of Lennox. The plates are filled with worm guts and green slop. Samuel, not particularly hungry, eats the green slop for energy before pushing his plate forward. Lennox, on the other hand, does not even look at his food before he tears into it like an excavating machine tearing new ground. He licks his plate clean, then moves on to Samuel's plate to finish his leftovers. Lennox's tongue licks every inch of both plates, making sure they are as clean as they were before food was placed on them.

"It's tasty, right?" asks the king. He is intrigued by Lennox's insatiable appetite. "I see you're a fan of worm guts."

"Worm what?" asks Lennox. His face turns even greener than usual.

Izadora licks her lips. "Worm guts. You're clearly a fan like I am. First, you rip the skin from the worm. Then, you mince up the insides and mix them with some green kelp and barnacles to add a little crunch. It's really quite tasty, don't you think?"

Lennox hocks up any traces of remaining food that hasn't passed through his gullet to the pit of his stomach. He spits chunks of food in every direction. The others watch as Lennox acts like a fool. They choose to ignore his bad manners and move on.

King Zedorious feels it is time to discuss the reason for Samuel's presence. "Let's get down to business, shall we," says the king, addressing Samuel, Lennox and the other council members. "So, Samuel, I'm assuming my daughter has shown you the Wall of Prophecies by now?"

"She has."

At first, Samuel's answers are succinct. The less he says, the quicker he feels he can leave. It is still a lot for him to take in, and he is not sure he belongs here.

"My friends," the king says to the council. "Samuel visited the Wall of Prophecies and glimpsed his future and the future of the Aquatanian race. Our entire world, as we know it, is in danger of extinction. This we know. Clatheron and his army destroyed our way of life. He captured Queen Mizbeth. He enslaved our loved ones, who now exist solely to gather Clatheron's next meal. He seized our homes and peaceful kingdom, where we once lived as hunters, gatherers and tradesmen. His reign of terror over our world cannot last. It shall not last! That is why we must take charge of our destiny for once and for all. The time has come for us to take a stand and reclaim what is rightfully ours. It is time to free our people and all those who depend on us. We must return to the kingdom where we lived in peace, harmony and happiness. We must restore our lives to the way they were before Clatheron's insidious rule!"

"But King Zedorious, he's too powerful and our numbers too few," says one of the members timidly. "What can we do?"

"Ahh, yes. What can we do? What it is that we...can...do?" King Zedorious turns toward Samuel. "I'm afraid that this is something only the boy can answer. Our destinies are entwined. It is up to him to find a way to defeat our enemies. That is why he has come here and why he has been summoned. What are your thoughts, boy?"

Samuel gulps loudly.

"I'm not sure what to say," he replies. Samuel is overwhelmed by the desperation he sees in the council members' faces. All he wants to do is swim away, return to his life on the surface and forget any of this ever happened. "A...a...are you sure I'm the one you've b...b...been waiting for?" he asks timidly.

Lennox interjects at the perfect time. "Listen up King... King...whatever your name is."

"King Zedorious," the ruler responds with a twinge of annoyance.

"Yes, of course, Your Royal Highney. As I was saying,

Samuel is not what you would call a hero. Somehow, you expect him to defeat your enemies, whom we know nothing about by the way, and restore your happiness and so forth." Lennox stands up and pulls Samuel to his feet. "Let's take a closer look at the boy whom you believe is destined to save your people."

He grabs Figlo's tail to use as a pointer. "Take notice of the boy's frail body. He's clearly underfed, and between you and me, he's not the most hygienic kid on the block." Figlo yanks his tail away from Lennox.

Samuel slaps Lennox on the back of the head. "Enough!" he scolds.

"What was that for?" Lennox asks as he rubs the hand print that Samuel left on his head. "I was only trying to help."

"Sit down, Lennox!" demands Samuel.

"But I…"

"I said sit!" barks Samuel, his nostrils flaring as he points toward Lennox's seat.

The princess releases a giggle and then covers her mouth with her hand to stifle her laughter. A humiliated Lennox lowers his chin down to his chest and returns to his seat. Samuel, taking quick breaths, returns to his seat to address the council.

"First of all, I'd like to apologize for my friend's rude behavior. Second, I'd like to thank all of you for your kindness. You've already done so much. You've fed us," he says, pointing to the empty plates on the table. "And…well, you've been very kind to say the least." Samuel nervously begins rubbing the back of his neck.

"You've already said they're kind," Lennox interjects.

Chapter Nine

Samuel shoots a peeved look at Lennox, then returns his gaze to the council. "As I was saying, I really wish I could help you. I'm just not sure I'm the right person for the job."

The council members' voices rise in anguish, the noise level reaching a point in which individual voices are drowned out by the cacophony. They are not sure why Samuel does not know what he can do to help them or why he decided not to try. But they are sure that what is written on the wall is true.

Samuel knows it is time to leave, but something inside him holds him back. He is torn between returning to the comfort of the lake house and finding out if he is really capable of saving an entire race. He yearns to find out more about the Aquatanians. He knows that Grandpa and his parents, if they were still alive, would want Samuel to do the right thing and help the Aquatanians in any way possible. Even so, he feels powerless.

"Quiet down, everyone!" the king demands, slamming his royal staff against the table. The members continue to debate Samuel's resistance, ignoring their leader's command. King Zedorious slams his fist and staff on the table. "I said quiet!" His eyes narrow as he clenches his jaw. Silence fills the room.

The king turns his attention back to Samuel. "I know you have a lot of questions, and these questions have filled you with doubts about your ability to save us."

Samuel nods in agreement.

The king continues. "We can at least agree that you're curious. You haven't fled. And the fact that you're still here and willing to hear us out, well, that to me speaks volumes."

Samuel tilts his head to the side and raises his eyebrows,

willing to listen a little bit more. "Please, Your Majesty. Continue."

"Thank you, Samuel," the king replies, acknowledging the respect that Samuel has shown him. "This is your destiny. Of that I'm sure. That's why I don't question your presence here today. I know in my heart of hearts that whatever has drawn you here is no accident. This meeting and the challenges that follow are part of your destiny. As for now, you must be patient. You must continue to feed your curiosity. The answers you seek will find resolution in due time."

King Zedorious senses that he is beginning to reach Samuel because the boy is still listening intently. He might not believe that he is capable of heroic feats, but soon he will.

"And what if the boy fails?" asks another member. "What will become of us?"

"Then I'm afraid we're all doomed," King Zedorious responds, lowering his head.

Gasps rise from the council members. Several members whimper, while others wipe their noses to suppress their sniffles.

Then King Zedorious lifts his head from his chest and says, "Promise me one thing, Samuel?"

"That depends," he responds, leaning forward in his chair.

"Promise me you'll meet with the Oracle. It's she who has the answers you seek. And it's she who will set you on the righteous path."

"Is she far from here?" asks Lennox as if he has somewhere more important to go.

"Not very," responds Izadora, gently biting her lip as she anxiously awaits Samuel's decision.

Chapter Nine

Samuel is unsure what he will gain from meeting the Oracle. He begins to think about his life before Pearl Cave remembering the overwhelmingly empty void that perhaps this challenge could help fill. When he is not being bullied by kids at school or struggling with the death of his parents, Samuel feels depressed about his lack of friends. But now, for the first time in his life, someone – a whole species – is looking to him for help. It feels good to be needed, and he is not in any real danger, at least not yet. Not sure why, he knows deep down inside that this is what he is supposed to do.

"Fine. I'll go. But I can't promise the Oracle will change how I feel," he warns.

"Thank you, Samuel. You've made me very happy. You've made us all very happy." The council applauds. "This is the right decision. I promise," adds the king with a wide grin.

"Wait. Just one second. Don't I have a say in this whole thing?" Lennox asks Samuel.

"Shush, Lennox!" Samuel places a hand over Lennox's mouth. "Trust me," he whispers so the others in the room cannot hear him. But the others are busy clapping and do not notice them arguing.

Zedorious then instructs Figlo to take Samuel and Lennox to the Oracle. "Please make sure they arrive safely," Zedorious says.

"Will do, sire," Figlo replies.

The princess then stands up, takes a deep breath, and turns to her father. "If Figlo is going, then so am I," she says sternly.

A hush falls over the chambers.

"Not if I have anything to say about it!" announces King Zedorious.

"Father, I'm old enough to take care of myself. I'm the one who found the boy and I'll be the one to help him find his way. I want mother back just as much as you do. Besides, no one knows Lake Aqueous like I do."

She has a good point. Izadora has been swimming off the the radar for years. She has learned every nook and cranny from the clear waters by the lake house all the way to Pearl Cave and then some. If anyone knows how to reach the Oracle without being detected by Malquars, it is Izadora.

"Daughter, please understand my concerns. I can't bear to lose you like I lost your mother. If something were to happen to you, I'd never forgive myself."

"Sire, if I may," Figlo interjects. "The princess has extensive knowledge of Lake Aqueous. More importantly, I would give my life before I ever let an enemy lay a hand on her."

King Zedorious takes a moment to consider their request. He knows she is stubborn and will surely sneak off. At least if Figlo is by her side, she will be protected.

"If I let you go, you must promise never to leave Figlo's sight," King Zedorious says to his daughter.

Izadora jumps with excitement. "Yes, father. Cross my gills."

"And promise to stay safe!" He grabs her cheeks and kisses her forehead.

"Yes, of course, father."

"Then it's settled. But before you head out, there's something I need to discuss with Samuel in private."

King Zedorious asks Samuel to accompany him to a back room. "I have something for you, something very near and dear to me. Something I think you might find useful."

Samuel follows the king into the room where the Aquatanians prepared the meals. The room is filled with mounds of worm guts, kelp and hundreds of fishing hooks that fell to the bottom of the lake with bait still attached.

"Those hooks look mighty sharp! They almost look like swords," Samuel thinks to himself. He breifly tries to determine why the Aquatanians hold on to the hooks after they remove the bait for food. King Zedorious quickly distracts Samuel's mind from wandering any further by moving a rock that covers a hole in a far corner of the room. He reaches into the hole up to his elbow and pulls out the most beautiful sword Samuel has ever laid eyes on. Other than images that he has seen on television or in books, Samuel has never seen the real thing in person, so this is a real treat.

"I hold in my hand the Royal Sword of Luminescence. It has been in my family for centuries," King Zedorious says.

Samuel admires the fine craftsmanship. He can tell that the sword is intended for use by a mighty warrior. With a long sharp edge, it can slice through the toughest body armor. Below the sword's wing-shaped hand guard is a silver-tipped hilt. A radiant blue crystal is embedded in the pommel, or knob, at the tip of the hilt.

"It's a fine sword, the finest in Lake Aqueous," says the king, raising the sword high as he thrusts out his chest.

"May I hold it?" Samuel asks, his eyes aglow.

"Of course, but do be careful. The sword is extremely sharp," King Zedorious warns.

Samuel takes the sword in his right hand. He tosses it quickly back and forth from his right hand to his left and back again. The sword is heavy at first, but Samuel adapts to its weight rather quickly. "It's remarkable," he says.

"Please repeat after me," King Zedorious requests. "Luminous."

"Luminous," Samuel repeats. Nothing happens.

"Try it again. This time, from the diaphragm, my boy." The king pushes on Samuel's stomach, causing Samuel to blurt out the magical word with more emphasis.

"LUMINOUS!"

The sword flickers, then glows brightly. When the sword's light is at full strength, Samuel squints. Everyone in the next room can see the bright light streaming through the openings around the closed door. Then the glow quickly fades out.

"Spectacular, even if only for a few seconds," Samuel says, his shoulders drooping with disappointment.

"Don't worry, my boy. You'll get better at it in due time," assures King Zedorious. "You cannot lift yourself from darkness without the proper light to guide your way."

Samuel hands the Royal Sword of Luminescence back to King Zedorious, but the king declines.

"Please, I insist. Take it," King Zedorious says, pushing Samuel's hand down. "This will help you on your journey. Remember to take good care of the sword, and the sword will take good care of you when needed."

King Zedorious then hands Samuel a leather belt with a holster to hold the sword. Wraping the belt around his waist and fastening it tightly, he uses the very last notch to secure the belt around his skinny body.

"I'll return the sword just as I received it, without a scratch. I promise. Just one question. If I get it to work, how do I shut it off?"

"Hee hee hee. Why the same way you turned it on, my boy."

Samuel repeats the magic word "luminous." And just like that, the sword flickers but fizzles out shortly thereafter. Slightly discouraged, Samuel decides to try again later and slides the sword into its holster.

"Now go with haste. Time is of the essence," commands King Zedorious.

"I'll try not to fail you, Your Majesty. And I'll keep an open mind."

This is Samuel's chance to prove to everyone that he truly is capable of accomplishing something of great consequence. From this day forward, Samuel will no longer be the child who is picked on or pushed around by bullies. From this day forward, he will embark on his quest to become a hero.

A Kingdom of Despair and Desolation

Before Clatheron imposed his brutal tyranny, there stood a beautiful underwater kingdom called Aquatania ruled by the peaceful Aquatanians, but you already know that. What you do not know is that the kingdom was once a place within the vast waters of Lake Aqueous where all of the friendly inhabitants were welcome to exchange goods and share happy times. This was a magical place, a shining symbol of freedom, trustworthiness and equality. It was a safe haven where sunlight from the heavens penetrated down to the depths of the lakebed, illuminating all areas within the kingdom's protective walls with a soft, pleasant light.

In the center of the kingdom is the Great Castle, which was constructed in ancient times from massive, rough-hewn stones. Long ago, flags emblazoned with the Aquatanian Crest of Unity undulated in the water's current as they hung from the castle's ceiling and from poles along the walls. A sense of pride used to fill the hearts of community members as the flags rippled in harmony with the waves.

The Aquatanian flag is white with a blue circle in the center, and in the middle of the circle is a golden heart. The emblem appeared throughout the kingdom to remind everyone of the peace and goodwill that the kingdom extended to all. The Crest of Unity welcomed everyone with open arms, providing them with a sense of security. Those who entered the Kingdom of Aquatania did so with good intentions and a heart of gold.

From two lofty watchtowers perched high on cliffs inside of the kingdom's walls, guards could peer for miles into the distance. King Zedorious always stationed one in each tower to spot intruders. If the kingdom were to come under attack, the royal guards would sound the alarm and notify the troops to prepare for battle.

The alarm had never been sounded before, not even on the fateful day that Clatheron and his army of Malquars invaded Aquatania. When the kingdom was besieged, the guards assigned to the watchtowers were absent from their stations. They had joined others from all over Lake Aqueous to commemorate the birth of Princess Izadora. Large creatures, small ones, tall inhabitants, short ones. All were friendly and in a celebratory mood. Capitol Hall was filled with laughter and joy.

The kingdom's citizens danced and sang to the lively sounds of seashell horns and drums made from pots and pans found in wreckages scattered along the lake floor. No one gave it a second thought when the watchtower guards participated in the festivities, leaving the kingdom vulnerable to attack.

***

When Clatheron was just a baby, he was taken in by the Aquatanians and cared for as if he were a native. Much like Samuel, he too grew up without his parents, but for very different reasons. Clatheron's mother and father decided to abandon him and disappeared without any explanation as to why they left him behind. One day, two patrolling units found Clatheron at the foot of the kingdom's gates in a baby basket with a simple note pinned to a blanket woven from kelp. When they first discovered him, the guards were not sure what to do with Clatheron, so they quickly brought the baby to King Zedorious and Queen Mizbeth. Zedorious read the note out loud to his wife, "Please take care of our baby as if he were your own." The king and queen, being kind and generous in nature, did exactly as the note asked, without question.

Unfortunately, as Clatheron grew older, other children his age began to poke fun at his awkward size, weight and ghastly features. The adults tried their best to stop other children from picking on Clatheron, but whenever they turned their backs, some of the children would tease and taunt him. There were other children his age that were not full-blooded Aquatanians, but none were as unique and grotesque in appearance as Clatheron. This made him feel like an unwanted outsider. Eventually, the teasing and abandonment of his biological parents took a toll on Clatheron, causing him to grow coldhearted and isolate himself, often hiding from the other children to avoid ridicule.

Throughout his childhood, Clatheron blamed those around him for his misfortune. When he was old enough to do so, he decided to run away from it all. He vowed that one day he would raise an army, return to the kingdom and seek his revenge on all those who ruined his childhood.

When the elders discovered that Clatheron had run away, it was already too late. They sent search parties out into the open waters of Lake Aqueous to try and retrieve him, but they failed and were unable to track him down. Some inhabitants of Aquatania suspected that one day Clatheron might return to the kingdom, and that if he did, it would not be on good terms.

That brings us back to the birth of Princess Izadora and her celebration that took place in the Capitol Hall. Halfway through the festivities, a dark cloud formed over the kingdom. The sunlight that always had shone upon the kingdom suddenly disappeared. Everyone grew quiet. Everyone, except King Zedorious, assumed a storm was approaching. They were half right. A storm was brewing, only it was one of unprecedented violence and mass destruction, the kind from which they might never recover. Little did they know that Clatheron had returned with a vengeance and spent his time away growing in resentment and anger toward his tormentors and raising an evil army of Malquars bent on retaliation. Wherever Clatheron and his army went, darkness followed.

The merriment came to an abrupt halt. At that moment, before the gates came crashing down, King Zedorious sensed danger and ordered two guards to take the newborn princess and her mother the queen to a hidden cave outside of the kingdom's walls. His instincts told him that he had very little time to evacuate the entire kingdom, but he at least could withdraw the council and other close allies to what would become the secret hideout in which they would live for years.

Zedorious was right. Immediately after the king issued his command, Clatheron and his Malquar soldiers crashed through the kingdom's gates on chariots pulled by long, snake-like black lampreys, with sharp teeth that looked like those of an alligator.

With overwhelming numbers and the element of surprise on the Malquars' side, Clatheron himself did not need to take to the battlefield. All he had to do was give the order and watch the kingdom fall as if he were watching the action on a movie theater screen.

If Clatheron had participated in the battle, it would have taken six Aquatanian soldiers to bring him down due to his size and strength, and they would have taken him out of commission only for a few moments. Wearing bottle-cap helmets and body armor, the spear-wielding barbarian army stormed the castle walls, destroying the unity and serenity that had been long enjoyed. The Malquars replaced the Aquatanian flags with their own, which are as black as Clatheron's reign is dark. In the center of the flags is the white outline of a long-fanged piranha.

Chariots cut through the crowds, firing cannons filled with jagged mussel-shell fragments that indiscriminately injured innocent bystanders in the line of fire. The surprise attack overwhelmed the Aquatanian army, which was caught completely off-guard. By the time troops gathered to fight back, it was too late.

During what later became known as the Great Invasion, many innocent children and adults were taken captive and thrown into the Coral Jail, which never had been used before. Some citizens escaped, although they were forced to live a life on the run.

Somehow during the chaos, the two guards assigned to escort the princess and the queen to safety became separated. The guard entrusted with the newborn princess made it safely to the secret hideout, but Clatheron's army captured

Queen Mizbeth and her escort. They tortured the guard for many moons in a futile attempt to learn the location of the secret refuge. He died bravely without betraying his people. Clatheron knew that if a lowly guard would not divulge the secret, neither would Queen Mizbeth. She was faithful to Zedorious; not even torture would break her spirit.

The king and his subjects fought valiantly for as long as they could, holding off the Malquar's until he knew his loved ones had escaped beyond the kingdom's walls and out into Lake Aqueous. When he realized he had lost the battle, Zedorious retreated to the secret hideout, leaving behind a kingdom now ruled by ruthless oppressors who would never compromise.

When King Zedorious reached the sanctuary, he expected to meet his daughter and wife, but to his dismay, his queen never arrived. For weeks after the attack, he looked hopefully at the hideout's entrance, waiting for Mizbeth, but she never showed. Distraught, the king directed all of his love and affection for Mizbeth to Izadora.

The kingdom fell in just one day. Since then, sunlight no longer bathes the kingdom in a warm glow. Clatheron sits on a throne in dark chambers inside of the castle, waiting gleefully for anyone with the audacity to challenge his rule.

***

"Where's that worthless servant of mine?" asks Clatheron as he impatiently sits on his throne, clicking his sharp pointy fingernails against the throne's gold armrests. Click Click Click Clack. Click Click Click Clack.

"SQUUUUIIINNNCH!" Clatheron shouts, summoning his servant with a beastly growl. His voice stirs the waters inside the castle, flapping all of the flags hanging from the walls and ceilings. The white outlines of the flags' long-fanged piranhas undulate as if the piranhas were swimming in search of prey.

Squinch is not the only one who fears Clatheron; all of his minions are terrorized by their mercurial leader's explosive temper and frightening appearance. He has gigantic red hands, razor-sharp fingernails and two long tentacles attached to the ribs of his enormous body, which is held up by nine spider-like legs with pointy tipped feet. No one dares challenge Clatheron's merciless wrath unless they want to meet their maker.

Because of his diminutive size, Squinch is way too scrawny to be a soldier. He is even smaller than the average Aquatanian, who is half the size of the average Malquar. So Squinch was forced to become Clatheron's personal assistant.

Squinch approaches his master with caution. His breath deepens the closer he swims toward the throne. He never knows whether Clatheron will be in a good mood or a bad one; Squinch always assumes he is in a foul state. "Yes, my king. How may I be of assistance?" he asks with a shake. He always shudders in Clatheron's presence.

"Can I ask you a question?" Clatheron asks cunningly so he can lure Squinch closer to the throne. He softens his voice just enough to make his servant believe he is in a good mood. However, the tactic is not very effective as Squinch stays on edge out of habit.

"But of course, sire," he replies, lips trembling. Squinch

slowly inches towards Clatheron, slouching with his head hung low.

"Come closer. I don't bite…most of the time," the evil ruler says with a smile, revealing rows of sharp yellow-stained teeth.

Squinch obeys but tries his best to maintain enough distance from Clatheron so he can flee at a moment's notice. He stands at the foot of the throne, nervously anticipating a verbal lashing.

"Now be completely honest, Squinch. Do I look fat to you?" Clatheron asks, stroking Blob's head. Blob is the evil ruler's pet, which often sits on his lap without a care in the lake. He spends most of his day purring contently while his squishy body is caressed. His name accurately describes his appearance; he is a yellow-and-orange striped, slimy, simple-minded gelatinous blob. He constantly licks his face near his wavy lips, probably in search of any food that he might have left on his face from an earlier meal.

"Fat? Why of course not, sire. Wh…Wh…Why would you ask such a thing?" Squinch asks with a noticeable stutter.

"Are you questioning my question?" Clatheron's eyes widen and bulge.

Squinch shakes his head from side to side. "No, of course not, sire."

Clatheron rolls his eyes, which then return to their normal evil stare. "As I was saying," he continues to speak softly. "If I were fat, it would mean I ate well. If I ate well, I would be fat and wouldn't have to ask you if I looked fat. So why do you think I'm asking you if I look fat?"

Squinch looks down at the floor, his eyes darting about.

"Gosh. I don't know, sire. I'm not as smart as you. Please, tell me." He braces himself for what might come next.

"I'm asking because I want to be fat, but how can I get fat when SOMEONE AS LAZY AND WORTHLESS AS YOU CAN'T GET MY SLAVES TO CATCH ENOUGH WORMS FOR ME TO DEVOUR!" Clatheron thunders. He squeezes Blob, who lets out an ear-splitting screech.

Squinch falls to his knees out of fear and from the pain inflicted by Blob's yelp.

"Look at me, Squinch," Clatheron says pointing to his ribs with one of his tentacles. Squinch continues looking down at the floor. "LOOK AT ME, I SAID!" His roar echoes throughout the castle, striking fear in all who are within earshot of his thunderous bellow.

Squinch jerks his chin up from his chest, his eyelids blinking rapidly. "I'm look...look…looking, sire," he responds as his teeth begin to chatter from fear.

"I want you to understand. No, I need you to understand that I'm withering away into nothing. Now, is that what you want? Really? Is that what you want for your beloved master?" Clatheron leans back in his throne and pets Blob gently.

"Of cour...cour...course not, Your Ma...Ma...Majesty," replies Squinch.

Clatheron continues his rant. "Do you want your master to become as scrawny as you are? What will everyone say about me, Squinch, if I'm nothing but skin and bones? My minions will start talking about me behind my back, saying things like, "Why should we follow him?"" He leans forward again. "Next thing you know, I'm the laughing stock of the kingdom, and no one will respect me. No one. Is that what you want? Do you want me to be small, skinny and worthless like you?" He leans back in his throne.

The complaint is nothing but a blatant lie and Squinch knows it. Clatheron is not starving; he is the most well-fed being in the lake. His needs are met before anyone else's. In fact, most Malquars are perplexed at how his massive body can be held up by only nine spider-like legs. And Clatheron's rear end just keeps getting wider and wider. No Malquar would ever stand up to him.

"Of course that's not what I want. You still look amazing, sire. You're a picture-perfect depiction of health, power and greatness." Squinch puts his hands together to beg Clatheron for forgiveness. "Please. Allow me the chance to make this right, my liege."

"THEN MAKE IT RIGHT AND STOP WASTING MY TIME, YOU STUTTERING SIMPLETON. GET OFF YOUR KNEES AND GET YOUR SCRAWNY BUTT BACK TO WORK!" Clatheron shouts. Blob lets out a devious laugh.

"Right away, my king. Right away." Squinch tries to leave, but his body is frozen with fear. He cannot get one leg to move in front of the other.

"Well...WHAT ARE YOU WAITING FOR!" Clatheron screams as he wraps one of his tentacles around his assistant's neck and tosses him through the doorway leading to Capitol Hall.

Squinch swims off to the worm vault, upset again at the way he has been treated. No one takes him seriously. The soldiers scoff at him as he passes by. The guards tease and taunt him about his stature. He has grown tired of being treated like a bottom feeder and wants to be appreciated for his services and respected for his brain. He wants to be recognized as someone important. However, he knows that as long as he remains under Clatheron's thumb, he will never get the respect or recognition he deserves.

Though the others are unaware, Squinch never approved of Clatheron's treacherous plan to take over the kingdom. At first he sympathized for the way Clatheron was treated, but now fears what Clatheron has become and he feels bad for the good-hearted Aquatanians who suffered during the Great Invasion. It was never Squinch's desire for anyone to be enslaved on that dark day. In fact, he tried to save a few himself but bowed to the inevitable.

As Squinch approaches the worm vault, a large bubble emerges from a crack in the lake floor. He sees his reflection in the bubble, hating who stares back at him. At that moment, he feels numb. He cannot remember what it was like to feel alive inside. "Is this all there is?" he asks himself. "Is this how I'm supposed to live out the rest of my days? As a nothing, a nobody?" Squinch pokes the bubble with his claw, releasing his reflection from servitude. "My reflection can escape, but I'm trapped here forever."

Squinch stops in front of the worm vault's large, rusty door and reaches for the keys attached to his belt. The vault contains all of the worms that Clatheron's slaves toil to retrieve for him, including many that curiously fall from the sky loosely tied to some wire just when they are needed. He inserts a key into the keyhole and turns it clockwise while pulling down on the rusty handle with all his might. Though he struggles to open the door, Squinch eventually gets it to budge. As it opens, the hinges squeak, causing seemingly endless piles of live squirming worms to quiver when they realize they might become Clatheron's next meal.

"Take *him*!" squeaks one of the worms as he points to another next to him.

"No! Take *him*! I've got a family," begs the other.

Squinch reaches in and scoops up a claw full of live worms. In an act of defiance, he also picks a batch of decomposing worms that died of fright and places them in a brown pouch attached to his belt. Then he spits into the pouch. Clatheron will not know the difference once the worms are minced into tiny pieces and mixed with kelp.

Squinch struggles to pull the rusty door closed with one claw while holding a handful of live worms with the other. With his empty claw, he locks the door.

"Go now, little ones. You're free!" Squinch says as he opens his claw to release the live worms. All of them scatter but one. It looks up at Squinch with grateful eyes. "Go, I said! Are you deaf? Don't you understand? You're free now!" Squinch shouts.

The little worm does not listen. Instead, it swims up to Squinch's cheek and gives him a warm kiss.

Squinch begins to cry. "Thank you, my little friend." He pats the worm on the head. "But you really must go now."

The worm wraps his little pink tail around Squinch's claw and tries to pull Squinch along with him, insisting that he follow him to freedom.

"Oh, how I wish I could join you little buddy, but this is the life that fate has forced me to live. Now go before someone sees us and we get caught. GO!" shouts Squinch, pointing the way to freedom.

The little worm rubs its body against Squinch's cheek and speeds off.

Squinch hopes that one day someone will come along and set him free too. But freedom is not in his future, until Clatheron meets his demise. Squinch feels trapped, but maybe he needs only to look within himself to achieve the freedom he longs for.

The All-Knowing Oracle

As Samuel, Izadora, Lennox and Figlo approach the Oracle's lair, Samuel cannot help but feel a sense of déjà vu. There is something familiar about the way the rocks rest on the muddy lake floor and the way the plant life sprouts from recognizable nooks. Even the wooden posts supporting a dock in the distance seem familiar, as if he had swum in this area before. Only Lennox notices the look of bewilderment on Samuel's face.

"What is it?" Lennox asks.

"It's this place. There's something about it." Samuel steadies his hand on Lennox's shoulder. "Stay with the others. I'll catch up with you in a minute."

Samuel swims swiftly to the surface and pokes his head above the water. Sure enough, in the distance, he can see the lake house, which is much larger than he remembers it. Then again, everything above the surface looks gigantic after his transformation into a smaller version of himself. Samuel concludes that they are heading toward his boat dock, which means that the Oracle lives somewhere beneath it. He is reminded of just how far from home and Grandpa he is right now. Samuel is curious if his grandfather is sad and misses him.

Plunging back underwater, Samuel rejoins the group. He wonders if the Oracle always resided under the dock. When he was growing up, this was one of the few places where he had been allowed to swim. Grandpa would supervise as Samuel swam around the boat dock. In all those years of swimming, he never noticed any peculiar creatures roaming around. A large fish, however, did frequent the dock from time to time. "Maybe that's the Oracle," Samuel thinks to himself.

"Do you guys hear something?" Samuel asks, cupping his hand to his ear. He hears faint voices as he swims closer to the dock. It sounds like a barbershop quartet singing in melodic harmony. Grandpa used to sing in a barbershop quartet with a group of his buddies. Each man in the group would sing in a different pitch and together they harmonized.

Samuel smiles as he looks toward the dock. He has to admit that whoever or whatever is singing sounds pretty decent, almost as good as Grandpa and his singing group.

"Yes, of course, the voices," Izadora responds. "What you're hearing are the singing mussels."

"Look closely at the wooden posts at the end of the dock," Figlo says as he points to the splintered posts.

"Well, that's something you don't see every day!" Samuel exclaims with a chuckle. Lo and behold, the posts are encrusted with tiny mussels whose little muscular arms protrude from their sparkling silver shells. "I've never met singing mussels before. Then again, I've never had gills and webbed feet before either," Samuel says to himself. "I guess this shouldn't be too hard to believe." He shrugs his shoulders, accepting yet another strange encounter with the mystical inhabitants of Lake Aqueous.

Figlo instructs everyone to stop at the end of the dock and wait for the mussels to finish their welcome song. Lennox rolls his eyes, finding all of this to be somewhat ridiculous.

"Hello. How are you? Hello. Hello. How are you? Hello. In order to pass, you must answer fast. Why are you here... here...here?" The mussels sing in unison. There are approximately 25 of them, sparkling magically and reflecting the comforting, orange glow of the summer sunset.

"They're so adorable," Lennox says, reaching his hand out to pet one of the mussels, which unexpectedly jumps off the post and tries to bite his hand. He quickly retracts his arm into his shell before he is bitten.

"Whoa! Back up, you cannibals!" screams Lennox. His brow furrows, and his pale green lips tighten in anger.

"Careful!" warns the princess. "They mean business. One bite and you'll lose a finger, or two, or five."

"Yeah. Thanks a lot. I can see that for myself. How about a little forewarning next time?" Lennox shakes his head in annoyance. His near-death experience gives him another reason to engage in melodramatic behavior.

Samuel, the princess and Figlo struggle to hold back their laughter.

"These are the singing guardians," explains the princess. "They're the all-knowing Oracle's muscle, if you will. They protect her. Once they latch onto your skin, it's almost impossible to get them off. Their beauty is meant to attract enemies who are unaware of their ability to kill. As you've found out, they'll lure you in and, without hesitation, attack intruders with a viciousness that belies their cuteness."

Figlo then turns to the singing mussels to answer their

first question. "We're here to see the Oracle. I've brought her the boy."

"The boy, the boy, the boy, the boy" the singing mussels sing in perfect harmony.

The lead singer detaches itself from the wooden post and sings, "I'll be right back after these messages." He speeds off under the dock to inform the Oracle of her visitors' arrival. Seconds later, he returns and pulls from his shell what looks like a tuning fork. He smacks the tuning fork against the exterior of his shell. It produces a humming noise with a steady pitch. Samuel has seen this device before and knows it is used by singers to stay on pitch.

The lead singer then launches into another song. "Before you go, I want you to know, the Oracle has agreed to see you. Beware of your fate, her lives she has eight, it best be that way when you leave her."

"We come in peace, my friends," states Figlo, reassuring the guardians that no harm will come to the Oracle.

"Her lives she has eight. What does that mean?" asks Samuel, scratching his temple.

"Be patient, and you'll find out," Figlo replies. "I'm afraid the rest of us must remain out here. The Oracle will want to speak with you alone." He pats Samuel on the back and pushes him in the direction of the Oracle's lair. Izadora wishes him good luck and waves goodbye. She can hardly wait to hear what the Oracle will say about saving her mother, her species and the entire kingdom.

The mussels let Samuel pass without harm. His nerves are on edge because he does not know what to expect when he enters. He takes a deep breath, looks over his shoulder at his companions and presses on.

It is dark under the dock, and Samuel can barely see where he is going. Surprisingly, little sunlight seeps through the cracks between the wooden planks of the dock above. He follows the path of the planks, which lead him to a hole in the lakeshore. He enters the hole, which leads to a spacious well-lit room. The light comes from little tiny glowing balls floating almost motionless in the water. Everywhere Samuel looks, he sees books stacked high, piles of junk and weird contraptions. As he reaches out to touch a glowing metal sphere, which sits on an algae-covered stone countertop, Samuel knocks over a pile of books. The books crash to the floor. Behind the books is the Oracle, a grayish heavyset catfish. On the tip of her nose, she wears spectacles made from the broken bottoms of two glass soda bottles. The two round pieces of glass are held in place by braided twigs. Her glasses almost take up her entire face, reminding Samuel of Grandpa. She appears ancient and disheveled, her milky white whiskers flowing from her upper lip all the way down to her age-worn tail. She is wearing a long, flowing purple-plankton robe that covers most of her silver scale-covered body.

"Please. Don't touch that," she says in a soft voice.

"Oh…whoops…my sincerest apologies." Samuel places his hands in his pockets to stay out of trouble. "Wait a second...are you the Oracle?" he asks with a dazed look.

"That I am. Why? Am I not what you expected?" She swims close enough to Samuel that her whiskers tickle his chin, causing his body to twitch.

"A catfish?" he asks with a chuckle.

"I don't get it? What's so funny?" asks the Oracle as she

pushes her glasses from the bridge of her nose toward her eyes with her fin.

Samuel clears his throat. "Um...well...It's just that everyone I've met so far has looked like something from a dream that I had…almost mystical looking. Then, I meet you. I guess I thought the Oracle would be the most mystical looking creature of all, not a fish."

"So sorry to disappoint you. But sometimes the most effective approach is not always the most obvious choice," she says. The Oracle begins coughing violently. She covers her mouth with her fin.

"I didn't mean to offend you ma'am," he replies, realizing how rude he has been.

The Oracle continues coughing harshly.

"Gosh. Are you okay?" Samuel asks patting her on the back. "I'd ask if you want some water, but considering where we are, I don't see the point."

The Oracle stops coughing long enough to answer him.

"I'm okay," she says with a final cough as she hocks up a hairball. "Ahh. There it is. I've been working on that pesky thing all morning. I do, however, appreciate your concern."

Samuel flinches at the sight of the gross hairball. "Anytime," he says, wrinkling his nose in disgust.

She signals Samuel to take a seat at the large stone table in the center of the room. She spends a few minutes clearing off what appears to be a slew of useless junk: old car parts, clock gears, abandoned kitchen tools and broken bottles. The Oracle swims to the corner of the room and begins rummaging through another pile of junk that includes a nonfunctioning boat motor, broken fishing poles, rusty reels and more books. Various objects from the collection fly in every direction while she mumbles repeatedly, "Where is it? Where is that darn thing?" When the Oracle surfaces from behind the junk, she is holding a pot full of fish bones.

"A little help, Samuel, if you please." She struggles to lift the heavy pot onto the table.

"How do you know my name? I don't believe I ever mentioned it."

"I'm the Oracle, my dear. I know everything." She winks. "Now come over here and help me with this. It weighs a ton."

"Of course." Samuel lifts the pot with one hand and places it on the table.

"What a strong boy you are. Strength like that is hard to come by." She signals for him to return to his seat. "Now, let's get to it, shall we?"

The Oracle places Samuel's hand on one side of the pot and her fin on the opposite side. Together, they shake it back and forth until she dumps the pot's contents on the table. The fish bones scatter in a pattern that seems random to Samuel but seems to mean something to the Oracle.

"How peculiar," she says, examining the bones closely. "Oh, no! What's this?" she adds with apprehension. Her eyes widen with surprise.

"What? What do you see?" The anxiety in her tone makes Samuel uneasy.

She waits for the right moment and begins to laugh. "Just as I thought. What we have here..." She pauses. Samuel hangs on her every word, eager to hear the results of the Oracle's odd ritual. "What we have here...are a bunch of bones spread out on a table." Samuel looks puzzled.

"Gotcha!" she says with a playful giggle.

It takes a moment for Samuel to realize that she is only toying with him. "What's with all you underwater creatures and your jokes? That was plain mean," Samuel responds as he folds his arms.

"I had you going though, didn't I? What kind of Oracle would I be if I didn't have any fun from time to time," she says as she clears the pot and bones off the table.

"Does that mean you can't help me, then?" Samuel asks in desperation, unfolding his arms.

"I'm a little out of practice, but I can help you if you're willing to help yourself."

"Thank goodness," he replies with a sigh of relief.

"As you can see from all of the junk lying around here, I'm more of an inventor these days than an oracle. It pays the bills, but my true passion is inventing. Oh, how I love to create new and interesting gadgets." She begins to go on and on about her contraptions but notices that Samuel is growing impatient and wants answers.

"I hate to be pushy, but I need to know why I'm here." Samuel picks up a rusty horn-shaped apparatus. With a look of intrigue, he rotates the object in his hands, trying to determine what it is or used to be.

"I know. I know. We're getting to that. The Oracle is supposed to guide those who are lost, and you're as lost as a runaway catfish." She rips the rusty horn from Samuel's hands and places it back on top of one of her junk piles. "I guess it's time to begin."

Samuel settles down into a chair, anxiously awaiting answers. He twiddles his thumbs.

"I'm assuming you've seen the wall?" she asks.

"Yes, I have."

"Then you already know what it is you have to do."

"That's it? That's your advice? I don't understand," he replies with a hint of frustration.

"All you have to do now is simply choose," she replies.

"Choose? Choose what?"

"Choose to find what is already inside of you," she answers with a wide smile.

Samuel has no idea what the Oracle is talking about. In fact, he gets the feeling she is not going to be much help at all.

Though the Oracle is old and her eyesight is fading, she is not blind. She can tell from Samuel's posture and facial expressions that he is having trouble understanding her words of wisdom.

"Let me explain," she says. "You chose to answer my call when I visited you in the tree house."

"That was you?" He had a sneaking suspicion that he had heard the Oracle's voice that day in the tree house. Before meeting her in person, he thought it was his mother's voice, but the minute the Oracle asked him not to touch the glowing sphere, he thought her voice sounded familiar.

"Of course that was me!" she replies. "As I was saying, you chose to follow your instincts and find Pearl Cave. You chose to listen to King Zedorious and seek me out. Soon, you'll choose to display the great courage that we all know you possess and become the hero that you're destined to become."

"But that still doesn't explain how I'm supposed to defeat Clatheron and regain the kingdom for the Aquatanians."

"Don't you see? It's right in front of your face. The most important choice you have to make is accepting the responsibility to lead your new friends to victory. Accept this and you'll succeed." She makes it seem so simple, but Samuel is not quite yet sold.

"I'm afraid there's one more thing," she adds.

"What is it?"

"You have to make the most dangerous choice of all."

"Which is?" he asks with eyebrows raised.

"You must choose the impossible journey." She shudders at the mere mention of his quest.

"If it's impossible, then why would I choose to accept it?"

"Because of what lies at the end of it," the Oracle says.

Samuel knows from the way the conversation is going that he will have to ask what is at the end of the journey before she finishes explaining what's so impossible about it.

"And what lies at the end of this journey?"

"Impossible journey," she says, interrupting Samuel.

"Right. What lies at the end of this impossible journey?" he asks, moving his finger in a circle to get her to move the conversation along.

"At the end of the impossible journey is the Hall of Mirrors, which holds the Mirror of Truth. It's not easy to get to, and this journey has taken many lives, but there's always a chance that those seeking the right answers will survive. Understand, Samuel, that I'm here only to guide you in the right direction, the direction of the righteous path. It's the Mirror of Truth that will definitively answer your questions."

"I have a feeling I'm going to regret asking this, but has anyone ever survived the impossible journey?"

"Not exactly, but it just so happens that I've done extensive research on how to reach the Hall of Mirrors, and I believe I can get you there safely. Besides, you won't go it alone. You'll have your friends Figlo, the princess and Lennox to help you." She begins searching through a pile of books. "I know it's around here somewhere…Ahh, here it is." She pulls out an ancient-looking map tucked securely inside a frail notebook.

"See here," she says, pointing to the map. "It has diagrams and coordinates of a far-off place that resides in Lake Aqueous." At the top of the map, written in script, is the title, "The Impossible Journey."

"So encouraging," Samuel says, mocking the map's title.

"Never mind that," the Oracle says. "According to this map, the Hall of Mirrors is somewhere at the tip up here. Unfortunately, you and your friends will have to pass through many life-threatening obstacles to reach it. I can't tell you exactly where the Hall of Mirrors is because, even though I drew the map, I never got close enough to the Hall without… well, you know. Don't worry. My calculations should be correct as to the Hall's general whereabouts."

All Samuel can do is worry after hearing what the Oracle shared with him. "I see," he says, only slightly comforted in knowing that the Oracle made it back alive.

Then Samuel grows confused. "I thought you said no one has ever survived the impossible journey, and yet you returned." Before the Oracle can respond, Samuel realizes what the mussel meant about the Oracle having only eight lives. She must have had nine lives, lost one during the impossible journey and took it as a sign that she was never destined to complete it.

"Now I get it," he says as a light bulb goes off over his head, though it turns out to be one of the Oracle's glowing balls floating above him.

"If it's any comfort, there's one difference between you and me that gives you an advantage," the Oracle says while rubbing Samuel's back with her fin.

"And what's that? That I'm not a fish?" he asks.

"No. That you're the boy from the prophecy, and unlike me, you have a great team that will help you succeed on the impossible journey," the Oracle replies. "For these reasons, I know you can complete this quest."

"And if I decide to walk away from the challenge?" he asks.

"Well, you always have a choice in life, but will it be the right one? If you decide to walk away from this, you'll return to your normal life unchanged and unfulfilled. However, if you decide to go through with it, you must take each step without hesitation and with the utmost confidence. Dig deep and begin your journey wholeheartedly; otherwise you won't find the answers you seek, or worse, it could mark the end of your journey inside and out."

Such decisions are not to be taken lightly. The expectations for Samuel are high. After all he has heard and seen so far, he is beginning to believe that the king, the princess and everyone else in this upside-down world might actually be right about him. Is he just a visitor passing through, or was he sent here to put it all on the line to save the kingdom?

Samuel fears that something horrible might happen to him and Lennox. Grandpa already lost his daughter. What will happen if he loses his grandson too? What would

Grandpa say he should do? He always taught Samuel to be brave and trust his gut. Too bad his gut is all tied up in knots.

One thing that Samuel knows for sure is that in this world, he is someone special, someone with purpose, someone who is needed. He realizes he has already made his decision. He knows he has to follow this journey through to its end, whatever that end is.

"I'll do it," Samuel says, nodding his head.

"Wise decision, Samuel. You can't win the fight if you never step inside the ring," the Oracle says, clapping her fins with excitement.

She is proud of Samuel and is not afraid to acknowledge her appreciation with a hug. With little time to prepare, she releases Samuel from her embrace and begins to prep him for his mission.

"Now that it's all settled, I have just the right inventions to help you and your friends along the way." The Oracle is excited to show them to Samuel and what better way to test her inventions than to use them in the field.

Samuel follows her to a long table filled with strange gadgets. On display are some of what the Oracle believes are her greatest accomplishments. She lifts a glowing metal orb from the table, much like the one that Samuel saw when he first entered her lair. On top of the orb is a bright red button. Samuel reaches for the button, but the Oracle slaps his hand away with her fin.

"Don't!" she screams. "That was close! You would've blown us to smithereens!"

Samuel gasps. He places his hand over his mouth. He does not realize what the orb's powers can do.

"Just kidding, Samuel. Gotcha again," the Oracle says with a giggle.

Samuel is already on edge and unsure of how many more jokes he can endure. He releases the breath that he had been holding since imagining himself splattered all over the room.

"I call this object Blaze. And please, don't worry. It's not a bomb of any sort. Inside this intriguing metal orb are hundreds of Scorchers."

"What are Scorchers?" asks Samuel.

"I'm glad you asked. Scorchers are nothing more than tiny glowing spheres. They're very much alive and will help light your way on the first part of your journey. Here, let's look at the map." Samuel helps the Oracle spread the map out on the table, placing stones on all four corners to prevent it from floating away.

"See here," she says. "This is where the impossible journey begins. It's called the Abyss. It's a dark area and not the safest of places."

Samuel grabs a chunk of his hair and begins twirling it nervously.

"How are you going to see where you're going and what's lurking around you so you can stay out of harm's way? Well, not to worry, Samuel. That's where Blaze comes in." She lifts the orb up with both fins. "There are many dangerous and hungry creatures lurking in the Abyss, and they've grown accustomed to darkness. Much like Malquars, they hate light. When released, the Scorchers will not only guide your way, but predators will be blinded by the brilliant light that each Scorcher emits. All you'll have to do is press the red button." The Oracle places Blaze on the table and continues to instruct Samuel.

"First, Blaze will squirt out a liquid that attracts Scorchers. Next, it'll release the Scorchers themselves. Be careful not to get the liquid directly on your clothes or skin. The Scorchers are attracted to the liquid and will follow the liquid's trail. Think of the liquid as food. You'll have to press the button more than once to release the magnetic liquid. If any gets on you, the Scorchers will stick to your body, and you'll shine brightly. I suggest you find a sturdy object to spray the magnetic liquid on, like a stick. Eventually, though, they'll consume the liquid, and the Scorchers will drop off onto the floor until you release more liquid. Rinse and repeat. Got it?"

"Got it!"

"I'm afraid the danger will grow with every obstacle encountered, so let's move on to my next invention." The Oracle makes sure to stress the mission's risks so Samuel will always keep his guard up.

"My next creation is extraordinary," the Oracle says as she reaches inside a bag next to the orb and pulls out what seems to be nothing more than an average looking metal bracelet shaped like the cuff of a sleeve. It is the kind of bracelet that lacks a latch, so it can easily slip on and off a wrist or a fin.

"Taa-daa!" she says, as if she is performing a magic trick. However, there is no rabbit, pigeon or bouquet of fake flowers. All Samuel sees is a tarnished-metal bracelet that looks as if it has been worn thousands of times. He is convinced the Oracle has been spending way too much time alone because he cannot see anything special about a dented piece of jewelry.

"Umm…I'm not sure what I'm supposed to be looking at here," Samuel says, trying to hold back his disappointment.

"Of course you don't. That's the point. Those around you aren't going to see anything either." The Oracle acknowledges Samuel's befuddled expression with a tiny nod. "Allow me to explain. I've created a special device called the Aquacuff. When worn, the Aquacuff bonds with its bearer, creating a small reflective field that's large enough to make the person who wears it practically invisible or at least appear that way in water."

"Let me get this straight. That rusty hunk of metal is supposed to make me invisible?" asks Samuel, his voice filled with doubt.

"Practically invisible," she corrects. "Think of it more like blending in with your surroundings like a chameleon, camouflaging yourself to look as clear as water." She begins to demonstrate. "Just slip the Aquacuff on your wrist like so and..." Right before Samuel's eyes, the Oracle's body fades in and out like a flickering yellow light until poof, she disappears. Her entire body, including her glasses, disappears into thin air, instantaneously taking on the appearance of the water around her.

"That's incredible!" Samuel says.

Then all of a sudden, the Oracle's body begins to flicker, fading in and out of sight like a strobe light.

Samuel bites his lip. "I think I may have spoken too soon."

"Why? What's the matter?" asks the Oracle, unaware that the Aquacuff is on the fritz again.

"I think there's something wrong with your Aqua thing. You appear to be flickering in and out of sight," he replies with concern.

"Don't you worry about that," says the Oracle as she slams

the Aquacuff on the table. "It acts up every now and again." She brushes off the device's defect as if it were no big deal.

"Now pay attention!" the Oracle orders, clapping her fins together to get Samuel's attention. She puts on the Aquacuff again and then vanishes before Samuel's eyes. She swims around Samuel while invisible, then pulls the cuff off her fin, reappearing behind Samuel.

"Hee hee. I'm right here," she says, tapping him on the shoulder. Samuel turns around, but she has already put the Aquacuff back on, making herself invisible again. A few seconds later, her visibility begins to flicker in and out. She takes the cuff off her fin and slams it hard against the surface of the table. "All you need is a little patience and a hard surface, Samuel. Don't worry. I'm sure the Aquacuff will come in handy," she says with a smile.

"Sure it will. Just as long as it's working." With slight apprehension, Samuel takes the Aquacuff from the Oracle and places it in his backpack. "So, is that it?" he asks politely, wondering if the Oracle has any other tricks up her purple-plankton sleeves.

"Of course not. I've saved the best for last." She reaches for a necklace with a peculiar-looking whistle attached to it. The whistle looks as if it were carved from an oversized awkward shaped brown and white snail shell.

"This is the Whistle of Obedience." She gently places it around Samuel's neck as if awarding him with a medal for bravery.

"Just one blow on this whistle, and the sound will tame even the wildest of beasts," she explains.

"Then why not just use it on Clatheron?" he asks.

"I had a feeling you were going to ask that, but I'm afraid the whistle only works on creatures of lower intelligence." Samuel looks disappointed. "Still, it'll prove to be quite useful. I promise, Samuel."

Samuel places the whistle to his lips, blowing ever so lightly, and almost immediately Lennox rushes in with mussels attached to both of his arms.

"Ow…ow…you rang." Lennox says in a monotone voice, ignoring the fact that he is covered in mussels.

"Mussels, release," commands the Oracle. The mussels let go and swim back to their posts.

Samuel and the Oracle look at each other and chuckle.

"If that's all, I suppose we'll get going," says Samuel.

"Wait. Before you go." The Oracle places her fin on his shoulder. "Remember to trust your instincts. The war has already been won. All you must do is fight the battle."

"Thank you, Oracle. Thank you for everything."

Samuel grabs Lennox by his arm on the way out. He is still disoriented from the sound of the Whistle of Obedience and needs help finding his way out from underneath the dock.

When Samuel reaches Figlo and Izadora outside the Oracle's lair, he decides to wait until they return to the council's secret hideout to share the news with everyone at once. His decision perturbs the ever-so-curious Izadora, who repeatedly nags him for information on their way back to the hideout.

Believing in Yourself

King Zedorious and the other council members rejoice when Samuel, Izadora, Figlo and Lennox return to the council's secret hideout. Like everyone else, Izadora is eager to hear what the Oracle foretold about her people's future. She insists that the council members quickly take their seats around the stone table, and as soon as they do, the room grows silent. Everyone turns uneasily toward Samuel.

Samuel shares the distressing news that he will have to pass through the Abyss to reach the Hall of Mirrors, where he will find the answers that will lead the Aquatanians to victory. All have heard about the dangers of the Abyss and know that no one has ever survived the impossible journey. The council members and King Zedorious stare at one another, their brows creased with worry. Some bite the tips of their webbed hands. King Zedorious is reluctant to send Samuel to the dark depths of no return.

Samuel shares the news and waits for King Zedorious to respond. The council members turn their heads toward him in anticipation of his decision.

King Zedorious lifts his head and draws a deep breath as

his eyes blink rapidly in distress. Everyone grows as quiet as the lake's waters at first light.

"I have listened to what the Oracle had to say," says the king. "Although I've never questioned her judgment before, I'm afraid I can't let Samuel follow the Oracle's wishes."

"But you must allow it! You have to!" shouts a council member, quickly lowering his head after realizing that he is speaking to his king. The council member slouches in his chair.

"No! I don't have to do anything!" shouts King Zedorious. He shoots an angry piercing look at who spoke out of turn. "It's much too dangerous. And I could never put the life of a young boy at such great risk."

King Zedorious turns to Samuel. "Surely the Oracle must have mentioned another path?"

"I'm afraid not, King Zedorious. This is what the Oracle said we must do to win back the kingdom and free your people."

"We?" the king asks, the distress rising in his voice.

"Yes. The Oracle mentioned me, Lennox, Figlo…and the princess," Samuel replies, bracing himself for the king's reaction to the mere mention of his daughter's involvement in their quest.

"Absolutely not!" King Zedorious yells as the purple veins pop out from his blue scaly neck. "Is the Oracle mad? I could never allow my daughter to risk her life on this mission! Do we have an understanding?" he asks in a powerful yet non-threatening tone.

"I hear you loud and clear, Your Majesty, and I completely understand your fear. But before you say no, consider this," Samuel responds, joining hands with his new friends. "Maybe this destiny that you claim is mine is meant to be shared. Maybe this journey is ours to fulfill as a team."

"No!" the king interjects. "There's no way I'm going to let my one and only daughter risk her life. This ends here! It is out of the question!" He slams his fist on the stone table, which shakes despite its massive weight. The bottles on the table almost tip over. The luminous fish inside them swim nervously in circles. The hanging bottles sway as they are hit by the currents created by the table's vibrations, casting shadows that sway ominously. King Zedorious is as tense as a newly tuned set of guitar strings. He folds his arms and curls his lips in anger.

"Father, please hear me out," Izadora says softly as she swims to the head of the table. She places a webbed hand gently on the king's shoulder. "You know better than anyone that when it comes to one's own destiny, resistance is futile. That is what you have taught me. If this is what I must do, then so be it. The Oracle has spoken. I must fight by Samuel's side."

The king unfolds his arms as he gazes at Izadora with an apprehensive look on his face. He takes her hand and places it between his own webbed hands. "My daughter, my only child, what if I lose you? I don't know what I would do. How could I continue to live?" The king's eyes swell with ink-like tears. His stomach tenses. A single tear rolls down his cheek, which Izadora catches with her fingertip. The tear spreads throughout the water like a drop of blue food coloring in a swimming pool. Her father wipes his eyes with his pointy blue tail.

"Shhhh. Don't say such things," Izadora says. "Trust us. Have faith in us. The four of us will reach the Hall of Mirrors. Samuel will find the answers we seek. You've taught me to be strong and to survive. Together, we will survive this, too." She wraps her arms around her father and holds on tightly.

King Zedorious grows depressed at the thought of losing his only offspring, but he concludes that Aquatanian principles demand that he follow the Oracle's advice. His mind tells him this is the only way, but his heart says otherwise.

Although Zedorious strongly doubts his decision, he knows that not even a king can stand in the way of destiny. Without explicitly giving his approval, he lets Izadora join Samuel and the others on the impossible journey.

A strained silence fills the dimly lit cavern. Not another word is spoken by council members as they get up from their chairs and leave the table. Their minds are overwhelmed by the horrific thought that Clatheron's evil reign of terror might never end. They fear for the lives of their two new friends as much as they fear for the lives of Figlo and their princess. Still, they have always trusted the Oracle's guidance and know they must have faith that Samuel will restore the kingdom to its glorious past.

The night sky grows dark. Calm fills the waters. Samuel, Lennox, Figlo and Izadora realize they must rest before embarking on their dangerous quest. There is not much space to sleep in the secret cave, so the four brave souls bunk together in the princess' sleeping quarters, which happens to have plenty of spare beds. She is more than happy to share her room with her new friends.

Lennox rudely pushes his way through the others and is

the first to enter the princess' quarters. The room has four sleeping cubbies of various sizes, carved out and embedded deeply within the cave walls. Each sleeping cubby is padded with lake debris and fresh leaves for cushioning and comfort.

"I call the top bunk," says Lennox, as he hops into a mid-sized elevated cubby.

Figlo selects the oversized cubby right beneath Lennox's. The princess' sleeping cubby is carved inside the wall adjacent to Figlo. The remaining compartment is for Samuel and is directly above the princess'. In the center of the room is a gaping hole in the ceiling that reveals an awe-inspiring black sky filled with stars so densely packed that they seem to shine together as one.

Everyone settles comfortably into their beds for the night.

"Sleep tight, everyone," says Izadora.

With Lennox and Figlo already half asleep, Samuel is the only one fully awake to answer, "Good night, Princess Izadora."

As the room fills with silence, Samuel's mind fills with doubt. He is nervous and hopes that he is making the right decision by embarking on such a dangerous journey. And now Samuel is worrying about Grandpa, figuring that he must be worried sick about his whereabouts. He then begins to wonder if he is going to get back home in a reasonable amount of time.

Samuel has never fallen asleep underwater before. He rests his head on a rock covered in moss and kelp that acts as a pillow. As he lies on his back, he looks up at the cave's ceiling, trying to clear his mind and drift off to sleep. The princess, who is directly beneath Samuel, is also having a tough time getting to sleep. She tosses and turns, eventually giving up on sleeping all together. In a fit of frustration, she sits up-right. Samuel can hear her restlessness from above.

"Is everything all right, Izadora?" Samuel asks in a whisper to not wake the others.

She sighs. "I'm just anxious about tomorrow."

"Don't worry. Everything will be all right," he says softly, trying to console her while convincing himself that everything will in fact be all right.

"How do you know that? How do you know everything will be all right?" she responds with a hint of dread in her voice.

He pauses for a moment to collect his thoughts, hangs upside down over the side of his cubby, and looks into her eyes.

"Because I believe."

"Believe in what?" she asks.

"Us. I believe in us," replies Samuel with sincerity.

She is touched by Samuel's words. They stare into each other's eyes, wondering what the other is thinking at that very moment.

Just then, Lennox begins to snore loudly from across the room, ruining their tender moment. Samuel and Izadora re-lease a quiet chuckle.

"Princess, can I tell you something that I've never told anyone before?" Samuel asks.

"Please do. Anything to take my mind off tomorrow."

"This is sort of a confession, one that I'd like to make to you, but I don't want to frighten you. Agreed?" She shakes her head and listens intently. Lying back down, Samuel wig-gles around until he finds a comfortable position.

"Back in my world, I'm not what you would call brave or a hero of any sort. I usually back down from a fight. I often run the other way, but not this time, princess. Not this time," he says firmly as he shakes his head from side to side with conviction. "Sure I have my doubts. But this place, everyone I've met, Figlo, you...especially you...it all makes me feel...it makes me feel like anything is possible. It makes me feel invincible. It's as if the Wall of Prophecies, the Oracle, all of my new friends – and my grandfather – have been right about me all along."

"How can you be so sure? What if we don't make it out of this alive?" she asks.

"I promise you this, Izadora. Whatever dangers await us, we'll face them together, and together we'll defeat Clatheron once and for all!"

Overcome by emotion, the princess buries her face in her moss and kelp covered pillow to hide her blue-ink tears, but Samuel can hear her sobbing.

"Why are you crying, princess?" he asks as he returns to a hanging position so he can get a clear view of Izadora's face. The princess lifts her head from the pillow and Samuel quickly shoots her a funny face, crossing his eyes and sticking his tongue out. She giggles, stops crying and gently wipes away her tears. "There now. Isn't that better? Why bother crying when it feels so good to laugh," he says with a smile.

She remains quiet as she stares at her reflection in his eyes, and at that moment, she feels loved. Uncharacteristically shy, she blushes.

Samuel is mesmerized by the princess' charm and strength and has been from the moment he laid eyes on Izadora. They are both around the same age and though neither of them will admit it, an unspoken mutual crush has begun to develop between them.

Lennox turns over on his shell, this time mumbling something about a savory meatloaf. Samuel and Izadora look at one another with a smile and share a laugh at Lennox's expense. Samuel returns to a lying position in his bed and quiet once again fills the room.

"Samuel?" asks Izadora, breaking the silence.

"Yes, Izadora."

"I believe in us, too," she says.

Samuel smiles and then suggests they get some rest. "We have a big day tomorrow. Close your eyes and try to get some sleep," he says.

"I suppose you're right," she says with resignation, lying down and turning on her side. They slowly drift off to sleep.

Figlo was awake during the entire conversation between Samuel and the princess. Through his half-closed eyes, he witnessed the spark between them, but neither their budding feelings for each other nor their convictions matter to him. He has not changed his decision to take matters into his own hands.

Figlo waits patiently for the two of them to fall asleep so he can embark on his own mission, which is to save the only other living creature of his kind, his only living relative, his sister Alaina.

During the Great Invasion, Clatheron captured both Figlo and Alaina. Although Figlo managed to escape, the Malquars threw his sister into the Coral Jail with the other prisoners. Since then, Figlo has wished he could trade places with her and has searched for a way to free her. Unbeknownst to the others, Figlo thinks relying on a 13-year-old boy to save the kingdom and thus free his sister is too risky, so he has decided to strike out on his own. Even if he must betray his friends and the princess, he feels he has no other choice.

As soon as he is sure that his companions are sleeping, he swims swiftly and stealthily through the gaping hole in the cave's ceiling. He must be back before morning to avoid arousing the suspicions of his friends, or soon-to-be former friends, once they find out what he is up to.

A Traitor in Their Midst

Figlo arrives at the kingdom's front gates, feeling uneasy about his planned face-to-face negotiations with Clatheron. He is uneasy not because he is afraid of the barbarian, but because he is overcome by guilt and self-loathing. Figlo feels responsible for his sister's capture and feels compelled to get her out of prison even if it means betraying his Aquatanian family, which has always treated him like one of their own species.

Figlo wants to offer a fair trade: Princess Izadora for his sister Alaina. He is sure that after turning the princess over to Clatheron, he will rescue her later on and ease his guilt. Figlo also hopes that, somehow, he will be able to keep his betrayal a secret from his family. His plan, however, is a little like Swiss cheese; full of holes. But Figlo is overwhelmed with guilt and emotion. He is thinking with his heart, not with his mind.

Figlo is certain of one thing. He will never divulge the whereabouts of the council's secret hideout, even if tortured by Clatheron. If he did reveal the location, and his plan backfires or fails, no one would be left to regain the kingdom and free his sister. Figlo will endure any pain to keep the secret.

He will meet with Clatheron to make one deal and one deal only: his sister for the princess.

Clatheron has heard rumors that a hideout exists far from the kingdom's walls and that many of the subjects live secretly near it. He has been on the prowl for the council and its members.

To keep the hiding place secret, Figlo will arrange for the Malquars to intercept the princess at a place far from the hidden Aquatanians. Figlo will offer Samuel and Lennox to Clatheron as a bonus if he needs to sweeten the deal. If they must be captured, so be it.

Figlo nervously repeats his plan over and over in his mind as he approaches two guards stationed at the castle's front gates. The guards are fearsome in appearance and hideous to look at. A hard green exterior covers their muscular bodies. Slime oozes from the pores of their wrinkled faces. Dark circles below their eyes make their oversized yellow pupils all the more prominent. Thick snot pours from their nostrils as they breathe heavily through their pug-like noses.

It has been a while since Figlo has seen a Malquar up close. He is still disgusted by their appearance, but he fearlessly approaches the guards with both paws raised high in the air, claws retracted. He wants the guards to see that he is not carrying weapons and has no hostile intent. As he gets closer, the guards draw their spears.

Malquars are trained to be ruthless, to show no mercy to anyone, not even their mothers. It is forbidden to show weakness except when facing Clatheron. To toughen them up, Malquar army recruits are locked away in a dungeon for a week without food or drink. They receive nightly visits from guards who beat them with wooden clubs until they beg for mercy, night after terrifying night. If they survive their initiation, they are allowed to join the ranks of the Malquar army, but not before the words "Property of Clatheron" are burned into their necks as if they were being branded like cattle.

"Halt!" one of the guards exclaims, using his massive paws to thrust his razor-sharp spear at Figlo's chest. Figlo stands still while the second guard examines him from the two fins on top of his head to his snake-like tail, searching for vulnerabilities.

As he looks Figlo over, the second guard recognizes the intruder. "I know who you are! You are Figlo, the warrior beast in the court of King Zedorious. You have some nerve showing up here, beast," the guard shouts. As he speaks, his open mouth reveals two fangs, one larger than the other, protruding from his upper lip.

Both guards have heard about Figlo's notoriety as a fierce warrior and know it will take more than the two of them to overcome him. Figlo established his reputation during the Great Invasion, when five Malquars piled on top of him but were flung in every direction as if a bomb had exploded underneath. If only Figlo had been able to take on the whole army that terrible day, then maybe he would not be in his current predicament.

"A warrior I claim to be, but a beast I am not," Figlo responds, offended by the guard's hypocritical characterization. He remains calm, using his fearsome reputation to his advantage. "If you recognize me, then you and your partner know what I can do to you, but do not be afraid. No harm will come to either of you — if you honor my request." Figlo speaks with utmost confidence.

Chapter Thirteen

"And what request might you be making?" asks the first guard while continuing to press his spear against Figlo's chest. He laughs in contempt.

"I came here to speak with Clatheron. I advise you to inform him of my presence – NOW!" Figlo shouts. He doesn't appreciate being mocked. He snarls, and sharp claws shoot out from the end of his right paw. In a flash, his claws slice off the spear's tip with a single stroke.

"I'd retract those claws if I were you," the guard snarls back. "All we have to do is sound the alarm and an entire battalion of Malquar soldiers will appear within seconds. Then we'll see if you're the great warrior beast that we've heard so much about. Besides, King Clatheron is asleep and doesn't like to be disturbed at this hour."

The guard reaches for a second spear that he keeps next to the castle door. "Whatever this is about must wait until morning," he says. "Until then, we have a cozy cell waiting for you."

"We suggest you come with us," says the second guard as both of them thrust their spears against Figlo's throat, hoping he will acquiesce quickly.

"And I will come with you if you take me to Clatheron," answers Figlo, retracting his claws. "I'm not frightened by you or your jail. In fact, your jail is why I'm here. Someone very near to me is being held captive in the Coral Jail, and I want her back."

"And you think Clatheron is going to hand her over to you?" Both guards break into synchronized cackles. "What, are you crazy?"

"Maybe I'm foolish, or maybe I have information that Clatheron will want in exchange for my sister's freedom."

"I'm afraid it will have to wait until morning," replies the second guard.

"I urge you to reconsider, for this cannot wait until the morning. If I don't return before dawn, the information I have will be of no use to Clatheron. It's about a serious threat that could mean the end of his rule. Your master will surely hold both of you accountable if you don't let me bring this information to his attention immediately."

The guards seem unconvinced, but Figlo continues to play on their deep-seated fear of Clatheron. "Clatheron will have your heads for withholding vital information like this. Hmm...I wonder if he'll put you in jail to rot for eternity or roast you alive for dinner?" Figlo asks confidently while stroking his chin. "Judging from your size, he'll have a hearty meal."

The guards' resolve begins to waver. Fear begins to show in their yellow pupils. The formidable-looking Malquars look nervously at each other, wondering if they should risk Clatheron's wrath by waking him from his slumber. A chill rushes through their bones.

"Clatheron should have enough meat between the two of you to last for weeks," Figlo continues with a laugh.

"Give us a moment," the first guard says. They step back to confer, and when they return, they tell Figlo they will take him to their fearsome leader. Figlo isn't surprised. He knows that Malquars live in fear of their ruler's volcanic temper.

"But if Clatheron is in a foul mood, and you make us look bad...let's just say you'll have an unfortunate accident on the way to the dungeon...an everlasting accident, if you catch my drift," adds the second guard with an evil sneer.

"Fair enough," he replies with a slight grin.

The guards escort Figlo to Clatheron's sleeping quarters, keeping their spears pressed against Figlo's back the entire way. They tell him to remain outside the royal bedroom, then timidly enter to wake their master. Through the stone door, Figlo hears Clatheron scream at the guards, who yelp like dogs as he lobs objects at their heads.

"What?" screams Clatheron. "You morons left him alone in the hallway? What in Lake Aqueous were you thinking?"

"B...b...b...but sire," the first guard says nervously. "He says he has important information."

"It can wait until tomorrow! Blob and I need our beauty sleep." Blob, Clatheron's pet, slithers toward Clatheron's hand, nudging him to scratch his gelatinous belly.

"It's Figlo, the great warrior beast," replies the first guard.

"He said it can't wait until morning," the other guard quickly interjects while turning his head away from Clatheron's hunger-filled gaze.

"Great warrior. Ha!" Clatheron scoffs. "If Figlo is such a great warrior, then why do I hold the key to this kingdom? Great warrior? I should say not. Bring him to me this instant!"

Clatheron grabs Blob with his tentacle and throws his quivering gelatinous body at the door. The first guard reacts instinctively, jumping in the air to catch Blob. Clatheron gets out of bed, his nightcap securely fastened to his head and slithers on his nine spider-like feet across the bedroom to sit on the bedroom throne. The first guard places Blob on Clatheron's lap and pats him on his head.

An impatient Figlo continues to listen outside and decides to enter at his own risk before the guards come for him.

He pushes the door open and enters cautiously but with his head held high.

"Excuse me for barging in unannounced, Clatheron. But I…"

Clatheron jumps from his throne. "How dare you guards allow our enemy to waltz into my bedroom chambers!" he shouts. "It's like I'm not allowed to feel safe in my own home. Unbelievable! Grab him this instant!"

Both guards, knowing they are in big trouble, swim toward Figlo. They stand on opposite sides of him, each with one arm so tightly wrapped around one of Figlo's whitish-gray arms that green veins bulge from them.

"I mean no harm. There is no need to restrain me," says Figlo.

"I'll decide when to restrain you. Now state your business! What brings you here at this time of night?" Clatheron coldly asks.

"My name is Figlo."

"Yes. I know. You're Figlo, the so-called great warrior. Blah, blah, blah," Clatheron responds contemptuously as his large blood-shot eyeball attached to the end of a long red tentacle on his head examines Figlo from head to toe.

"I've heard stories, but I have to say, you don't look like much of a warrior to me," Clatheron says. "We handily defeated you during the Great Invasion. And with warriors like you fighting against us, I can see why we won so easily." Clatheron lets out a chuckle.

"Please, Clatheron. I don't have much time," Figlo interjects.

"You get down on one knee when you address the king of this castle!" Clatheron demands.

Figlo hesitates but decides to humor Clatheron in hopes of improving his chances of striking a deal. Figlo slowly drops to one knee. "Please listen carefully to my every word. My sister Alaina resides in your jail, and I want her freed."

"Your sister is in my jail and you want me to free her? Well, why didn't you just say that at the outset. No problem at all. Guards, go to the Coral Jail and release his sister at once!"

The guards look at each other and then at Clatheron with puzzled looks on their faces.

"Really, sire?" asks the first guard.

"Are you serious?" asks the second guard.

"No, of course I'm not serious, you dimwits." Clatheron is annoyed by the guards' stupidity. His anger builds up like lava in a volcano ready to explode. He then shoots a fierce glance at Figlo. "How dare you make demands of a king! Who in Lake Aqueous do you think you are? You've got gumption. I'll give you that. Now stop wasting my time and get on with it."

Figlo begins to second-guess himself, wondering if his scheme will free his sister, but there is no turning back now. "I'll make you a deal," Figlo says.

"A deal? I like deals, but only ones that are in my favor." Clatheron is amused by the prospect of making a deal that he will most likely break. "Continue. I'm listening," he adds with a hint of deviousness in his voice.

"In exchange for my sister, I'll deliver Princess Izadora to you."

"That's all you offer me?" Clatheron sneers. "Take him to the Coral Jail and place him in solitary. You'll be all alone with nothing but thoughts of your former freedom to haunt your every waking moment." Clatheron releases the most horrible evil laugh, which no one has ever heard before. The guards begin to laugh nervously to curry favor with their king.

"Silence, you imbeciles!" Clatheron shouts as he squeezes Blob tightly until his eyes protrude from their sockets.

Silence returns immediately to the cavernous chambers. The guards' faces turn ashen. They begin to haul Figlo off to the Coral Jail.

"Wait!" Figlo begs. "There's more."

Clatheron raises his hand and instructs the guards to stop. The guards push Figlo down on his knees.

"There's a boy," Figlo says, brushing each guard's claw from his shoulders.

"A boy?" Clatheron repeats. The words echo eerily off the bedroom walls.

"Yes. The boy's name is Samuel Waters."

"Go on," orders Clatheron, unsure what a *boy* is.

"Ancient prophecies foretell of a boy, a savior, who will descend to Lake Aqueous to rescue the Aquatanians from an evil being. This boy, Samuel, has arrived with his friend Lennox to take you down and win back the kingdom."

"Is this some kind of joke? There isn't a creature in Lake Aqueous powerful enough to defeat the almighty Clatheron and my ruthless army. What an entertaining bedtime story. Go on, tell me more." Clatheron has no idea what a Samuel Waters or a Lennox is or what they look like, but he assumes they cannot be that powerful if Figlo is offering to sacrifice them in exchange for his sister.

Figlo sighs as the guilt begins to weigh down on his shoulders. "At dawn tomorrow, the princess, the boy, his friend Lennox and I will embark on a journey through the Abyss to reach the Hall of Mirrors. Samuel is searching for the knowledge he needs to defeat you and return the kingdom to its rightful inhabitants. The Mirror of Truth in the Hall of Mirrors will provide the answers he seeks."

"That's preposterous!" Clatheron exclaims. "No one who has ever journeyed to the Abyss has ever lived to see another sunrise. Everyone knows that."

"And if we do survive?" Figlo asks. "What then?" Figlo figures Clatheron will leave nothing to chance to maintain his reign over the Kingdom of Aquatania. "Isn't it worth it for you to be on the safe side? You have a chance to capture the princess, the boy and his friend in one fell swoop. It will only be them and me, only the four of us." Figlo is trying to spell it out for Clatheron.

"Interesting point." Clatheron strokes his chin with his blood-red hand.

"If you free my sister, I promise that I won't stand in the way of you capturing all three of them at a prearranged location. You'll surely foil Samuel's plan to overthrow you."

"I do like the sound of that," says Clatheron. He pets Blob as he mulls Figlo's fate. "But all of this depends on whether I let you leave here and return to your friends."

"Trust me. If I wanted to, I could have easily escaped by now," Figlo says with a steely, low-key confidence. He flashes his claws, and both guards back away. He gazes directly into Clatheron's eyes, and for a moment, Clatheron's eyes seem to show fear.

"If I don't return before morning, they'll never leave on their journey. Don't you see? You must let me return. You'll miss your opportunity to capture them." Thoroughly disgusted with himself, Figlo retracts his claws into his paws and extends one paw to Clatheron to shake on the deal. "So do we have ourselves a deal?"

Clatheron takes a moment to think it through. "I suppose so," he whines, shaking Figlo's paw with his hand. "It's settled. I'll deploy a dozen of my finest Malquar soldiers to meet you at the prearranged location of your choice."

Unbeknownst to Figlo, Clatheron won't order his soldiers to capture his enemies at the agreed upon location. Instead, Clatheron will order his soldiers to follow Figlo and his friends until they reach the Hall of Mirrors. Clatheron wants to know what the Mirror of Truth will tell Samuel. Knowledge is power. Clatheron reasons that gaining knowledge from the Mirror of Truth could work to his advantage.

Clatheron also wants to delay the capture to satisfy his demented sadism. He wants to torment Figlo, who will not hear or see his special-operations soldiers follow stealthily behind him on the journey through the Abyss. Figlo will not know when they will strike. Clatheron expects the prolonged anticipation of a surprise attack to drive Figlo mad.

Because Figlo and his friends will be the first to encounter the dangers of the Abyss, Clatheron anticipates his soldiers will remain safe if they keep a proper distance. The heartless monster really does not care for his soldiers' safety, but he needs them alive to capture Samuel, Lennox and the princess.

Figlo begins to feel sick to his stomach. If only he could have found another way to free his sister. Instead, he sold his soul to Clatheron and sold out all of his friends in the process.

"Oh, don't look so sad, great warrior. We'll make it look like you tried to defend your friends. I don't want to ruin your precious reputation. But you will suffer the pain of betraying your friends and family for the rest of your life. This brings me much joy in and of itself. Just remember to play nice with my boys, and I'll free your sister. When I receive delivery of Princess Izadora, the boy and his friend, your dearest sister will be set free. You have my word."

"Promise me you won't harm my friends," Figlo responds.

"Oh, I promise." Clatheron crosses his tentacles behind his back. "If it helps ease your mind any, the princess will reside in a cage beside my throne, where she'll remain on display as a reminder that King Zedorious will never defeat the almighty Clatheron. Never!" He belts out another evil laugh. The guards remain silent.

"Laugh, you blockheads!" Clatheron commands. The guards begin to laugh hysterically. "As for the boy and his friend, they'll live the rest of their lives in the Coral Jail, never to be heard from again!" He breaks into a final round of laughter, and the guards chime in again as if on cue.

"Enough, you two numbskulls!" Clatheron roars. Both guards immediately stop laughing and stand at attention, straight as rulers.

Figlo is nauseated by the sound of Clatheron's laugh and by his own betrayal of his friends. He loathes himself. Still, it is getting late, and he knows he must return to the council's hideout.

"I must return to the princess before she notices that I'm gone," Figlo tells Clatheron.

"I'll let you return to your so-called friends, but before

you go, you must kiss my hand and profess your allegiance to me as your king."

Figlo cringes, but for the sake of his sister's freedom, he obeys. "As you wish…my king." Figlo puckers his lips and quickly kisses Clatheron's blood-red hand, afterward spitting the vile taste from his mouth.

"That's more like it," says Clatheron. "Guards, remove this worthless being from my chambers. Blob and I require sleep before tomorrow's festivities."

The guards escort Figlo to the front gate and push him to the ground. He lands on the lake floor with a thud, kicking up dirt that swirls about him like a tornado. Figlo picks himself up and swims back to the secret hideout as expeditiously as possible, constantly glancing back to make sure Clatheron or his soldiers are not following him. As the kingdom grows smaller and slowly vanishes in the distance, Figlo hangs his head down low, asking himself over and over, "What have I done?"

By sunrise, Figlo and the others will set forth on their sojourn. The outcome of the journey, his friends' fate and the freedom of his sister Alaina are completely out of his paws. He hopes that Clatheron will uphold his word and not harm his friends. That would give him the opportunity to somehow free them once his sister is safe. For now, Figlo will have to hope for a miracle and pray that everything works out in the end.

Deep into the Abyss

In the morning, King Zedorious and the other council members give Samuel, Izadora, Lennox and Figlo a grand send-off complete with a feast to fill their stomachs.

As the four swim toward the sliding rock to leave the secret lair, they find themselves flanked on both sides by grateful supporters. The crowd cheers and tosses the glittery remains of discarded candy wrappers at their heroes to show their appreciation. Samuel, Izadora and Lennox bask in the glory of their praises. The cheers boost their courage, which they will need to overcome the many obstacles that they will surely encounter.

Figlo, however, is not celebrating. The festivity makes him feel even guiltier about his secret pact with Clatheron to free his sister from the Coral Jail. He struggles to hide the guilt from his face as he follows his friends from behind.

After the raucous send-off, the four adventurers swim as fast as they can toward the Abyss. On the way, Samuel and Izadora exchange a few flirtatious smiles and occasionally reach for each other's hand.

"Are we there yet?" asks Lennox, struggling to keep up with the rest of the group.

"Yes. We're almost there, Lennox," replies the princess with narrowing eyes. "Stop your whining and keep up! You're slowing us down."

"Did you remember to pack some food, Samuel?" asks Lennox, his stomach already beginning to growl. Even though he just devoured a huge meal at the send-off feast, he always thinks about his next meal.

"Yes, of course I did, Lennox. Now do as Izadora said and keep up," orders Samuel, irritated by his friend's self-centered concerns.

For his part, Figlo has been pretty quiet thus far. He knows they have already passed the assigned interception point and not knowing the Malqaurs' whereabouts is driving him insane because they could attack unexpectedly at any moment. Figlo repeatedly peers over his shoulder to see if Clatheron's soldiers are near, careful not to look suspicious to his friends. But if the Malquars' special-operations forces are somewhere out there, Figlo cannot spot them.

Before long, the group arrives at the edge of a great rocky cliff. The area is dimly lit. The surroundings are barren, cold and depressing. Besides some jagged rocks, undisturbed soil and a few large plants, hardly any underwater life is present in this section of Lake Aqueous. The water itself is eerily still. Plants do not sway. No fish, crabs or eels stir up dirt from the lake bed.

A chill from the darkened waters hits the back of Samuel's neck, opening his eyes to the grim reality that awaits them. "It's exactly how the Oracle described it," he says as they look around.

Samuel peers cautiously over the edge of the cliff. He can

sense the dangers that exist below and knows they should not be taken lightly. Most of the lake's inhabitants have never dared venture this far. Those who did have never been seen again, except for the Oracle, of course.

Izadora and Figlo join Samuel at the edge and together they gaze over the side into the darkness that will be the starting point of their arduous journey. As they look down, it seems as if the ground beyond the cliff's edge has ceased to exist, as if it were bottomless.

Lennox stands a few feet behind his friends waiting for a sign that it is safe to join them. His eyes dart about at the lifeless surroundings, which send shivers down his shell. He is afraid of the dark, but to avoid ridicule, he pretends to guard the group from predators that might lurk behind them. Little does he know that they are being followed.

"This is worse than I expected," says Izadora as she brings her shaky webbed hand to her forehead.

"I'm sure it's not as bad as it seems," replies Samuel in a soothing tone. If only he could convince himself with his own words of encouragement.

Reality sinks in, and they join hands, fearful of the unknown.

"Everyone remain quiet," Figlo says. "Let's see how deep the Abyss really is." Figlo then wraps his paw around a rock and tosses it over the edge, waiting to hear how long it will take before the rock hits bottom.

Samuel sighs. He wishes the batteries in his flashlight had not died after he viewed the Wall of Prophecies in Pearl Cave. He would have used it to see if the Abyss had a floor.

If a nervous Samuel were thinking clearly, he might have

thought about using the Oracle's Scorchers to light the way, or try to figure out how to get the king's sword working properly to illuminate the darkness.

They remain motionless while waiting to hear the rock hit bottom. They hear nothing. This is not a good sign.

Lennox slowly inches toward the others to join them at the cliff's edge. "Did you guys hear anything? I didn't hear anything. Maybe there is no bottom to the Abyss. Maybe this is a bad idea after all. Maybe…," he hysterically rambles on as if his head is going to explode from panic.

Izadora swiftly reaches back with her webbed hand and smacks Lennox across the face. "Get a hold of yourself! Can't you see you're only making matters worse?"

Lennox snaps back to a semblance of normalcy, or as normal as he can get. "I'm sorry, princess," he says, rubbing the red mark that appears on his green cheek. "But was that really necessary?"

Samuel ignores the squabble and continues to look over the edge. He knows they cannot afford to waste any more time. "Jump!" Samuel shouts, abruptly breaking the silence like a gunshot in an open field. "That's what we'll do! On the count of three, we'll jump and swim our way to the bottom!"

"Say what?" Lennox cries. Samuel is not thinking clearly and cannot come up with a better plan. Lennox wonders if Samuel is mistaking bravery for foolishness. "You don't mean what I think you mean? Please, Samuel. Please think of some other way." He locks his palms together in mock prayer, praying that Samuel is not serious.

"I agree with Samuel," says Izadora. "There's no other way down. We'll have to jump and swim to the bottom. It's a risk we'll have to take," she says as she nervously twists the ends of her long black hair.

Lennox slowly backs away from the cliff's edge. "This is crazy! We don't even know if there is a bottom to the Abyss. We can't see what's down there from where we're standing!" cries Lennox, flailing his hands above his head. "Something awful could be waiting at the bottom with a taste for turtle soup. No way, Samuel. I'm not going!"

"Oh yes you are," an annoyed Izadora retorts loudly. "Whether you like it or not, you're coming with us, even if I have to throw you over the cliff and drag you down myself." She folds her arms. Her eyes widen and bulge. Her brow furrows. Izadora is willing to risk everything to see the journey through to the end.

Lennox backs away.

"I guess you could always stay behind," Samuel suggests.

"Finally, someone around here with some common sense," Lennox replies, sticking his tongue out at the princess. "I knew there was a reason we designated Samuel as our leader. I'll stay here and wait for you guys to return. I can protect the rear in case you need someone to karate chop any predators." Lennox spins around in a circle, flinging his arms and legs in every direction as if he were fighting off an army. But he is extremely uncoordinated.

Izadora and Figlo struggle to contain their laughter.

"That's perfect, Lennox," Samuel says in an even tone. "If a group of Malquars happens to be patrolling the area, you can take them on all by yourself." Samuel subtly winks at Izadora and Figlo.

"Wait, wait, wait. Malquars? No one said anything about

Malquars," Lennox says in a panic. "Do you really think they'd patrol this far away from the kingdom?"

"They most certainly would," answers Figlo. Even though he is simply playing along with Samuel, Figlo knows that a Malquar patrol must be close.

"They're stationed all over Lake Aqueous," Izadora adds. "Malquars, along with Aquatanian slaves, are instructed to spread throughout the lake so they can find savory meals and serve them up to Clatheron."

"They are?" asks Lennox, biting the tips of his fingernails.

Izadora nods in the affirmative.

"We've wasted enough time as it is," says Samuel. "We should get going, but you stay safe here, Lennox."

"And unappetizing," adds Izadora with a smirk.

"Hold up a second," Lennox interjects. "Come to think of it, how far do you guys think you'll get without my superior intellect and karate skills? On second thought, I think it would be best for all of us if I came with you."

"Well...If you really think so, Lennox," Samuel says, playing along. "I wouldn't want to pressure you."

"No pressure," responds Lennox as he nervously looks over his shoulder for Malquars.

"It's settled. On the count of three then," says Samuel.

They stand in a straight line beside one another along the cliff's edge, their hands cupped together, as they get ready to take their leap of faith together as one.

"Ready? One...two..."

"Wait!" exclaims Lennox as he turns to Samuel. "Do we jump *when* you say three, or *after* you say three?"

Izadora rolls her eyes and smacks her forehead.

Chapter Fourteen

"Is that really relevant?" asks Figlo.

"Yes, of course it is!" Lennox replies, his voice quavering as his stomach tightens into knots. "What if I jump before you and reach the bottom first only to face whatever is down there alone?"

"I guess you'll just have to use that superior intellect of yours to confront any dangers alone before we arrive," the princess says in a mocking tone. "If that fails, you can always rely on those fancy fighting moves you demonstrated earlier."

"Very funny. It's all a big joke until someone gets hurt," Lennox snarls, bearing his teeth.

"Enough, you two! It's three and then jump," Samuel says, shaking his head in frustration. "Okay. Let's try this again. One…Two…Wait!" shouts Samuel.

Lennox wobbles at the edge of the cliff, trying hard to regain his balance. He almost leaps over the edge alone when Samuel suddenly stops the countdown.

"Can you hear that?" asks Samuel.

"Hear what?" asks Izadora, cupping her webbed hand to the slit beneath her breathing tube.

In the distance, emanating from the water's surface, a familiar muffled sound approaches from behind. To Samuel, it sounds like a lot of motor-boat engines. He soon realizes a boat race is underway and figures out a plan to help everyone travel swiftly to the bottom of the Abyss without getting exhausted from what he expects would otherwise be a very long swim.

Samuel glances to his right and spots a large plant with oversized leaves, one of the few signs of life that they have noticed since they arrived. With little time to explain, Samuel swims toward the plant and breaks off four large leaves from its stalk. Samuel then hands one oversized leaf to each of the others, keeping the remaining leaf for himself.

"Use these and follow my lead," Samuel shouts enthusiastically.

The first boat begins to pass, its propeller slicing through the water's surface, whizzing loudly like a revving chainsaw. Then another boat and another pass overhead. All three propellers combine to create a strong downward current in the previously stagnant water. Samuel backs away from the edge of the cliff to get a running start. He grips each side of the green leaf tightly in his hands.

"One...Two...Threeeeee!" Sprinting as quickly as he can, Samuel leaps over the edge more daring than any banister stunt at the lake house could ever be. As he expected, the leaf captures the boats' current, opens wide like the mainsail of a sailboat, and pulls Samuel down like a shooting star toward the bottom of the Abyss.

The others watch in amazement as Samuel descends into the blackness. They can hear him cheer as the powerful current propels him toward the unknown.

"I'm next," shouts the princess. The others can barely hear her over the engine roar and strong current hitting their backs. Izadora backs up to get a running start. She holds on tightly to the leaf and extends her arms. But, before she takes flight, Lennox pushes her out of the way.

"Excuse me. I believe I was next," Lennox says as he wiggles his tail, takes a deep breath, and runs toward the cliff's edge. As he leaps over the edge, Lennox releases a high-pitched scream. He hurtles down into the Abyss, clinging to the leaf's edges as if his life depended on it.

More motor boats pass overhead. Izadora jumps, followed by Figlo. Together, all four adventurers hurtle into darkness, unsure of how long it will take to reach bottom.

Izadora notices eerily glowing eyes of all different shapes and sizes peering out from the cliff's overhangs and nooks. Her companions also notice the glowing eyes but stay focused on holding onto their oversized leaves. Whatever the creatures are, they are not in attack mode. Still, the glowing eyes give all of them the creeps, and they remain on high alert as they sail to the bottom.

Samuel is the first to see a whitish glow illuminate the ground beneath them. "We're almost there!" he yells to the others.

Lennox is so nervous that he does not realize that he caught a current stronger than Samuel's. He shoots by Samuel on the way down. Lennox shrieks when he notices that he is approaching the ground at high speed. He retreats completely into his shell for protection, lets go of the oversized leaf and smashes into the muddy floor of the Abyss. Luckily, the soft mud and Lennox's hard shell break his fall.

Samuel lands on top of Lennox, followed by Izadora. Figlo safely lands nearby in a large tree-like plant.

Lennox's muffled voice emerges from inside his shell at the bottom of the pile. He pleads with Samuel and Izadora to get off. "You're crushing me! I can't breathe. Get off!" he shouts in a panic.

Samuel and Izadora laugh hysterically as they climb off one by one.

Lennox pops his head out of his shell, which is covered in gooey mud. In a daze, he shakes his head rapidly from left to right, splattering mud all over Samuel and Izadora. "You guys never mentioned anything about a turtle pancake!" Lennox exclaims angrily.

Izadora wipes the mud from her face. Before she has a chance to get angry, she notices glowing flowers all around them. "They're so beautiful," she says, drawn to their whitish glow like a moth to a flame. The flower petals are a colorful collection of blues, yellows, whites and pinks, all attached to long purple stems sprouting from the lake floor. Each flower emits a faint white glow that helps light up the lakebed.

Izadora approaches one of the flower beds to smell their scent. As she gets closer, the flowers turn a reddish hue. Snarling teeth emerge from the center of each flowers' stamens. The flowers snap and growl, hungry for an innocent passerby. A startled Izadora jumps back and falls into Samuel's arms. Then, the flowers spray a cloud of gold dust particles into the surrounding waters like a long spritz from a perfume bottle. The dust cloud spreads around the princess, Lennox and Samuel.

Figlo, who is farther away from the trio, notices the dust cloud spreading and urgently shouts a warning. He assumes the dust is dangerous if inhaled. "Stop breathing this instant!" Figlo shouts. "Whatever you do, hold your breath and don't inhale!" But it is too late.

Samuel, Izadora and Lennox all breathe in the dust particles, unaware of the effect it will have. They swim frantically toward Figlo, who is still caught in the branches of the large plant in which he landed. As they swim toward him, the reddish hue fades, the cloud of gold dust particles dissipates and the flower's comforting whitish glow returns.

Chapter Fourteen

"Izadora, are you okay?" asks Samuel after they reach Figlo.

"Yes...I think so," she gasps, her heart racing. She bats her thick black eyelashes as she regains her composure.

"Look on the bright side," says Lennox, struggling to catch his breath. "At least now we'll be able to see where we're going." Lennox points to a pathway, lined on both sides by the hauntingly beautiful but deadly flowers.

Samuel rubs the princess' back to calm her down before they resume their search for the Hall of Mirrors.

The princess smiles while Samuel rubs her back. Then, suddenly, her eyes turn blood red, and her mood shifts to fierce anger. She grabs Samuel's hand and twists his arm behind his back, causing him to yelp in pain.

"Ow! That really hurts!" he screams. "Princess, what has gotten into you?" Samuel's mood just as suddenly shifts to anger. His eyes burn red as he fights her off.

Then Lennox's eyes turn from white to red. He jumps on top of Izadora, grabbing a wad of her long black hair. Lennox yanks violently on her thick black strands as if he is pulling stubborn weeds from a garden bed.

"Let go of my hair," she shrieks as she continues to twist Samuel's arm behind his back.

Samuel kicks Lennox with powerful thrusts from his webbed feet, knocking the wind out of Lennox, who struggles to regain his breath.

Figlo watches from high up in the plant, baffled by his friends' barbarous behavior. He can see that the whites of their eyes have turned bright red. He knows they are not themselves, that they are not thinking clearly. The cloud of gold dust particles must have altered their moods, he thinks to himself.

"I'll kill you if it's the last thing I do!" Izadora shouts as she wraps her free hand around Samuel's neck and begins choking him.

Lennox lifts his hand up high, extends his index and middle finger and lunges at Izadora, shoving his two fingers inside her nose and pulling upwards on her nostrils with all of his strength. Izadora howls in pain as Lennox continues to yank forcefully on her hair.

"When I'm finished, I'll have ripped every last strand of hair from your head!" Lennox yells.

"And when I'm finished with you, there will be nothing left but shards of broken shell!" Izadora shouts back.

Samuel screams as he repeatedly kicks Lennox's underbelly, each kick more forceful than the one before. He then wraps his legs around Lennox's neck, squeezing his legs together like pliers gripping the head of a stubborn bolt.

Lennox coughs violently, gasping for oxygen.

From above, Figlo knows he has to do something or his friends will surely kill one another. "ENOUGH!" he shouts at the top of his lungs. "ENOUGH!"

But Figlo's thunderous command goes unheeded. Samuel, Lennox and Izadora do not even blink. They continue to fight, their hatred strengthening with each passing second.

Figlo finally untangles himself from the plant's branches and dashes toward his friends. He uses his powerful strength to tear the three away from one another. Figlo grabs each of them with his monstrous paws and throws them in opposite directions. But as soon as they land in the muddy lake bed, they come swimming back with a vengeance toward Figlo from all three sides. Each swims with arms extended outward and legs kicking wildly to build up speed. Their eyes become a deeper red. With little time to react, Figlo takes drastic measures.

They come at Figlo with fists swinging wildly. They pound on his body, each blow increasing in force. Figlo reaches his paw back as far as he can and slaps Samuel across the cheek with all of his might. Samuel goes flying through the water, dazed as he lands on the lake bed with a thud.

Next, Figlo lifts Lennox high above his shoulders and throws him hard against the base of the rocky cliff. Lennox hits the wall and lands face down in the mud. He can barely move.

When Izadora tries to hit Figlo in his nose, he catches her fist with his paw, spins her around and wraps his arm around her neck. He puts her in a headlock and constricts her airway until she loses consciousness. Her arms and legs flail wildly for awhile, but she slowly loses strength. When she stops moving, Figlo gently places her down on the lake floor next to Samuel.

Figlo swims to Lennox and drags his body next to the others. He patiently waits until his friends regain consciousness, hoping they will snap out of their spell.

Samuel awakens first, moaning as he rubs his jaw with his hand. As he sits up, his eyes flutter. The area around his pupils are white again.

"Thank goodness, you're back to normal, Samuel," says Figlo, noticing the whites returning to his eyes. "Are you okay?"

"Wha...what happened?" asks Samuel, wondering why his cheek hurts and his arm is sore.

Lennox and Izadora begin to awaken at the same time.

"Don't you remember?" asks Figlo.

Samuel shakes his head. He remembers nothing about the fight.

"All of you were under some sort of spell caused by the gold dust ejected by the glowing flowers. If I hadn't stepped in when I did, you and the others would have murdered one another. Here, let me help you," says Figlo, lifting Samuel to his feet.

"My shell," groans Lennox as he massages his underbelly with his hand. "What happened? I don't remember a thing," he sits up slowly and brushes the mud off his face.

"Me neither," adds the princess. "One second I was smelling some beautiful flowers, and next thing I know, I'm waking up on the floor next to you. And why does my head hurt?" she asks rubbing her head.

"I think it's safe to say that beauty can be deceiving, princess," says Figlo. "Those flowers are dangerous. We can still use their light, but I suggest we keep a safe distance from them from here on out."

Samuel, Lennox, Izadora and Figlo take some time to collect themselves before pressing onward. None of them knows exactly where they are going, so Samuel reaches into his backpack in search of the map that the Oracle had given him. He pushes aside his dead flashlight and grabs the rolled-up map, unraveling it and using the light from the flowers to read it. The map points north. Samuel reaches into his backpack again, this time pulling out his compass. He waits for the compass needle to stop spinning.

Chapter Fourteen

"This way," he instructs. They follow their appointed leader, swimming close behind him.

After surviving their first brush with danger, they proceed with greater caution. At this stage, it is too late to turn back. They have committed themselves to finding the Hall of Mirrors, where Samuel will seek the answers he needs. Nothing can stand in the way of their mission, not even the dangers lurking ahead.

Judgment Day

For hours, the three brave souls and Lennox follow an underwater path lit by the white glow of the beautiful but deadly flowers. The glow, however, dims gradually as the flowers thin out until total darkness confronts the group. Samuel begins to worry. How will they be able to prevent potential dangers lurking ahead if they cannot see anything at all?

Samuel's backpack lets out a clanking sound. Blaze, the metal orb provided by the Oracle, shifts from left to right inside the backpack as the Scorchers stir within it. The Scorchers, which look like tiny glowing spheres with wings, are cranky from being cooped up for so long inside Blaze.

Samuel looks inside to find the source of the noise and spies the orb. He suddenly remembers the Oracle's demonstration of the Scorchers' ability to light the way.

"Gosh. I almost forgot," says Samuel as he smacks his forehead.

"Forgot what?" asks Izadora.

"The Oracle gave me a few things to help us on our journey," Samuel replies as he carefully rolls up the map and places it in his back pocket. "Allow me to introduce Blaze."

Samuel pulls Blaze from his backpack, handling the glowing metal orb with care and ogling its radiance. It is just like the first time he encountered the orb inside the Oracle's lair.

The others stare in wonder as the glowing metal orb pulses with a blue light. Samuel explains, in detail, how pressing the red button on top of Blaze will release hundreds of Scorchers.

"Can I press the button?" asks Lennox, raising his hand high above his bald green head. "Can I? Can I?"

"I don't know, Lennox. I'm not sure that's a good idea."

He looks at Samuel with irresistible puppy eyes and a puckered lower lip.

"Well...if it really means that much to you, Lennox. Here you go." Samuel caves in and presents the orb to the turtle, whose tiny stub of a tail wiggles enthusiastically.

"Be careful, " warns Samuel. "The orb might be danger…"

"I'll take that!" Lennox snatches it from Samuel's hands.

Samuel forgets to mention that magnetic liquid will squirt out from the orb, attracting the Scorchers that will then be released from Blaze's core. Lennox points the top of the orb toward his body. He closes his eyes and presses the orb's red button.

"Stop, Lennox, before...," shouts Samuel.

But it is too late. Just as the Oracle described, liquid bursts from the top of the orb. In a matter of seconds, Lennox is covered in a sticky solution that will remain on his green skin for some time before the glowing Scorchers finish lapping it all up.

Blaze then begins to vibrate as if whatever inside is eager to escape. Alarmed, Lennox lets go of the orb and watches it drop to the floor. The orb quivers faster and faster. A tiny door on the side of the orb pops open, releasing hundreds of small winged silver spheres, all glowing brightly.

"Those must be the Scorchers," says Samuel, his eyes fixated on one of the silver spheres as it quickly loops around him.

Izadora and Figlo have never seen such creatures before. Seeing Scorchers for the first time is, in fact, more of a surprise to Izadora and Figlo than it is to Samuel and Lennox because as natives, they thought they had met every type of living being in Lake Aqueous.

"Remarkable," says Figlo. He watches as the tiny Scorchers flutter all around them, creating a spectacular light show. Each Scorcher appears to have the curiosity of a child. They examine their surroundings as if this were the first time they have ever been released from Blaze.

"They're kind of cute," Izadora adds, giggling as their wings tickle her arms.

The Scorchers take one look at Lennox, detect the magnetic liquid and one by one cover his entire shell and body. Once they land, their wings stop fluttering, and they begin lapping up the liquid with their tiny purple tongues.

"You've got to be kidding me!" Lennox exclaims. "I look ridiculous. I mean come on. I could land an airplane on a runway at midnight." Lennox tries to brush them from his shell, but the little beaming creatures won't budge.

Izadora and Figlo laugh hysterically, almost falling to the ground.

"This is the first bright idea you've had since we've met," Izadora says with a chuckle.

Lennox tightens his lips.

"Good one, princess!" says Figlo. "At least we can't call him dim anymore." He gives Izadora a high-five with his paw.

Lennox does not enjoy being the center of attention, at least not when it involves others making fun of him. He picks Blaze up from the ground and hands the orb back to Samuel. "Here! Take it! I don't want to be in charge of this…this… whatever this is. You press the red button from now on," he shouts, throwing his hands in the air.

Samuel cannot help but join the others in laughter. "Don't worry, Lennox, the Scorchers will lap up the liquid in due time and fall off. Now that we know how Blaze works, let's be a little more careful next time. Life is about learning from your mistakes and trying not to repeat them."

Samuel keeps on laughing as he gently returns Blaze to his backpack. He signals for Lennox to take the lead so that his shell lights the way. Lennox is mortified but complies.

Time passes and eventually the Scorchers devour so much of the magnetic liquid, that they begin to fall to the ground one by one. Each Scorcher sits on the ground, refusing to move and waiting patiently for more liquid to lap up.

Samuel remembers the Oracle's suggestion on how to get the Scorchers to move along with him and his friends. He instructs everyone to stay put while he goes on a quick side mission. The others agree.

While Samuel is away, the light from Lennox's shell continues to fade as more Scorchers drop to the lake floor to wait for more magnetic liquid. It becomes hard for Figlo, Izadora and Lennox to see one another in the dim surroundings.

After he breaks off from the group, Samuel finds four

sturdy sticks. He pulls Blaze from his backpack and presses the red button, soaking the ends of each stick with the magnetic liquid. Scorchers approach from every direction, swarming like bees to honey and landing on the end of each stick, fighting to claim a comfortable spot. Samuel returns with a handful of illuminated sticks and hands one to Figlo. Samuel brings the remaining three sticks to the spot where he last saw Izadora and notices the princess is gone.

"Where's the princess?" he asks.

"What do you mean? She was right here standing beside me just a second ago," replies Figlo, waving his stick in all directions to find her.

"Princess!" shouts Figlo. "I don't understand it? She was right here. Princess!"

Figlo begins to worry that maybe the Malquars have taken the princess captive. But if they captured the princess, why didn't they take Samuel and Lennox as planned? Wracked by guilt and worried that the princess has been harmed, Figlo is about to confess the deal he made with Clatheron when Lennox has a meltdown.

"We can't catch a break. Now we have to waste even more time looking for the missing princess!" cries Lennox. "As if we aren't under enough pressure! Why couldn't she just stay put like the rest of us until Samuel returned!" Lennox snatches his light stick from Samuel and begins searching for the princess.

"She couldn't have gotten far," says Figlo. They agree to search the surroundings and meet back at their current location in 30 minutes. With any luck, one of them will return safely with the princess. Samuel marks their current location by using some of the liquid from the end of his stick to draw an "X" that attracts some Scorchers.

Though they search near and far, there are no signs of Izadora anywhere. They search uncharted territory that does not appear on the Oracle's map, cognizant that danger might lurk in the dark corners of the Abyss.

After a fruitless search, Samuel and Lennox rendezvous at the spot where they lost the princess. They wait patiently for quite some time before realizing that Figlo has disappeared without a trace.

"FIGLO!" shouts Samuel. Lennox chimes in, shouting the names of Figlo and Izadora one after the other.

"This is plain nuts! First the princess, then Figlo. From now on, we stick together. Agreed?...Samuel...Samuel?" Lennox turns around only to discover that Samuel has also disappeared into thin air.

"I can't believe this is happening!" shouts Lennox. "'Save the kingdom,' they said. 'Travel to the Abyss,' they said. 'Survive the dangers as one.' I told them this would happen. I warned them, but no one listened to me."

"I'm sure they're somewhere nearby," Lennox says softly, speaking to himself aloud. "Maybe they're playing a joke on me. If they are, it's one cruel joke. How did this even happen? We're supposed to stick together. We're a unit, and a unit never splits up. This is crazy. This is making me crazy. Maybe I was always crazy. Nah...it's crazy to think that."

Lennox places his hands on his forehead. "I feel like fresh bait, like a worm on a hook. YOU GUYS! THIS ISN'T FUNNY!" he yells, but there is no reply, just forlorn silence.

"Face it. I'm defenseless. Whatever captured my friends is

still out there. It's watching me. It's toying with me. I can feel its eyes piercing the back of my head."

Then, Lennox hears something move nearby, almost like a rustling noise. "What was that? Samuel is that you? Figlo? Princess?" He spins around, looking in every direction, waving his glowing stick as if it is a weapon.

"Show yourself, whoever you are," he demands.

Then, in answer to Lennox's pleas, the ground begins to shake violently beneath his feet. Two vines lined with rows of tiny suction cups slice through the dirt. As they slither out from under Lennox's legs, they wrap themselves around his entire body, their suction cups sinking tiny sharp teeth into Lennox's tough skin.

"Let go of me!" Lennox begs, his heart pounding against his chest. Lennox tries furiously to tear off the vines. One by one, he yanks the suction cups off his skin as his body writhes in pain. For every suction cup he removes, however, two more take its place. The vines continue to twist themselves around his legs and sink in their teeth. They begin to pull him under the soft ground of the lake bed. He struggles to shake them loose, but their grip is too tight. Struggling is futile.

Soon, Lennox finds himself pulled deep underground as if he were sliding on a chute, which eventually leads to another perplexing water world. He twists his torso left and right, terrified of where the vines are taking him. The pain from the suction cups' tiny teeth is unbearable. He cries in agony.

When Lennox reaches bottom, the vines hurl him into a large transparent container. He lands in an uncomfortable position, his body leaning against the container's wall like a wilted cucumber in a clear refrigerator bin.

The vines' suction cups let go, leaving behind a horrific stinging pain and circular black-and-blue spots. The vines slide a latch on the container's door to lock Lennox inside. He is now a prisoner in an unusual sort of jail.

Next to his holding cell are four other containers. Three of the cells hold his friends, who are as motionless as Lennox.

The fourth cell holds a strange-looking creature about the length of the princess' arm. It appears malnourished. It has fluffy purple feathers and an elongated purple beak. Its beady little black eyes are lifeless. The creature must have a serious cold because every few seconds, it sneezes violently, releasing tiny bubbles into the water.

Lennox is grateful to be reunited with everyone he cares about. However, the reunion does not change the fact that they are in serious trouble.

"Princess," Lennox says as he tries to move his head, arms, and legs. "What's going on? Why can I hardly move?"

"It must have been those teeth-sucking things," Izadora responds. "I can barely move my body either. Their venom must have weakened us." The princess looks like a lifeless doll left to collect dust on a child's bedroom shelf.

"Look at this place. Where are we?" Filgo asks as he slowly scopes out his surroundings using the limited mobility he has in his neck. "It seems we've been deposited in some kind of a courtroom. Although the kingdom never had to use a courtroom, the council had a room like this in case it had to hold trials for anyone suspected of committing crimes against the Aquatanians."

The room contains a jury box, two tables, a witness stand,

endless rows of pews for observers and a judge's bench. The walls are painted black, and the same glowing flowers that earlier lit their path line the walls to dimly light the room. Behind the large bench is a painting of a heavyset slug-like creature wearing a curly white wig. The painting's frame is lined with the glowing flowers, illuminating the decomposing face. The slug's eyes are black and sunken. Its wrinkled skin is gray like a corpse's. It lacks a nose; in its place are two black holes shaped like sideways mushroom caps. Floppy wrinkled ears hang low on each side of its head like an elephant's.

"I think we should determine who or what captured us," Samuel states. They are far from the Hall of Mirrors without any clue as to what they are dealing with.

"Hachoo!" The purple creature releases a sneeze so loud that it does not seem possible to have been expelled by such a frail being.

"I believe I can help answer that question," the feathered stranger says in a weak voice. It squawks, then sneezes again, the sneeze echoing off the walls of its cell. "Those who wind up on food row face a courtroom trial for trespassing on private grounds. The good news is that the Windershanks give everyone a fair trial...at least before they find them guilty."

"The Windershanks? What in the world is a Windershank?" asks Samuel.

"A Windershank...you know. Ha...ha...ha...ha...hachoo!" It shakes its head from side to side to regain its composure. "A Windershank is a slimy, grimy bottom feeder that eats everything and everyone it captures. They're strong, unforgiving and always hungry." The purple creature sighs as if it knows its own time is nearing its end.

"If Windershanks aren't fearsome enough," he continues, "they have pets called Binderluts, a species so ferocious they can tear you in half with one bite. Good thing they're as dumb as bricks." Once again, the tiny purple creature lets out a sneeze that belies its size. "Hachoo!"

"So what do we do now?" asks Figlo.

"There's not much you can do," it responds. "In fact, I'm kind of glad you four showed up when you did. Now that you're here, they won't bother with me. I'm too unappetizing," the creature says as it wipes its nose with a stroke of its feathery hand. "Who knows? Maybe you'll get lucky, and they won't like the way you taste…one can hope."

Then the purple creature begins to sneeze again, "Ha… ha…," but this time it catches its sneeze by placing its feathered finger under its beak. When it feels the sneeze has passed, it lowers its finger away from its beak. "Choo!"

Samuel notices that the creature is able to move its limbs. "How long will it take before we're able to move our limbs again?" asks Samuel.

"That all depends. It's really hard to say. Sometimes the loss of mobility lasts a few minutes, and sometimes it lasts a few days."

"You sure do know a lot about this place, especially for someone who's in the same boat as we are," Izadora points out.

"Well, as I said before, I've always been considered unappetizing. So far, the Windershanks have had bigger, better and healthier meals to choose from, and they've left me alone. I've been here for at least a month now. I've seen so many come and…not go. All were eaten right here in front of me in this very courtroom after they were found guilty. One never gets used to watching a gruesome Windershank feast and seeing the Binderluts fight over the leftovers. No siree. That's a sight that never gets easier." Recalling the scenes makes the prisoner feel sick to its stomach.

Lennox yells. "Guys! We need to get out of here now. I mean NOW!" He tries with all his might to move his limbs, but he cannot.

Samuel, on the other hand, remains composed. As his limp body sits scrunched up, leaning uncomfortably against a corner of his cell, he realizes it is important to remain calm so he can focus on solving their dilemma.

"What about escape? There has to be a way out. Has any-one ever escaped...dinner time?" Lennox asks their inmate, hoping for a positive response.

"Can't say I've ever seen anyone leave this place in one piece, or in many pieces for that matter. At least not as long as I've been here. Windershanks don't believe in wasting food. Eyeballs are like cherry tomatoes to them." The little critter does not seem too sympathetic to the group's plight.

Then, somehow, Figlo manages to wiggle the tip of his snake-like tail. "Samuel, look," Figlo says. "Whatever has weakened us seems to be wearing off. Go ahead. Try to move."

Samuel's eyes look down at his hand. He pictures himself bending his fingertips to touch his palms as if he were grip-ping a baseball bat. He is about to give up when one of his fingers twitches. "You're right, Figlo. Look at that!" Samuel says excitedly. "The paralysis is beginning to wear off!"

As Figlo and Samuel focus on moving their limbs, doors at the back of the courtroom fling open with great force and bang against the blackened walls, shaking the cells as if a powerful earthquake triggered an aftershock. Two slimy legless Windershanks slither down the main aisle toward their seats at separate tables. They leave behind trails of slime on the courtroom floor.

One table is labeled prosecution and the other defense. One Windershank sits on each side of the courtroom. Just like the painting on the wall, the two slimy slug-like creatures have sunken death-filled black eyes and elongated ghost-white faces. Their bodies are wrinkled, their arms covered in saggy skin.

Both Windershank attorneys are accompanied by their snarling Binderlut pets, which they keep on leashes. The Windershanks struggle to control their bloodthirsty pets as they slither down the aisle.

"Relax, Snarfels," says one lawyer, yanking on his Binderlut's leash.

The ravenous Binderluts foam at the mouth as they stare at the delicacies locked up in the holding cells, eager to enjoy their next meal. Their fur is slimy and coal-black. They too have sunken black eyes. Razor-sharp teeth protrude from their mouths, ready to dig into some tasty flesh. Despite the copious amounts of gray snot dripping from their noses, they can smell their prey from miles away, which makes them indispensable in alerting Windershanks to trespassers way up above on the lake bed.

A second door in front of the room swings open, creating a thud against the dimly lit wall. The force causes the painting behind the judge's bench to tilt to the left. More Windershanks, each with their own vicious Binderlut, file into the courtroom one by one. Each Windershank is as ugly as the next, with streams of white pasty slime oozing from their pores. They fill up all of the jury seats and observer pews.

Then the ugliest Windershank of them all enters the room. It appears to be the judge, who is twice the size of the other Windershanks. Before taking its seat, it leans on the bench next to the witness stand and licks its lips as it stares at the wonderful cuisine locked up in the holding cells.

A Windershank standing next to the judge's bench addresses the court. "Hear, ye. Hear, ye. All rise as the honorable judge takes his seat."

They all stand in unison while the judge takes his seat. Upon sitting, he pounds his gavel and instructs the other Windershanks to sit as well.

It is like watching the courtroom television shows that Samuel watched when he stayed home sick from school. He tries to avoid panicking by concentrating on moving his limbs, which are still useless, but he finds he can move his head. Samuel shakes his head to loosen the Whistle of Obedience, which is wrapped securely around his neck, tucked out of sight in his shirt. If only he could pop the end of the whistle into his mouth without the assistance of his useless arms. The minute the whistle touches his lips, he will blow it to see if the Windershanks are dumb enough for the whistle to have any effect on them. From there, he will find a way to free himself and help everyone flee this dangerous underworld.

As Samuel formulates his plan, the courtroom remains silent. The gluttonous Windershanks wait for the judge to begin the proceedings. The judge looks around the room as he places his glasses on his floppy ears.

"This court is now in session," says the judge as he wipes some slime from his chin. He slams his gavel down on the bench and turns his attention to the prisoners on trial.

The judge prefers to skip right to the verdict, or in this case, the feast. He is bored with performing pointless trials, but trials have become a tradition, which is important to the Windershank species. The judge's duty is to keep tradition alive. Others see no purpose in delaying the inevitable, but they are lower in rank and have no real say in the matter.

"You four have been charged with trespassing. How does the defense plead?" the judge asks in a bored, monotone voice.

To show the court respect, the Windershank representative sitting at the defense table gets up from his chair. "Guilty, your honor. My clients plead guilty."

"That's not true, your honor!" Izadora interjects loudly. "The four of us plead not guilty. As for the little guy, if you ask me, he does not look guilty either." Izadora refuses to sit idly by and watch this injustice unfold. Her father expects her and her partners to succeed, and that will not happen if these hideous creatures digest them before they even have a chance to reach the Hall of Mirrors. She fights with the only weapon she has: her voice.

"Your opinion is irrelevant, little girl. What says the defense?" The judge shuts her down quickly and asks the legal representative to finish his response.

The defense attorney remains standing and continues speaking. "As I was saying, they plead guilty on all counts." He shoots a sneering look at Izadora, sticking out his wet black tongue at her. Then he licks his lips in anticipation of the coming feast. He sits back down in his chair and begins to pet his Binderlust.

"This is an outrage!" Figlo yells, struggling to move. He wants so badly to fight his way out of the holding cell. He has never felt so helpless before. "I have never seen such a dishonest and unjust proceeding in my entire life. You act as if we asked this...this thing to represent us and speak on our behalf."

Figlo manages to move a paw, which means it might only be a short time before he regains full mobility. If that happens, the Windershanks will surely pay for what they are doing.

"Order in my court!" the judge yells as he slams his gavel down on the bench.

"Order? You want order? This is completely unfair!" Figlo answers with intense anger. "If I could move...I swear, I would tear you limb from..."

"One more outburst from you, and I'll hold you in contempt," squeals the judge, jumping out of his seat in outrage. "No one has ever spoken to me with such disrespect for the law." He slams his gavel over and over. Clack. Clack. Clack. "I will have order in my courtroom!" Clack. Clack. Clack. The judge retakes his seat and wipes away the slime that seeped out of his mouth during his fit of rage.

He turns to the prosecutor's side of the courtroom and asks, "Do you have anything to add to this mess?"

The lawyer stands. "The prosecution rests your honor." He looks toward the holding cells and taunts the prisoners with a huge grin plastered across his slimy face. He knows that he has already won the trial. He has never lost a case yet.

Chapter Fifteen

"Then it's settled," says the judge in an authoritative manner. "We'll have a short recess while the jury deliberates."

The judge addresses the jurors before they leave the courtroom. "You have been chosen on this day to make a very serious decision, one that should not be taken lightly. The fate of these four trespassers rests in your hands." Banging his gavel twice, he signals for the jurors to leave the room. "Now go. And may you show no mercy on their souls."

"What the heck kind of court is this?" Lennox yells. "Is this some kind of sick joke? This is more like a circus than a courtroom!" Lennox is highly worried. Being that he was the last to join the others, he still cannot move his body, so he has no way to escape. The others, however, are beginning to regain control of their bodies, little by little.

"As far as justice goes, their legal system isn't much different than the system in our world," Samuel says to the others. "I mean, sure, we don't eat people who are found guilty, but there are many times people are found guilty when they're really innocent."

At this point, Samuel is able to move his hands and wrists in a complete circle.

Izadora has just begun to regain motion in her arms. The paralysis is definitely wearing off on all three of them. If Samuel can just get to the whistle, he will get a chance to see if it will work its magic on the Windershanks. All Samuel has to do is command the Windershanks to release everyone and demand they be guided safely back to the waters above the underworld. The plan is fool-proof, if it plays out the way he hopes it will.

While Samuel continues plotting their escape, the judge

slithers back to his chambers, and the jurors leave the room to discuss their prisoners' fates.

"Good grief. What now?" asks Lennox, as he notices some new additions to the courtroom.

A group of Windershanks wheels in four black, oversized cauldrons filled with boiling liquid. One cauldron is placed in front of each of the cells so our heroes can be tossed unceremoniously in after the jury delivers its verdict. This is how it is done: all prisoners are found guilty and cooked alive.

Each cauldron holds a thick, heavy acid, which mixes with the water in the room to create a corrosive white foam that boils over the sides. The acid is heavier than water, so it stays inside the cauldrons, ready to cook their next victim.

The acid, called flectron juice, is derived from the waste of the Windershanks' pet Binderluts. Because flectron juice comes from Binderluts, it has zero effect on the Binderluts themselves. They can take a bath in flectron juice without harm, but their masters must be careful not to get any on themselves or they will face the same fate as their victims.

As for Samuel and his friends, flectron juice will make them crispy or extra crispy, depending on the cooking time.

Samuel whispers to the others softly so that no Windershanks will overhear his plan. "You're all going to have to trust me. I'm breaking us out of here."

"But how will you open the door to your cell when it's locked shut?" asks Izadora with a hint of skepticism.

"You'll see. Just be patient, and when I say so, follow my lead and make a break for it."

Unaware that the purple creature has been listening in, Samuel prepares to blow the Whistle of Obedience. He pretends that his mobility is still limited even though he regained all of his strength after the jury left the room.

Once again, the Windershank standing next to the judge's bench instructs the court to rise. "Hear, ye. Hear, ye. All rise as the honorable judge takes his seat. Please prepare to feast after the jury delivers a guilty verdict."

Everyone stands out of respect as the judge enters the room and takes his place at the bench. The jury members enter next, one behind the other, and fill their respective seats.

"Well?" asks the judge. "Has the jury reached a guilty verdict?" His evil grin could chill the warmest of hearts.

A female juror stands up from her seat to represent the jury. "Yes, your honor." She takes a deep breath. "We the jurors find the defendants...guilty of all charges." The courtroom fills with thunderous applause. The Windershanks splash slime in every direction as they clap their hands. Some have already begun to tie large napkins around their necks so they can eat without getting chunks of the defendants stuck to their slimy bodies.

"Then, by the powers vested in me, I sentence all four of our prisoners to dinner. Prepare the stew and get ready for the feast. Let's eat!" the judge says as he ties a napkin around his neck. He slams his gavel one last time to close the trial and begin the culinary phase of the proceedings.

Four Windershanks approach the cells. They position themselves directly in front of the latches on each cell door. In unison, they fling open the latches. Samuel continues to play possum, as do the others. As the Windershanks open the doors, the purple creature decides to tell the court about Samuel's escape plan in return for freedom.

"Wait, your honor! Wait! I have something important to tell you," the tiny traitor shouts.

"Speak then, already. We're starving!" demands the judge.

"Only if you grant me my freedom," begs the tiny creature.

"Fine, fine. You're not much to snack on anyway. You're not even worthy of feeding to our Binderluts. Get on with it." The judge accepts the creature's demands so he can start eating.

"The minute you transport your prisoners from their cells to the cauldrons, they plan to escape. They've been conspiring in your absence."

"Why you little…," Lennox mumbles under his breath in response to the purple louse's betrayal.

Samuel has no other choice but to improvise and take action a little earlier than planned. With the doors of their cells cracked slightly open, he quickly reaches for the whistle tied around his neck and blows it as hard as he can. Just like before, Lennox's eyes glaze over, as he enters a trance.

In his hypnotic state, Lennox awaits his first directive from Samuel, controller of the Whistle of Obedience. Unfortunately, the Windershanks are not affected by the whistle's magic. Samuel thought for sure that it would work on them, but he is dead wrong. Their eyes do not glaze over the same way that Lennox's do. Samuel quickly notices, however, that he has gained control over the Binderluts, and he improvises one more time.

"I command you to attack your masters…now!" Samuel shouts authoritatively at the pets, who begin to growl ferociously at the Windershanks. The Binderluts encircle the Windershanks, forcing them to retreat toward the bubbling cauldrons. The slug-like creatures form a back-to-back circle to fend off their disobedient pets. The Windershanks have never seen their pets act like this before and wonder why their faithful sidekicks have suddenly turned on them. The Windershanks scream and yell at their pets, but they ignore them and continue their attack.

The distraction creates an opportune time for Samuel and the others to slip away.

"Quickly! We must go now," Samuel says as he kicks open the door to his cell and points to the door leading to the judge's chambers. Samuel has a gut feeling the chambers will lead back to the surface.

"Wait, what about me?" asks the feathery purple squarler. "Please, I beg you. Don't leave me here to rot. Hachoo!"

At this point the Binderluts have begun to attack the Windershanks, tossing them one by one into the acid-filled cauldrons, turning the slug-like creatures into crispy Windershank escargot. One by one the Binderluts cook the Windershanks to perfection and then tear their crispy bodies apart before swallowing them.

Figlo, having emerged from his cell, stands outside the traitor's cell. "On this day of all days, I will show you mercy," says Figlo. "I will do this out of compassion so that one day you'll remember this moment and show mercy on someone who deserves a second chance." He opens the door of the traitor's cell. "Go now. You're free to do as you will, but do not follow us. Dwell upon what you've done while you make your own escape."

The feathered creature does not understand why Figlo has taken pity on him, but is very grateful. "Thank you. Thank you so much. I'm so sorry for what I did," replies the creature, jumping up and down with excitement despite its debilitated state.

"Just remember our agreement, little one. One day, you must pass this good fortune onto someone else," says Figlo.

The others are confused by Figlo's act of kindness. They do not feel the creature deserves their help. But they are unaware that Figlo hopes to set an example so that one day his friends will have mercy on him if they discover that he betrayed them.

Lennox is still in a trance, so Samuel commands him to head for the exit. They flee quickly into the judge's chambers, leaving the horrific sound of Windershank screams behind.

Lennox trips clumsily over a dingy sofa in the middle of the chambers and falls on top of a marble statue of a female Windershank. He slams into one of the statue's arms, bending it backward. The arm turns out to be a control arm that causes a bookcase across the room to swing open like a door, revealing a hidden staircase.

"Well done, Lennox," says Samuel as he pats his friend on the back of his shell. If it were not for Lennox's lack of coordination, they might never have found a way out of this underwater underworld.

Lennox, Samuel, Izadora and Figlo swim up the staircase as quickly as possible, hoping it will lead to the surface. They stop intermittently for short periods of time to catch their breath. It is a long staircase, but anything that leads to freedom is welcome.

By the time Lennox snaps out of his hypnotic state, they have already returned to the surface right where they had dropped their Scorcher-covered sticks.

Chapter Fifteen

Lennox has no recollection of how they escaped. "I don't know how we got back here, and to tell you guys the truth, I'm not sure I even care. All I know is that we're safe and uncooked."

They pick up their sticks, which are still shining brightly. Lennox holds his stick high up and forward to light the way. He wraps his other arm around Samuel's shoulder as the group quickly continues on with their journey. No one realizes that their close encounter with death is not nearly as close as it will be when they encounter what is waiting ahead.

The Boneyard

In the distance, a seemingly infinite wall comes into view as the four heroes proceed through the dark, murky waters. The wall extends from left to right until it disappears over the horizon and rises so high that they cannot see the top. The wall is too wide to swim around and seems too high to swim over. They stare with their mouths agape at the towering obstacle, which makes their tiny frames seem all the more insignificant. They wonder how they will get to the other side so they can reach their final destination, the Hall of Mirrors.

"Great. Now what?" asks Lennox.

Because of their previous encounter with death, Lennox quickly urges everyone to turn back and call it quits. He wants to go home to curl up in his tank and watch Samuel read adventure books. Even turtle food is beginning to look appetizing to him.

Meanwhile, Figlo looks around for Malquars. Just as Clatheron expected, the suspense of not knowing when his troops will strike is driving Figlo mad. He hopes the soldiers will arrive soon before he and his friends meet their likely doom during their dangerous journey.

"We can't give up," says Izadora, biting the corner of her lower lip. "We must find a way to the other side! Any suggestions, Samuel?"

"According to the map, there's some kind of graveyard behind this wall," replies Samuel. The map shows a wall and some tombstones behind it circled in red with an exclamation point. The Oracle must have drawn that to remind her and others of danger.

"Let me see that," Lennox says, grabbing the map from Samuel's hands. "Precisely," he concludes. "The map indicates that this is some kind of graveyard."

Izadora rolls her eyes.

Then everyone notices two massive wood doors in the wall, each with elaborate but peculiar carvings. All four swim cautiously toward the doors to get a closer look.

"These carvings are so creepy," says Izadora as she places a trembling webbed hand over her heart. Large bone-chilling skulls are chiseled into the edges of the wood, outlining the door frame in a spooky pattern. In the middle of each door, two lifeless faces carved into the wood seem to stare vacantly at the visitors. The face on the left is rectangular with a small pointy, bald head. The face on the right is rounder and meatier with a full head of hair and stubby nose. The faces are encircled by a carved pattern of tiny bones linked to one another.

"Should we knock on one of the doors?" asks Izadora with a curious tone.

"I don't know, princess. It might be dangerous," warns Figlo.

"They're wooden doors, people," Lennox snaps. "When

has knocking on a door ever been considered dangerous? Now step aside. I'll do it." He pushes his way past Izadora and Figlo and begins knocking loudly and persistently with a closed fist on the right door. Knock, knock, knock. Knock, knock, knock.

"Who goes there?" asks a voice, which seems to be coming from the face on the right.

"Is it me, or did that door just talk?" Lennox asks as he runs his fingertips over the eerie face.

"How would you like it if I ran my dirty fingers over your face without asking first!" snaps the face on the right. The face yawns, stretching its jaw wide open as if it had not spoken in years.

"My dear brother, you don't have any fingertips, or hands for that matter," squawks the face on the left.

"I guess that would make touching that ugly head most difficult," the face on the right responds. The two ghostly faces begin laughing hysterically.

"Who are you calling ugly?" asks Lennox, raising his fists.

"Please, green one. There's no need for violence," says the face on the right.

"No need at all," agrees the face on the left. "Allow me to apologize for our rudeness. We are the Guardians of the Boneyard."

"Gulp! Did he say Boneyard?" Lennox lowers his fists. He does not like the sound of the word "Boneyard" and what it might imply. He is not sure he has the fortitude to face another near-death experience.

"That is correct. My brother said Boneyard," confirms the face on the right.

"How can we be of service?" asks the face on the left.

"I am Samuel, and these are my friends, Izadora, Figlo and Lennox. Together we seek the Hall of Mirrors. Can you open the doors and give us directions and safe passage to the Hall of Mirrors?"

"Pleased to meet you both," the princess says as she curtsies before the seemingly supernatural faces.

"The Hall of Mirrors...hmmm. The Hall of Mirrors...unable to place the name," says the face on the right.

"Why, of course...The Hall of Mirrors. We know it very well," says the face on the left in a joking manner. "Can't say we've ever been there, of course, but we know it well."

"Ah yes, now I remember," says the face on the right. "I haven't heard that name in quite some time. We don't get many visitors here at the Boneyard."

An unnerved Lennox silently wishes the animated faces would stop saying Boneyard.

"Well…living visitors, that is," adds the face on the left.

Lennox's face turns a paler shade of green. "What's that supposed to mean?" he asks.

The group hears howls and moans emanate from the other side of the wall through the doors. They feel queasy.

The two faces begin whispering to each other, debating whether to help their visitors in their quest to find the Hall of Mirrors. Samuel and the others wait nervously.

"We talked it over and we've reached a verdict. We think we might be able to help you," says the face on the right.

"That's great news!" Izadora yells in excitement.

"That is good news, but maybe we could avoid statements with the word verdict in them," Lennox chimes in. He still does not know how he escaped from the Windershank's "trial" but would prefer not to relive the nightmare.

"Fair enough," replies the face on the left.

"There's just one thing we need you to do before we can help you," the face on the right demands with a hint of deviousness in his voice.

"Yes, one tiny thing," adds the face on the left.

The group is willing to do whatever the faces want to get on with its mission after facing so many challenges in the Abyss.

"One of us is a truth teller," says the face on the right.

"And the other is a fibber, an outright liar," says the face on the left.

"If you can guess which one is the trickster," instructs the face on the right.

"And which one of us is the truth teller," adds the face on the left.

"Then we will help you get to the Hall of Mirrors," both say in unison.

"You will be allowed to ask only one question," continues the face on the right. "And that question will help you determine which of us tells the truth and which of us lies. For obvious reasons, you can't ask either of us who lies or who tells the truth. But guess correctly, and we will let you pass through the doors, where you will be safely transported to the other side of the boneyard, unharmed, close to the Hall of Mirrors."

"I hate to ask, but what happens if we guess incorrectly?" asks Lennox as he nervously rubs the back of his neck.

"Guess incorrectly and you and your friends will be sucked through these doors against your will and transported directly into the middle of the Boneyard," says the face on the left with an evil grin.

"Oh. You don't want that. No, no, no," warns the face on the right. "That would be most unfortunate for you, most unfortunate indeed."

The group decides to humor the faces and consent to their terms and conditions. They will do almost anything to proceed with their journey.

The two faces then toy with Samuel and his friends, trying to confuse them. "Allow me to save you the effort," says the face on the right. "I am the truth teller, and my brother is the liar."

"Don't be silly. I am the honest one. He is the liar," responds the face on the left.

"That would be true if it weren't you who lies all the time," replies the face on the right.

"And if that weren't an outright lie, then maybe it would be the truth," the other brother says.

The two brothers argue back and forth until the group becomes flustered.

"That's enough!" interrupts Samuel. "We can't waste another minute listening to your bickering. This mission determines the fate of an entire race of good and honest creatures. They deserve their freedom. Please, I beg you, let us through and help transport us safely to the Hall of Mirrors."

"No," the two brothers say in unison.

"To gain safe passage, I'm afraid you'll have to ask us a question to determine who is the liar," adds the face on the right.

"What are you afraid of? Take a chance," tempts the face on the left as his eyes sparkle with mischief.

Figlo and Samuel look at each other, both at a loss for

words. They discuss swimming around the wall but know that it appears endless. Samuel misses Grandpa, figuring his grandfather is worried sick about his whereabouts. If Samuel is going to get back to Grandpa in a reasonable amount of time, he knows he has to make a decision and make it soon.

Izadora then takes it upon herself to ask the brothers a question. "Leave this to me," she insists with a glimmer in one eye.

"I hope you know what you're doing, princess," says Lennox. "I'm not in the mood to find out what's lurking in the Boneyard. The turtle is always the first to get eaten, or so I've heard." Lennox cringes at the thought.

"Princess?" asks Figlo. "Are you sure you can handle this?"

"Trust me," she replies.

Samuel and the others brace themselves while the princess begins her interrogation.

Holding her hands loosely behind her back, she looks the brothers straight in their cold carved-wooden eyes. "Answer me this," she smiles with confidence. Izadora is sure she has already defeated the brothers. "How many of us do you see standing in front of you?"

"One, two, three, four. Four," replies the face on the right.

"One, two, three, four, five. Five," replies the other.

"That was easy enough. The truth teller is most definitely the brother on the right. You answered four, and we are most definitely four travelers in search of the Mirror of Truth." Izadora is proud that she outsmarted the faces. Samuel and the others celebrate. Lennox is not sure why he had not thought of asking it himself.

"That isn't fair," replies the face on the right. "You tricked us!"

"Very sneaky, indeed," says the face on the left.

"That's too bad. You told me I could ask one question, and that's just what I did. Now, if you don't mind, I think we'll be on our way." The princess gestures with her hand to order the brothers to open the door.

"She is correct, brother. It is only fair that we keep our promise," says the face on the right with a subtle grin. The doors slowly open with an eerie creak, revealing a glowing light. "Don't be afraid. Step on through to the other side."

Samuel enters first and the others follow closely behind. They can hear the brothers wishing them luck.

"Do come back and visit us soon," says the face on the right.

"Yes, do come back and visit. That would be lovely. Good luck to you all," wishes the face on the left.

Once they pass through, the doors slam shut behind them, and they are instantly transported into the middle of the Boneyard. From a distance, they can hear both brothers laughing in a malevolent tone.

"Too bad we're both liars. The trick is on you!" yells the face on the right, his voice echoing from behind the door.

"Neither of us is a truth teller. You were doomed from the beginning. Good luck. You're going to need it," says the face on the left.

"Oh, you're so deliciously evil, my dear brother," utters the face on the right.

The doors then disappear into thin air, and the brothers' evil laughter fades away.

Lennox turns to the princess to complain about the predicament. "You said to trust you, that we should leave it to you. Well a lot of good that did us. Look at us now!" he shouts, pointing at hundreds of crumbling tombstones surrounding them. The graves are coated in algae. They're too damaged to make out any inscriptions.

"She meant well, Lennox," intervenes Figlo. "How was she to know that both brothers were liars?"

"If she didn't know, she shouldn't have taken the lead. If she really wanted to help us, she should have kept her trap shut," Lennox retorts. He is furious and frightened.

"Lennox, is that fair?" asks Samuel. "The princess was doing what any of us would have done in a tough situation, and that is to try your best. I mean, how bad could this really be?" he asks with no conviction in his voice.

"I'd say our current situation is pretty BAAADDD!" he shouts, pointing to all of the gravestones.

A cold mist suddenly spews forth from the ground in front of each grave. The howling sounds of restless spirits fill the air as ghostly apparitions emerge with the mists from their resting places. The Boneyard, it turns out, is the not-so-final resting place of all ancient, dangerous creatures from Lake Aqueous.

Long ago, before the Abyss was filled with danger, the ancient ones of Lake Aqueous, the same ones who etched their predictions on the Wall of Prophecies, buried their most fearsome enemies in this graveyard. With the burials came an unexplained curse on the dead. Little did the ancient ones know that their enemies' spirits would live on in a constant state of restlessness, anger and hunger to consume the souls of anyone who wanders nearby.

Chapter Sixteen

After their enemies were buried, a few Aquatanians and other inhabitants unexpectedly disappeared. The ancient ones sent out a search party to investigate, and when the searchers reached the graveyard, they found the withered lifeless bodies of the missing. The hungry spirits had consumed their souls.

The ancient ones then ordered the construction of a massive wall around the Boneyard to contain the spirits. They added two magical doors, each with its own animated face to warn people away if they tried to enter. From that day forward, the Boneyard was considered a no-man's land, totally off limits.

As time passed, the two animated faces turned evil, vowing their eternal loyalty to the spirits and dedicating themselves to luring innocent travelers into the Boneyard so the spirits could consume their souls.

Some say the faces turned evil because they were in the presence of malevolent spirits for such a long time. Others blamed the change to feelings of abandonment and neglect after they were left alone, cut off from the rest of the lake.

Samuel yells to the others to form a circle. "Quick, everyone, get back-to-back so we can see them from all sides."

The wraiths creep slowly toward them, moaning and groaning.

"So this is it, then. This is the end!" cries Lennox as he places his hand across his forehead. "I always pictured myself starving to death. Never in a million years did I think I would die in a graveyard full of vicious ghosts."

Izadora reaches for Samuel's hand as the spirits close in. "Samuel, what do we do?"

"I'm not sure, princess, but we have to do something. The inhabitants of Lake Aqueous are depending on us." Samuel tightens his grip around her webbed hand.

From up above, they hear a voice screaming for help. "SOMEONE...ANYONE...HELP ME!" Figlo is the first to look up, spotting a worm tightly knotted around a fishing hook. The worm is holding on for dear life as the hook and the fishing line are whipped out of the water, then tossed back in.

The pink worm issues another piercing cry for help. "Please...You down there...You've gotta help me!" The worm is suddenly yanked again toward the surface of the water, temporarily disappearing from sight.

"Someone on the surface must be fishing. It's just like Grandpa and I did the other day. They're casting their line in and out of the water," says Samuel. He quickly begins to formulate an escape plan. A spirit is inches away from snatching the princess and sucking the soul out of her.

"Listen up, gang. I have an idea. It's so crazy it just might work," says Samuel.

"Crazy is all we have right now," yells Lennox, squeezing his shell into Figlo's back to avoid the oncoming spirits.

"The next time the worm appears, we have to act quickly," Samuel says, trying to appear calm. "I want everyone to hold hands, and whatever you do, don't let go until I say so." They all join hands, forming a chain. Samuel, Izadora, Figlo and then Lennox.

One of the spirits grabs Lennox. A strong underwater current swirls forcefully around them. The evil spirit wraps its mouth around Lennox's lips and inhales. He freezes as the spirit begins to suck the soul from his body. Lennox's grip on Figlo's paw loosens, but Figlo tightens his grip, refusing to let go. Figlo sees a ghost-like double of Lennox emerge from Lennox's shell. The current swirls faster.

"Whatever it is you plan on doing to get us out of here, Samuel, you better move quickly," shouts Figlo as he sees the life fading from Lennox's eyes.

"Just hold on tight, and whatever you do, don't let go!" shouts Samuel fighting to be heard over the sound of the heavy current. Samuel does his best to ignore the spirits as they attack. He gazes intently on the waters above, waiting for the worm to reappear. Just as he predicts, the worm is submerged once more.

"For the love of God, don't just stand there! Please do something!" cries the worm.

Samuel takes his free hand, stretches out his arm, and grabs the worm's tail. Linked together, Samuel and the others shoot up toward the surface of the water at lightning speed as the fisherman quickly reels back his line, assuming he caught something big.

Lennox's lips break free from the wraith's mouth, and his ghost-like soul snaps back into his body. He quickly awakens and wails with his usual high-pitched scream as he finds himself speeding through the water like a shooting star.

Water gushes around them as they soar over the Boneyard.

"Now! Everyone, let go!" Samuel shouts before they reach the surface.

As the others let go, Samuel yanks on the worm's tail as hard as he can, undoing the knot and bringing the worm with them as they hurtle down into the Abyss beyond the Boneyard and out of harm's way, at least for now.

Samuel and his friends pick themselves up from the lake floor and shake off the mud covering them from head to toe. The worm, grateful for his rescue, wraps himself around Samuel to embrace his savior.

"Thank you! Thank you! Thank you! You saved my life. I was worm bait, literally," he gushes, squeezing Samuel tightly.

"You're very welcome, but I can't breathe," Samuel says, gasping while he tries to free himself from the worm's lung-constricting embrace.

"Oh, I'm terribly sorry," the worm responds. "I'm so grateful. You have no idea how scared I was. I am forever in your debt."

"That's okay. We sort of saved each other. If you hadn't come along, we wouldn't be having this conversation," reasons Samuel, extending his hand to shake the worm's tail.

"I'm Samuel. This is Lennox, Princess Izadora and Figlo." He exhales a sigh of relief and brushes the rest of the mud off his hooded blue sweatshirt.

"Nice to meet you all. I can't thank you enough for saving my life. My friends call me Crawler, so I guess that means you can call me...well, Crawler," the worm says, shaking each of their hands with his tail. "I vow to follow you to the ends of the waters for I am now your humble servant."

"Speaking of the ends of the waters," Lennox says, now fully recovered.

"He's right. We must press on, Samuel," advises Figlo. The fishing line propelled them closer to their final destination, but they still have a little way to go.

Lennox glances at the map. "We're really close now. The Hall of Mirrors should be just over that ridge, somewhere in the distance," he says, thankful that they have come so far without being harmed.

As the group climbs the ridge, the princess explains their mission to Crawler. After hearing their astonishing tale, Crawler does not back out of his commitment to repay his debt. He is excited to participate in their adventure. Even with the additional help, however, nothing can prepare Samuel for what happens next.

The Hall of Mirrors

Samuel and his friends are still somewhat in shock after their encounter with the treacherous spirits of the Boneyard. Was their success pure luck or were they destined to escape? Either way, they survived what could have been a most unpleasant ending to their search for the Hall of Mirrors.

They stop to rest for a few minutes while they contemplate their next move.

"How far away are we now from the Hall of Mirrors?" asks Figlo, stretching his torso and releasing a great big yawn. He begins scratching his ear with his hind leg. His eyes roll farther and farther to the back of his head with each scratch.

"Your guess is as good as mine. Lennox is the one holding the map," replies Samuel as he sits on a rock rubbing his aching webbed feet. He tilts his head back and gazes upward. He still cannot believe they have made it this far without a scratch.

Lennox is sitting next to the princess, examining the map and trying to figure out how long it will be before he is safely back in his turtle tank. He holds the map open with one hand, tracing and retracing their current route with his stubby index finger.

Chapter Seventeen

"Give me that!" snaps the princess, snatching the map from Lennox's hand. She turns the map two times to the right. "You ninny! You had it upside down." Izadora smacks Lennox on the back of his bald green head.

"Ow! Why do you have to keep hitting me?" asks Lennox. "If you keep it up, I'll have no other choice but to start hitting back."

Izadora throws a fist at Lennox's stomach, stopping right before it hits him. Lennox cringes and yelps as if Izadora followed through with her punch.

The princess giggles.

"I knew we should have left Samuel in charge of the map from the get-go," says Izadora. "We might have bypassed the Boneyard all together. Then maybe you wouldn't have blamed me for our near-death experience."

Izadora hands the map back to Samuel.

"Well, at least I got us a little farther. That's more than you can say, princess," Lennox shoots back.

"Barely!" she answers, placing her hands on her hips.

"Do you guys always argue like this?" asks Crawler, their new friend and faithful follower.

Izadora and Lennox respond simultaneously.

"Yes," Lennox says. "No," says Izadora.

"You should be happy you're alive," Crawler interjects. "We could all be fish food, but instead we have a chance to live, breathe and taste life's many offerings." Crawler's eyes drift upward as his thin pink lips form a smile. He daydreams about warm, moist soil and burying himself deep in the earth while feasting on a smorgasbord of fallen leaves and fungi.

"Crawler is right, you two. That's enough!" orders Samuel.

"We must remain focused. The fate of the Aquatanian race depends on the outcome of our mission. Enough resting for now. We have to keep moving."

Samuel, frustrated by his friends' behavior, grabs the map from the princess and examines it to calculate their current location. They continue moving forward while he examines the map. "It looks as if Lennox hasn't done such a bad job after all. According to this mark, the Hall of Mirrors should be somewhere over..."

"There!" Figlo interrupts. "Look. Even with an upside-down map, we made it. It's there in the distance." He is over-whelmed with relief yet nervous for he knows the Malquars might arrive anytime. Figlo looks around once more to see if he can spot them, but they still are nowhere to be found. Maybe Clatheron has changed his mind and decided to keep his sister Alaina locked up. If so, at least his friends will remain free and safe, Figlo hopes.

Izadora, lost in a moment of celebration, decides not to wait for the others. "Come on, guys! Last one there is a rotten piece of kelp!" she shouts. She speeds off, challenging the others to keep up.

"No fair!" cries Lennox. "Of course she's gonna win; she had a head start!" He pouts like a four-year-old not getting his way.

They all chase after the princess, but she swims too fast for them. Of course, Figlo is not swimming at top speed. He falls behind, constantly looking over his shoulder for Malquars.

When Izadora reaches the front entrance, she stops dead in her tracks, stirring up a thick cloud of lake debris. By the time the others reach her, the debris clears and she sees wide smiles plastered across their faces.

With all they have been through, it is hard to believe they have finally reached the destination that would help them solve their problems once and for all. This magical place holds all the answers to the questions that have remained unanswered for so long. How can they defeat Clatheron and his soldiers? Will they survive and regain their freedom, or will they falter?

The building is not much to look at. The Hall of Mirrors is surrounded by large boulders that form a fence. Its exterior is decorated with festive red lights strung together and attached to the roof's eaves. Some of the lights are broken, and the ones that do work flicker as if they are ready to die out.

The roof is made of yellow and brown leaves that sank to the bottom of the lake long ago. The leaves rest on top of sturdy branches held in place by logs that also fell from above. Dirt-covered mirrors wrap the upper portion of the exterior walls, reflecting the building's surroundings. The lower portion of the walls are made from stone and mud, creating a sturdy foundation. No one alive today in Lake Aqueous knows who built the Hall of Mirrors, and no one has ever had the opportunity to see it up close. This is a rare experience.

Samuel and his friends stand side by side as they gaze at the building.

"Pretty awesome lights," says Crawler.

"Astounding," Izadora chimes in.

"Wait. This is the Hall of Mirrors?" Samuel asks with a disappointed tone. "It looks more like a run-down funhouse at an abandoned amusement park."

"I'm not sure what a funhouse is, Samuel, but if it's anything like the building that stands before us, it must be extraordinary," says an awestruck Figlo, mesmerized by the blinking lights that adorn the building. To him, the building is strange and mysterious.

"This just isn't quite what I was expecting," Samuel says with a heavy sigh.

"Well, what are you guys waiting for?" interrupts Izadora. "Let's go in."

"Hold up a second. Shouldn't we take a look around first?" insists Lennox.

"For once, Lennox might be right," says Figlo.

The front door is a mirror with a glass knob. But there is something very odd about this particular mirror. Even though they all are standing in front of it, the mirror reflects only Samuel's image, as if it is sending a message.

"What do you think that means?" asks Crawler.

"Really, Crawler? Could it be any more obvious?" Lennox replies in an obnoxious tone. "It means that only Samuel can enter. I mean really. Use your brain!"

Crawler doesn't understand sarcasm and lets out a goofy giggle.

Samuel catches the sarcasm just fine. "You don't have to be so mean to our new friend," he says, scolding Lennox. "However, you may have a point about my reflection. I think I'm supposed to do this on my own, guys."

As Samuel reaches for the door knob, the glass flashes blue like the other glowing pearl he found in the cave. He pauses for a moment before gripping the knob.

"Here goes nothing." Samuel touches the flashing blue

knob and turns it clockwise. He expects the worst as the mirrored door swings open, revealing a corridor that leads to a dark room.

"Oh, come on. It can't be this easy," says Samuel.

"One should never take a gift for granted, Samuel," Figlo says. "Maybe easy is all it needs to be. Enter with pride. Seize your destiny. There's no need to be afraid."

Samuel looks back at his friends and takes a mental picture just in case he does not return. They look back at him with eyebrows raised and sympathetic looks on their faces. If he never sees his friends again, or anyone else for that matter, he hopes that their mission will have been worth it all. From the flesh-eating plants to the soul-sucking graveyard spirits, even the courtroom trial that almost ended in his culinary demise, Samuel feels his next step will be his most dangerous of all. What if he came all this way to gain nothing in the end? Worse, what if this is the end?

Samuel takes his first step inside the Hall of Mirrors, crossing the threshold to the corridor. The others remain outside. As soon as Samuel enters, the glass door quickly slams shut with a thud, creating a strong gust of current that knocks his friends down onto the lake floor.

"Hey! What's the big idea?" Samuel pounds like crazy on the door, but it does not budge. He is cut off from the rest of the world. His friends cannot hear him banging on the soundproof glass. They quickly get up and pound on the door from the outside although Samuel cannot hear their pounding, either.

Figlo, being the wisest of the group, instructs the others to save their energy and stop pounding. He somehow knows that Samuel will be okay; he can feel it inside. He trusts the Oracle and knows that she would not have led Samuel to the Hall of Mirrors without good reason.

The rest of the group, however, begins to second-guess their decision to let Samuel go alone.

"All we can do now is wait for Samuel to return. Try to be patient, and let fate take its course," Figlo says in a deep, soothing voice.

"That's easy for you to say, Figlo. You're not in there. Samuel is my best friend," Lennox whimpers. Even though he is anxious, he has no choice but to await the outcome of a situation over which he has no control. He sits down against the wall and bites his nails.

Meanwhile, Samuel gives up trying to escape from the Hall of Mirrors. But before he begins to explore the interior, a mysterious voice booms from every direction, echoing off the walls.

"Relax, Samuel. Your friends are outside and safe…for now," says the voice. The voice is deep and powerful. While not threatening, it is not that comforting, either.

"Who said that? Reveal yourself!" commands Samuel.

"I cannot reveal myself, for I am just a voice, a guide if you will."

"What did you mean when you said 'my friends are safe for now'?" Samuel shouts back, demanding an explanation. In his estimation, the voice threatened the safety of his innocent friends. He looks around in panic, searching for the voice's source.

"That all depends on what you do next, Samuel. Complete your journey and save their lives," answers the mysterious voice.

"I swear, if you harm one hair or scale on their bodies…," he says, trying his best to intimidate the disembodied voice.

"You'll do what?" it responds angrily. "I am but a voice. You cannot harm something that is intangible…unless you know something that I don't," the voice says, mocking Samuel's empty threat. "As I said, if you complete your journey, then your friends will remain unharmed. Do not focus on them; focus on the task at hand."

"And if I fail? Then what?" asks Samuel. He is not even sure what his task is yet, but he has already begun to doubt whether he will succeed now that he is on his own. The presence of his friends bolstered his confidence, but now he is alone.

"Do not worry about the consequences, my dear boy. If I were you, I wouldn't fail. When you eliminate failure as an option, you eliminate the ability to fail." Though his words are wise, the voice has not convinced Samuel that it speaks with benevolent intentions.

"Lennox…Crawler…Figlo…Izadora…," Samuel calls out their names in desperation. He wants more than anything to be by their side so they can face the next obstacle together.

"It's no use, Samuel. I told you. Your friends are safe. Need I mention that time is of the essence?"

Samuel releases a lengthy sigh and quits quarreling with the voice. "Fine then. Let's begin. What is it that you want me to do?"

"Now that I have your cooperation, I want you to follow this corridor to the end and wait for further instructions." The voice abruptly goes silent and will not say another word until Samuel reaches the end of the corridor, if he reaches it at all.

The Hall of Mirrors

Mirrors line the corridor's ceiling and walls, sparkling like the lake's surface at sunrise. They show Samuel from every direction, reflection upon reflection upon reflection. Samuel walks briskly down the corridor, knocking on the mirrored walls as he goes, looking for any potential exit, though none are available. He hopes that whatever the voice wants him to do, he can get it over with quickly. From there, he will make a swift exit and return safely to his friends outside.

At the end of the corridor is another mirrored door, this one without a door knob. The door slides upward quickly through the ceiling, revealing a tiny room dimly illuminated by light from the corridor. Samuel hesitates to enter.

"Do not be afraid, Samuel. Step forward and enter," instructs the voice.

"Wait. You want me to go in there. How do I know this isn't a trap?" Samuel clenches his fists and looks over his shoulder to make sure no one is behind him.

"I guess there's only one way to find out for sure. You'll just have to trust me."

"Trust you? Why should I trust you? I can't even see you. Grandpa always told me to look into the eyes of someone before deciding whether to trust them." Still, something in the voice's tone and the lack of alternatives persuade Samuel to proceed. "As if I have a choice in the matter."

Samuel enters the room. "Now what?"

A bright light fills the room from overhead, illuminating five identical gold-framed mirrors, each with a black lever attached to the right side of their frames. While not the strangest thing he has seen since touching the magical glowing red pearl, it certainly is not normal.

"Do not touch the mirrors," the voice instructs.

"Trust me. I wasn't planning on it." Samuel is perplexed. He tries to formulate a last-minute escape plan while asking about the mirrors' purpose.

"So what's this all about?" asks Samuel.

"You are impatient. If you are to succeed in life, you will need to develop patience. Patience will change an outcome to your favor." Samuel rolls his eyes as he grows tired of the voice's advice.

"I saw that," says the voice.

Samuel's body stiffens.

"Let us continue. Of the five mirrors that you see before you, one is the Mirror of Truth. The Mirror of Truth contains the answers to the questions you seek. You must determine which one is the Mirror of Truth and then pull the black lever beside it to unleash its wisdom."

"Enough of these games! You're supposed to help me. Why don't you just tell me which is the right one?" Samuel pleads. But the voice does not answer. Instead, it repeats its instructions. "You must pull the correct lever! There is but one correct lever to pull. Doing so will yield the answers you seek."

"I'm curious. What happens if I pull the wrong lever?" asks Samuel.

"If you choose the wrong lever, you will find yourself trapped inside the Hall of Mirrors for eternity," the voice warns in a deep tone that rattles the mirrors.

The only thing certain is that if Samuel pulls the wrong lever, he will grow old trapped inside a funhouse without saying goodbye to Grandpa. He begins to worry about his friends, especially the princess, and wonders if he will get the opportunity to see her again.

"And my friends? What's to become of them if I make the wrong choice?" Once again, the voice does not answer, making Samuel feel even more insecure.

At that instant, four of the five mirrors display images of his friends, each occupying one mirror. He sees Izadora, Figlo, Crawler and Lennox, but they cannot see him. He cries out their names, but they cannot hear him.

In one mirror, Lennox is on both knees praying for the safe return of his best friend. In another, Princess Izadora is sitting with her head tucked between her knees. The next mirror shows Figlo swimming in circles, seemingly waiting impatiently for Samuel's return but in reality nervous about something else. The fourth mirror shows Crawler looking up warily at the surface of the water, probably searching for incoming fish hooks. The fifth mirror is empty as if it is waiting to be filled.

"Why is this mirror empty?" asks Samuel.

"If that is the mirror you choose, then pull the black lever," the voice responds. "Go ahead. Find out if your instincts are correct." Samuel senses the voice is provoking him, expecting him to slip up and make a mistake, but it actually is teaching Samuel to trust his instincts.

Samuel runs his hand over the black lever attached to the mirror that is displaying the image of Izadora, but he changes his mind and pulls his hand back. Then he thinks to himself that maybe he should choose the lever attached to the mirror that shows Lennox, his oldest and dearest friend.

Samuel is torn. None of this makes any sense. What would

Grandpa do? What is the logical choice? Samuel's chest tightens as the pressure begins to build inside. One wrong move and he will be trapped inside the Hall of Mirrors for eternity.

"There's no easy answer. I just have to go for it," Samuel thinks to himself.

He takes a deep breath and chooses the empty mirror, assuming that once he pulls the black lever, the answers to his questions will magically appear. As he pulls the black lever, Samuel squeezes his eyes shut, expecting something horrible to happen. His heart pounds. He can hear his breath grow heavier. He slowly opens one eyelid at a time, only to find that the mirror before him remains blank.

"I can't believe it! I'm trapped here forever," he says, assuming he chose incorrectly.

And then it happens. The overhead light in the room flickers several times as if a bulb is short-circuiting. Then the light disappears altogether for five seconds. When it returns, the other four mirrors have disappeared and an out-of-focus figure materializes in the fifth mirror. The figure appears to be the same size and build as Samuel. As the figures come into focus, Samuel holds his breath when he suddenly realizes who it is.

It is his own reflection!

He is overwhelmed with anger and disappointment.

"My friends and I came all this way, risked our lives on more than one occasion, and all to find this awful place just to see my own reflection?" Frustrated, Samuel had hoped pulling the lever would unleash something more profound, something that would help him find a way to fulfill his destiny.

"I promise, Samuel. This journey was not without purpose." Samuel's jaw drops. His reflection has developed its own voice and has broken free from mimicking Samuel's physical movements. Samuel's reflection looks identical in every way but has magically become its own entity. It stands tall with the prideful chest of a lion and speaks with the confident voice of a hero.

"And who might you be?" asks Samuel, slightly befuddled.

"I am you and you are me. I am the side of you filled with courage, passion and strength."

"Can you help me…I mean…can you help us?" asks Samuel.

"It is you who can help to repay our debt to the people of Aquatania," says his reflection with a smile, hoping it comforts Samuel. His reflection is about to share with Samuel all the unanswered questions that he has fought so hard to find, including all the memories he unknowingly blocked out from his childhood.

"Debt, what debt?" asks Samuel.

"Do you remember the shipwreck that we found at the bottom of the lake?"

"Yes, of course. How could I forget? We were almost eaten alive!"

"That's the one. And when we were inside the wreckage, do you remember seeing a photograph of two people holding an infant?" asks his reflection.

"Yes, but the photograph was hard to make out. The picture was damaged and covered with grime."

"Those people in the photograph are our parents and it was us they were holding."

"I don't understand," replies Samuel. His eyebrows furrow.

"What's there to understand?" asks his reflection. "That picture was hanging in mom and dad's boat."

"So you're telling me the boat once belonged to mom and dad?" Samuel wonders why he never heard this story before. What he does not realize is that Grandpa had tried telling Samuel on numerous occasions that the boat had been responsible for the death of his parents. Every time Grandpa tried to tell the story he found himself emotional and it was always too hard to talk about.

"And why are you telling me all of this?" asks Samuel.

His reflection releases a sigh. "Because, you need to know the truth. It seems you've blocked out or forgotten the bad memories of what happened on the traumatic day that mom and dad died."

The tears begin to flow heavily down Samuel's cheeks, mixing with the surrounding water. Samuel's reflection slowly fades away from the mirror. In place of his reflection, the mirrored glass begins to display a series of vivid images, as if Samuel were watching a movie.

"Let me see if I can help you remember. When we were just a toddler, mom and dad decided to take the boat for a spin on the lake. Mom was cooking, and dad was helping her in the boat's kitchen while you rested in the bedroom. A violent storm suddenly took hold, and lightning struck a hole in the side of the boat. The cabin rapidly filled with water. Our parents panicked. Then, out of nowhere, King Zedorious appeared. They didn't know what to make of him at first. It was a bit of a shock. He promised mom and dad he would carry us to safety and mentioned that the Oracle told him that we were destined to repay this debt. Our parents weren't sure what Zedorious meant, but considering the circumstances, they had to make a quick decision before their only child drowned. They agreed to his terms and watched the king snatch us up and swim through one of the portholes. The king was tiny enough to fit through the porthole with us in his arms. The kitchen door was blocked, and mom and dad couldn't fit through the porthole like we could. They...they didn't make it out alive."

Samuel's reflection reappears in the mirrored glass. "I know it's hard, Samuel. The story is a lot to digest, but you're brave. Just know that our parents did what any loving parents would do. Mom and Dad sacrificed their lives to make sure we were safe to live the life they always wanted for their one and only son."

"It's not fair. I wish I had drowned with them that day!" Samuel pouts, crossing his arms.

"Don't say that! That was not our destiny," replies his reflection. "Our destiny is to repay the debt for the day we were saved, to be courageous, and most important, to save the kingdom."

Samuel sniffles again, struggling to stanch the river of tears pouring from his eyes. "But how can I do that?" asks Samuel.

"Don't you see? You were once a boy, and now you're a man." His reflection places his hand on the mirrored glass, palm facing outwards toward Samuel. "Place your palm on top of mine," he instructs. Samuel complies with his request.

"You've known the answers all along, Samuel. Believe in

yourself. Believing in yourself is the only tool that you need to succeed in life."

"You're right," Samuel says as he wipes more tears from his eyes.

"Of course I'm right. Why wouldn't I be? I'm you," he replies with a smirk. "Together we are unstoppable." A mystical fog begins to pour excessively from the bottom of the mirror. His reflection then steps out of the mirror and merges with Samuel's body to unite them as one.

"I know what I must do," says Samuel, now standing tall with the prideful chest of a lion and speaking with the confident voice of a hero. At that moment, Samuel knows he is ready to take on anything that comes his way. He realizes that he must have believed in himself all along; otherwise he would never have made it this far.

Then the disembodied voice returns from its slumber. "Will you be needing anything else, my boy?"

"I suppose not. Just an exit," Samuel replies while trying to remain focused on the task ahead.

"Walk through the Mirror of Truth to reunite with what's left of your friends," instructs the voice.

"Wait! What do you mean 'what's left of your friends?'" The voice remains silent. Samuel backs up to get a running start and crashes through the Mirror of Truth, which transports him back to the front entrance to the Hall of Mirrors.

Crawler, Lennox and Izadora are nowhere to be found. All that remains is a barely breathing Figlo.

"Figlo!" Samuel swims swiftly to his friend's side, drops to his knees and embraces Figlo's head, lifting it gently off the lake bed.

"Figlo, stay with me!" Samuel begs as his friend fades in and out of consciousness.

Figlo begins to cough up green blood. "I didn't mean it, Samuel. I didn't mean for it to happen this way." He can barely get the words out of his bloodied mouth.

"You didn't mean for what to happen this way? Where are the others? What happened to you while I was gone?" Samuel frantically searches for answers. He should have been there to protect them. He should have been there to protect Izadora.

"They took them...they took them because of me," Figlo replies. "I wish I had never done what I did. I wish I could turn back time and set things straight. This is all my fault!" he cries in shame.

Figlo's garbled speech, mixed with coughing, is not making much sense to Samuel.

"Who took them, Figlo? Who took our friends? I need you to focus!" Samuel shouts, shaking his friends head.

"The Malquars. At least a dozen or more. They came out of nowhere. They did this to me."

"And the others? Where are they now?" asks Samuel.

"They took them back to the kingdom. They must have thought Lennox was you and Crawler was Lennox. I never told them what you or Lennox look like, so they...they...it's all my fault, Samuel. Clatheron knew. He knew and did this because of me. They left me for dead." Figlo continues to ramble on. "Deal...save my sister...betray friends..."

At first, Samuel doesn't understand what Figlo is talking about, but Figlo continues to ramble on and Samuel eventually fits the bits and pieces together. Luckily, the soldiers were extremely dumb and under the impression that they captured Samuel and Lennox when in fact they captured Lennox and Crawler. This gives Samuel an opportunity to set things right again.

Samuel feels sympathy toward Figlo but is upset with him. Samuel would do anything for his own loved ones if they were being held captive in Clatheron's jail. He understands why Figlo made a pact with the devil. He only wishes Figlo had talked to him about his sister Alaina's imprisonment so he could have reassured him about their mission's success and promised her safe return.

Now, Samuel must not only save the kingdom and the creatures of Aquatania but first free his friends, who he needs to help him defeat Clatheron and his army. The situation is more complicated than ever.

Samuel formulates another plan, caressing Figlo tightly as he regains his strength and snaps out of his daze.

"When you feel up to it, you must show me the way to the kingdom," insists Samuel.

"But Samuel, that's plain mad," he answers weakly.

"Oh, I'm mad all right, mad enough to gain control of the situation that you put us in!" Samuel does not intend to make Figlo feel worse than he already does, but he is angry with him.

"I'm so sorry, Samuel. I should have believed in you when we first met. Instead, I underestimated your abilities and made a grave mistake. I know it will take a long time before you can trust me again. Please, let me lead you to the kingdom. Let me help you save them," begs Figlo. "If it's worth anything, I believe in you now."

Samuel feels guilty for shouting at Figlo. "I didn't mean to yell at you. I know you feel bad. The truth is, I can't do this without you Figlo. I just can't."

"I'm here now. I won't make the same mistake twice. I promise."

Samuel strokes Figlo's head in a sign of forgiveness.

"If I take you to the kingdom, I'm just not sure how we'll get past all those guards. It's not like you'll be able to walk in, grab our friends and walk out without being pummeled by Malquars."

"You leave that part of the plan to me. They won't even notice me, not for a second." Samuel grins as he remembers the Aquacuff.

After resting awhile, they head off toward the kingdom. Figlo musters up his strength and insists that Samuel hold onto his tail. He is still in a lot of pain but does his best to ignore it because he has very little time to set things right again.

"We'll get there a lot faster if you let me pull you," says Figlo.

Samuel agrees. He is shocked at the speed at which Figlo can swim despite his suffering. It is ten times as fast as Samuel can swim, even with webbed feet. Figlo's speed will come in handy. Maybe Figlo will find a way to redeem himself for all of the wrong that he has done.

Under Lock and Key

There comes a time in everyone's lives when they see their reflection in a mirror and discern once-hidden truths. These truths are waiting to shine through when the right opportunity arises, and when it does, the clouds clear from above, unveiling the bluest of skies.

For Samuel, that moment has arrived. He finds in himself the courage and fortitude to overcome any challenge in his path. Discovering his true potential brings a deeper meaning to Samuel's life and a profound sense of self-worth. It does not matter what he was like when he lacked answers, direction, true meaning and purpose. That is all in the past. The future beckons.

As Samuel forges ahead, he focuses on the new and improved version of himself. The new Samuel is stronger and more focused, somebody on whom others can depend in dire circumstances. He has seen in the Mirror of Truth the tool to save his friends and the underwater kingdom. He is that tool.

To start, Samuel will have to restore his crew, including Figlo. Believing in second chances, he has already forgiven

Figlo. Samuel always tries to place himself in someone else's shoes so he can gain the perspective of the individual who made a poor decision. That is all Figlo did, make a poor decision, for which he can make amends by helping free his friends. Besides, Samuel has no choice but to forgive him. He needs Figlo by his side if he is to have any chance of regaining the kingdom.

In return for Figlo's help, Samuel intends to do the right thing and make sure Alaina is rescued along with the other Aquatanians who were enslaved after the Great Invasion.

Samuel and Figlo reach the outer walls surrounding the once beautiful Kingdom of Aquatania. After swimming over the city walls, they quickly take cover behind a nearby boulder that faces the front of the main entrance to the kingdom's castle. Shielded by the large rock, they remain undetected by patrolling Malquars and examine the entrance, searching for a way to infiltrate the castle while preserving the element of surprise.

Clatheron does not expect enemies to be so audacious as to enter his territory, so the element of surprise is already on Samuel's side, but there is one problem. Everywhere they look, Malquars are on guard, stationed from the front gate to the watchtowers and presumably in the inner hallways, as well. The guards are a lot uglier and intimidating than Samuel remembered them from his dream. He is thankful that, so far, the guards have not found them hiding inside the kingdom's walls, but he knows that soon enough, he will have to confront these monsters. Their large muscular bodies drip with gooey slime, fueling Samuel's desire to stand up to them as a representative of the Aquatanian race.

Although Samuel is still getting used to his newfound courage, the prospect of the coming battle barely fazes him now. All heroes fear their enemies, but they know how to control that fear and use self-control to their advantage. Thanks to the magical encounter with his reflection, the advantage is now Samuel's.

"If only we can sneak in through the front door undetected," whispers Samuel, "but those guards are standing directly in front of the door in our way."

Figlo scans the entrance with his keen vision. "If I remember correctly, a tiny door is embedded in the main door," says Figlo. "It swings open and doesn't have a handle or lock."

"Like a doggy door?" asks Samuel.

"I'm not sure what a doggy door is, but if it matches my description, then yes. The tiny door was never there in the old days, but I noticed it when...," Figlo says. He pauses and lowers his head in shame. "I noticed it the last time I was here, when I met Clatheron to betray my people."

"It's okay, Figlo. All that matters now is that you pay your debt to us, make things right and restore honor to your name." Samuel pats him on his furry back. The last thing they need is for Figlo to sink into depression. He needs to be alert and in prime shape.

Figlo lifts his head and focuses again on the main entrance. "There! Do you see it? Look toward the center of the door between the two guards standing side by side. Clatheron must have built the small door for one of his servants. It's too small for a Malquar or me to fit through, but I think you're just the right size to squeeze through." Figlo is so excited by his discovery that he almost blows their cover. He wildly wags his white tail, which pops out from behind the rock.

"Be careful. We don't want them to see us just yet," warns Samuel, quickly pushing Figlo's tail down to the lake floor.

Samuel then studies the doorway. "I can see it." He then reaches inside his backpack to grab the Aquacuff, which he will use to blend in with his surroundings and sneak past the guards.

Samuel then begins to worry about whether the Aquacuff alone will be sufficient to help him sneak in. As long as the guards stand side by side, they will surely feel Samuel's camouflaged body graze against their legs as he tries to get through the tiny door. Or worse. What if the Aquacuff suddenly stops working, as it did when the Oracle demonstrated its abilities in her lair? Samuel needs a good distraction to get the guards away from the door, but what kind of distraction?

"What if? Nah, that would never work," says Samuel. "However, if it does work…I suppose it's worth a try."

"What is it, Samuel?" asks Figlo. "Tell me! Tell me!" he insists excitedly.

"Are you feeling well enough for an old-fashioned chase and ditch?"

Figlo, still in pain from the beating he took at the Hall of Mirrors, smiles. He knows he is fast enough to outswim and abandon the two Malquars stationed at the castle entrance. They are no match for him, even in his current condition. All he has to do is endure the pain for a little while longer.

"I think I have enough energy left in me to do it. But where should I lead them?" asks Figlo.

Samuel remembers his family's boat that he encountered at the start of his adventure. If Figlo can lead the two guards to the monster inside the wreckage, then maybe they will wind up as the monster's breakfast. Given that Figlo is such a fast swimmer, Samuel is not worried that he would be caught and eaten.

Either way, Figlo will lead the guards away from the main entrance, giving Samuel enough time to squeeze through the doggy door into the castle.

Samuel describes what to expect at the wreckage and how he and Lennox evaded the monster. Then Samuel wishes Figlo luck.

"Ready?" Figlo asks, taking a deep breath before exposing himself to the guards.

"As ready as I'll ever be." Samuel counts in silence, using his fingers to count to three so Figlo can see when to make his move.

On three, Figlo emerges from behind the large rock. The guards do not notice him right away. "How can they not see me?" Figlo thinks, rolling his eyes. "You've got to be kidding."

"Hey dummies! Over here," he shouts, waving his tail left and right. The Malquars look at each other in confusion. They are not the same guards that Figlo encountered on his secret trip to meet Clatheron, so they do not recognize him. In fact, the guards never encountered an intruder inside the kingdom before, so they are not sure how to react.

"Do you think he's talking to us?" asks the guard on the left.

"I guess so? Should we capture him?" asks the guard on the right.

"Um. I dunno. I suppose so," says the first guard.

Figlo lifts a rock and throws it at the second guard, hitting him in the center of his forehead.

The chase is on.

The guards pursue Figlo as he takes off toward the wreck, swimming over the walls and disappearing into the distance with the guards on his tail. Samuel quickly slips the Aquacuff on his wrist before he emerges from behind the rock. His body begins to fade in and out with a flickering yellow light until he almost completely disappears by blending in with the water. Samuel seizes the opportunity to squeeze through the tiny doorway.

"I'm in!" he says with excitement. "Who the heck am I talking to?" he asks himself out loud. "Oops." He looks around to see if anyone heard him.

Samuel then heads down a long, dark musty corridor. It looks familiar, much like the corridor from his nightmare. He is careful to remain quiet and keep his thoughts to himself, switching back and forth between swimming and tiptoeing slowly on the floor, one step at a time.

While he moves forward, Samuel remembers why it is dark inside the castle. Malquars are extremely sensitive to light. Bright lights incapacitate them, or so the Oracle said.

Samuel begins to organize a plan to find the princess first and then hunt for his other friends, unless of course he finds them all in one place. He knows his rescue has to be quick or he will be captured himself.

"All right, if I were going to kidnap the princess, where would I keep her? What am I thinking? I wouldn't kidnap the princess. But if I did, where would I put her? I suppose I wouldn't want to keep her with the other prisoners. If I were in charge around here, I would keep her away from the other Aquatanians so she wouldn't inspire the other prisoners to revolt against me. So if I were Clatheron, I would keep a close eye on her. Maybe in my private quarters? Nah. She would keep me up all night with her crying. How about…"

Samuel suddenly stiffens. He hugs the wall as two rows of guards march toward him. They are on a regular patrol inside the castle.

"Please, Aquacuff! Don't fail me now," Samuel thinks to himself.

Samuel holds his breath. He remembers how he hid in the pool from the bullies in swim class. It made him a pro at holding his breath for up to three minutes if needed.

The Aquacuff almost does its job. It keeps him out of sight while all but one of the Malquars march by with a steady cadence. One of the last soldiers in the formation stops and takes a whiff of the water as if he could smell Samuel's fear. His face comes within inches of Samuel's cheek. He inhales through his snout as slime oozes out of his nostrils. Samuel turns his head to the side, pressing the back of his other cheek as close as he can to the cold stone wall to avoid detection. The Malquar snarls, exposing massive rotted yellow pointed teeth.

"Private! Where are you?" shouts a soldier from down the corridor.

"Hold your seahorses. I'm coming!" yells the Malquar private with a snarl. He continues on his way to join the other guards. Samuel lets out a sigh of relief. He quickly realizes his sigh is audible and covers his mouth with both hands.

The Malquar stops dead in his tracks. He whips around, his eyes exploring every inch of the corridor. He begins to drag his claws along the stone wall as he walks toward Samuel.

When the Malquar reaches him, Samuel tries his best to contort his body to avoid the private's claws. He moves slowly and steadily. Any swift move will cause a ripple in the water and surely expose him. Just then the Aquacuff malfunctions. Samuel's body flickers, fading in and out of sight like a strobe light. The Malquar grips Samuel's arm and begins growling loudly in anger. He slams the boy's flickering body against the wall, wrapping his claw around his scrawny throat. Samuel's wrist smashes against the hard wall and the Aquacuff falls to the floor, making him completely visible.

"Get off me!" cries Samuel.

"Intruder! Intruder!" shouts the Malquar, his grip tightening around Samuel's throat. The guards marching through the corridor come to a sudden halt. In perfect synchronization, they spin around, rushing back in tight formation.

Grunting and groaning, Samuel tries to reach for the Sword of Luminescence. He grows light-headed because the Malquar's claw is clutching his gills and sealing them shut. Before he can grab the sword, the Malquar throws Samuel to the ground next to the Aquacuff, puts his oversized foot on Samuel's chest and places a pointy spear on his neck. Samuel focuses on breathing and filling his lungs with cool water. His dizziness slowly subsides.

"I've got him! Over here!" shouts the private to the other guards.

The rest of the Malquars arrive. "Throw him in with the others!" the head guard barks.

"Release me this instant!" Samuel demands as he shakes wildly on the floor like a cluster of exploding firecrackers, trying to shake loose from beneath the large foot.

Chapter Eighteen

"Get up, prisoner!" barks the Malquar, pulling Samuel to his feet by the hood of his blue sweatshirt. He demands Samuel relinquish his sword. With no chance of escape, he removes the sword from his belt and hands it to the hideous guard. The others continue down the corridor as Samuel is escorted in the opposite direction. Every few steps, the Malquar pushes Samuel from behind to remind him who is in charge.

Samuel tries to remain calm and composed. This might be the end for him and his friends. Getting captured was not part of his plan. Figlo is long gone by now, which means no one is left to set him and his friends free. Samuel struggles to remain confident and find a way out of this mess.

"Maybe we can work something out. You seem like a decent Malquar," says Samuel.

The Malquar snarls. "Keep moving. No more stopping," he replies lightly pressing the tip of his spear into Samuel's back.

Samuel decides to cooperate for now, hoping the corridor will lead him to his friends. He begins to think that being captured might work to his advantage. Maybe they will have a better chance of escaping if they are all together in one place.

Samuel proceeds down the corridor, taking mental notes of his surroundings. After passing a stretch of wall, they come across a series of closed doors made from chiseled-stone. He hears a cry coming from behind one of the doors, sounding like a baby crying out in the night to be held by its parents.

"What's that?" asks Samuel with a curious look. The guard does not respond.

The cry grows louder as they approach the room. The Malquar twists the handle and kicks the door. It flings open and crashes hard against the wall.

"In!" orders the Malquar, pushing Samuel forward with all of his might.

"All right already. Enough with the shoving," says Samuel, stalling and struggling to make a connection with his captor.

The Malquar remains indifferent. "In!" he repeats in a cold raspy voice.

"I can see you're a Malquar of few words. Does someone need a hug?" Samuel asks, trying to lighten the mood.

The Malquar snarls again.

They quickly enter the room, where two upright tables stand before them. Lennox is bound by leather straps to one table and Crawler to the other. The straps are digging into their bodies, constricting their circulation.

"Crawler! Lennox! I'm so glad you're alive!" Samuel says excitedly.

"Are we glad to see you, Samuel!" says Crawler.

"Glad? Why are you glad?" asks Lennox sarcastically. "We're prisoners, you dope. It looks like Samuel got himself captured, too."

"The important thing is that we're all together and still breathing," replies Samuel.

"Not for long," threatens the Malquar. "Now be quiet! All of you!"

The Malquar continues to bark orders. "Take your bag and place it slowly on the ground. Keep your hands where I can see them!" With his every move, the Malquar's pointy spear follows Samuel's chest as if a bright red target were painted over his heart.

Samuel does as he is told to avoid confrontation. He slowly lowers his backpack to the floor.

"I'll take that," says the Malquar, snatching the backpack from Samuel's hand before it hits the ground. The Malquar leans the Sword of Luminescence against the wall closest to the door and places Samuel's backpack on the floor beside it.

At the opposite end of the room are two short rusty chains, each running through an iron ring anchored to the wall. Each chain is attached to an iron weight on one end and shackles on the other. The Malquar orders Samuel to place his tiny wrists in the shackles. Again, he does as he is told. The Malquar locks each shackle with a large key that clangs against others dangling from a large ring attached to his belt. Without another word, the Malquar leaves the room, closing the door behind him.

"Help! Someone! Anyone! Please help us!" cries Crawler as soon as the door closes.

"Would you please stop your shrieking!" snaps Lennox. "No one is going to hear us, and no one is going to save us. The least you can do is make my final moments peaceful!"

"Quiet down, you two. I need to think," Samuel orders as he looks for a way out.

The room is filled with torture devices, some hanging on the walls and others resting on the floor. Samuel notices that one instrument consists of a table, crank and ropes. He assumes the ropes attach to the prisoner's arms and legs and that the crank stretches the ropes until the prisoner's limbs are torn off. The other torture devices are just as terrifying.

"There must be a way out of here," says Samuel, fidgeting with his shackles. He musters up all his strength and takes one step forward. Samuel yanks on the shackles, lifting the iron weight on the other end of the chain off the floor. He takes another step forward, grunting and groaning as he moves toward the Sword of Luminescence.

"If I can just reach my sword, I think I can free myself," he explains as he takes another step forward. He believes he can use the sword to cut through his restraints and free the others.

The weights become heavier and heavier with each step he takes, but he does not give up. No matter how heavy the weights become, Samuel gives his all to reach the sword before a guard catches him.

Lennox and Crawler, bound to their upright tables, watch helplessly.

"I'm almost there. Just a few more steps." One foot after the other, Samuel slowly and haltingly moves forward, his arms and muscles trembling as he nears the sword.

"Come on, Samuel. You can do it!" says Crawler.

"I've got this," he says. But the weights become too heavy, flinging Samuel back against the wall like a slingshot. "I don't got this! I don't got this!" he cries in agony as he slams against the cold stone wall. The iron weights clang loudly as they hit the floor, echoing throughout the room.

Crawler remains silent for a few seconds. He then lowers his head and says, "We're not going to survive this, are we? If I don't get out of here soon, I'm going to go crazy."

"I think that ship sailed a long time ago, bud," Lennox replies as he closes his eyes and tries to forget where he is.

Samuel makes a few more attempts to free himself, but they are futile. His back cannot withstand another collision with the wall. He looks around the room, searching for anything that might help them escape. Nothing is in reach. Then, he thinks about the princess, where she might be and if she is still alive.

"Do either of you know where Clatheron took the princess?" asks Samuel.

"How would we know? We were split up when we got here," Lennox replies.

Then, the door to the room opens with an eerie creak. In walks Squinch, tiptoeing so as not to alert the guards on duty. He walks straight up to Lennox, believing, as did the captors, that Lennox is Samuel.

"This is it. This is the end of us all," cries Crawler, not knowing what Squinch is really up to.

"Shhh. Be quiet. They'll hear you. We don't have much time," Squinch says in a whisper.

"Who are you?" asks Lennox.

"My name is Squinch. I am a Malquar."

"You're a Malquar? Aren't you a bit undersized for the job?" asks Lennox.

"I'm not a soldier. I am a servant of Clatheron. A servant against my will," Squinch responds in a whisper. He begins to loosen the leather straps pinning Lennox's wrists to the table. "You must be Samuel," says Squinch as he addresses Lennox.

"Wrong," Samuel interjects. "I am Samuel. You're untying my friend, Lennox."

"I don't understand," says Squinch. "How can that be?"

"It seems your guards don't know who they captured," Samuel barks from across the room. "But that doesn't matter now because they've got me. Tell me what you're going to do to my friend!"

Squinch looks confused. "Can't you see? I'm trying to free him!" He continues to loosen Lennox's leg straps. "If the creature chained to the wall says he's Samuel, and this is Lennox, then who are you?" Squinch asks Crawler.

"I'm Crawler, and trust me, I taste really bad."

Squinch realizes that the soldiers who captured Lennox and Crawler outside the Hall of Mirrors had mistaken their identities. He continues to release Lennox from his restraints.

"Why are you setting us free?" asks Samuel.

"I'm setting you free because I need your help," replies Squinch. "I will free all of you and the princess as a show of trust in exchange for one favor and one favor only."

Samuel, excited to hear that the princess is alive, temporarily ignores the Malquar's request. "Then Izadora is alive. Thank goodness! What have you done with her?"

"Clatheron took Princess Izadora to Capitol Hall and placed her in a cage next to his throne," Squinch responds.

Lennox now free, sits on the table and rubs his wrists and ankles where the leather restraints left their marks. Squinch starts loosening Crawler's restraints, not worried about the consequences he might face if anyone enters the room and catches him in the act.

"You mentioned a favor in exchange for your help. What do you want?" asks Lennox, suspicious of the Malquar's intentions.

"You owe me nothing but friendship and your help in escaping. I no longer want to be part of this evil place. I want a new life, friends, meaning and purpose," answers Squinch.

Samuel nods his head. He understands.

"I no longer want to be bullied by the soldiers or treated

like dirt by Clatheron. I want my freedom. I want the respect I deserve," adds Squinch.

Samuel takes a moment to mull over Squinch's request while Squinch continues to free Crawler from his restraints.

With Crawler free, Squinch moves toward Samuel. "So, can you help me?" he asks while unlocking Samuel's shackles with a bronze key hanging from a ring attached to his belt.

"I understand where you're coming from," Samuel says, massaging his wrists. "I used to be picked on, too. It wasn't until recently that I changed into someone who no longer tolerates being treated like a lesser being. I am strong inside now, and you deserve to feel the same way." Samuel believes Squinch is sincere and decides to give him the opportunity to prove himself worthy of their trust.

"Does that mean you'll let me come with you after we save the princess?" asks Squinch.

"Hold up!" Lennox interjects. "Samuel, you're not seriously considering making a deal with the enemy? Are you?" Lennox is not nearly as trusting as Samuel.

"That I am, Lennox. Why would he help us escape if he weren't sincere? I believe him. I see something in Squinch that I can relate to. Besides, everyone deserves a chance. Everyone."

"Don't say I didn't warn you, Samuel," says Lennox in a snarky tone.

"Please, Lennox," pleads Squinch. "Give me a chance to prove my loyalty. And thank you for your kind words, Samuel."

"My pleasure. And thank you for setting us free," Samuel says. "You will have your freedom, Squinch, but first we must free the princess. Any suggestions?"

"It will be difficult, but I have an idea," Squinch says. "Clatheron is taking his afternoon nap. I'll sneak into his chambers. He's the only one with the key to the cage, and he wears it on a string around his neck. It won't be easy, but I think I can take the key from around his neck without getting caught. You three will have to stand guard outside his door and let me know if anyone comes. If any soldiers catch us in the act, we're all doomed for sure."

"Doomed? What exactly do you mean by doomed?" Crawler asks nervously as his body quivers at the thought of being strapped down again to the table.

"That table will be the least of your worries; Clatheron can eat a worm in one bite," replies Squinch.

"Gulp." Crawler does not like the answer one bit.

"Why should we trust you?" asks Lennox. "Who's to say this isn't some kind of trap?"

"I suppose you're right. It could be a trap; then again, what choice do you have?" replies Squinch.

Samuel chimes in. "The only thing that matters is saving the princess. None of us has ever been inside this castle before, and we need Squinch whether you like it or not."

Lennox realizes that Samuel is correct and that Squinch might be able to help after all. Still, he decides to keep close tabs on their new "friend" just in case he decides to double-cross them, like the purple traitor from the Windershank's courtroom.

After Samuel regains his backpack and sword, Squinch opens the door to the torture chamber, poking his head out into the corridor to see if the coast is clear. He looks back at the others who are huddled closely behind him. "Let's go.

It's now or never," says Squinch, using his tiny paw to signal them to stay close.

Samuel, Crawler and Lennox follow Squinch down the corridor. With every step they take, the danger grows, the greatest danger being Clatheron.

"I don't like this at all, Samuel," whispers Lennox. "It's too quiet. Something's up."

"Shhh. No more talking from here on in," Samuel says.

Samuel keeps an eye on Squinch, following his every move, staying alert for any possible danger, including any sign of betrayal from Squinch himself.

They reach Clatheron's bedroom chambers and hear snoring as they stand outside the stone door. Nervous tension builds up inside all of them. If Clatheron awakens, none will survive.

"Squinch, we'll stand here outside and if we hear something, we'll alert you," Samuel says.

"All right, I'm going in. Wish me luck." Squinch slowly turns the door knob. The door creaks and Clatheron's snoring ceases momentarily. Squinch freezes in his steps, waiting for the snoring to resume. It does.

"That was close," Squinch thinks. "Okay. Here I go." He creeps into the bedroom and looks toward the bed. Blob is fast asleep, tucked under Clatheron's claw. He approaches the king's bed and spots the key hanging around the evil ruler's neck.

Squinch reaches for the string's loosely tied knot when all of a sudden, Blob opens his eyes. Before he has a chance to alert Clatheron, Squinch grabs him by his slimy gelatinous mouth, shutting it tight so he cannot make the slightest noise. He carefully pulls Blob from under Clatheron's claw. Blob squirms, causing the evil ruler to roll over on top of the only key that will unlock the cage that holds Izadora captive.

Squinch slams Blob against the floor, knocking him unconscious. The sound almost awakens Clatheron, but his snoring resumes.

"What to do? What to do?" Squinch thinks to himself. Then he notices a feather poking out from Clatheron's pillow. Squinch yanks it free and begins to tickle his inner ear.

"Num. Num. Stop that, silly," Clatheron giggles, still asleep.

Once again, Squinch gently grazes Clatheron's inner ear with the feather, hoping that he will roll over again and expose the key. The plan works. He rolls over in Squinch's direction, briefly opening his eyes but remaining half asleep. Squinch begins to hum a lullaby.

"There once was a mighty king. Who wore a key tied to a string. He was handsome and smart, he was missing his heart and he had a powerful sting. La la la la la la la la. Hmm hmm hmm hmm hmm hmm hmm hmm."

And just like that, Clatheron falls back to sleep.

Squinch reaches for the knot and slowly unties it. The key slides off the string and almost hits the floor, but Squinch catches the key with his feet. He quietly exhales, wipes his brow and grabs the key from between his toes. He then begins to creep out of the room. On his way out, he provides one last swift kick in the head to Blob, who had begun to wake from his stupor.

Once safely outside, Squinch looks sad.

"What happened? Did you get it?" asks Samuel. "You

didn't get it, did you?" Samuel reads Squinch's facial expression, which seems to indicate failure.

Squinch then turns his frown into a huge grin. "Did I get it? You mean this?" He pulls the key to Izadora's freedom from behind his back. "Of course I got it."

"Great, Squinch! Absolutely awesome!" Samuel says as he struggles to keep his voice down.

"Yeah. Not bad," adds Lennox with a hint of jealousy.

"What are we waiting for? We don't have much time before Clatheron wakes up and finds the key missing. Let's get the princess!" says Samuel.

Squinch is pleased with his effort. He knows it marks the beginning of a new life without servitude. A life worth living.

Squinch leads the others to Capitol Hall. They remain as quiet as possible. As they enter, they see the princess curled up in a ball inside a rusty old cage next to the throne. She looks sad and weak as if this were the end of her days. Because she has not eaten in quite some time, her energy level is as low as her spirits.

Izadora is resting her head between her smooth blue legs, her black hair covering her sobbing eyes. "What do you want from me now?" she asks Squinch in a weak voice, unable to lift her head up.

"All I want is to help set you free," Squinch replies.

"Haven't you tormented me enough?" she asks, her head remaining between her legs. "Why would you be so cruel as to tease me like this?"

"Any chance you feel like getting out of here, Izadora?" asks Samuel. The princess quickly lifts her head when she hears his voice. The minute she sees Samuel and the others, her broken spirit is restored.

"You came for me. I can't believe it. You didn't forget me." She begins to weep again, this time in happiness. She stands up slowly and grips the bars with her webbed hands. Her wide smile makes Samuel feel good about himself.

"Forget about you? Not possible," Samuel says, blushing. They gaze at each other, frozen in a moment of bliss. This is not the right time for it, but Samuel hopes he will be rewarded with a kiss, just like in the movies and in his adventure books.

"Ummm. I don't mean to break up this romantic reunion, but we might want to spring her out of that cage and make a quick exit," says Lennox as he looks toward the Capitol Hall entrance for approaching guards. "It might benefit us all to remember that we're smack in the middle of a nest full of Malquars and minutes away from a gigantic monster waking to find his missing key. Isn't that enough to persuade you to get the heck out of here, and pronto? Then again, I'm a talking turtle. What do I know?"

Lennox, though sarcastic, has a point.

"He's right!" exclaims Squinch. "We've got to do this quickly."

Samuel grabs the rusty lock hanging from the cage door. "Give me Clatheron's key, Squinch."

"Please. Allow me the honor," Squinch says. Samuel holds the lock while Squinch inserts the key and turns it clockwise. The lock opens, but Izadora is too weak to move on her own. Samuel lifts her up into his arms, caressing her gently.

"You're safe now, princess. You're safe," he says, squeezing her tightly.

Crawler looks around the room for an exit. "How will we escape?"

The princess, though an infant at the time, remembers hearing detailed stories of how she and her Aquatanian guard escaped during the Great Invasion.

"Go to the throne. Push it to the left, and behind it you will find an underground passage that will lead us outside the kingdom's walls," Izadora says.

Squinch lowers his shoulder to help Crawler and Lennox push the throne to the left to reveal the secret passageway.

Reality hits when they hear a mighty roar echo from within the castle.

"Oh, no! He's awake," Squinch says in a panic. He signals for Lennox and Crawler to make a quick exit. "You two, go now before Clatheron finds us."

"Aren't you coming with us?" asks Crawler.

"Even though I want to come with you, I must stay behind to stall Clatheron so you have enough time to escape," replies Squinch.

"You don't have to do that. Come with us and leave this madness behind," insists Samuel.

"It's for the best. If I can provide you with even an extra minute to put some distance between you and Clatheron, it will be worth it. I now know my purpose. Don't worry about me. We will meet again."

The mighty roar grows louder and nearer.

"SQQQUUUIIINNCH!!!" yells the evil ruler Clatheron. "WHERE ARE YOU?"

"Go now, before it's too late," Squinch repeats as he pushes Lennox and Crawler through the entrance to the secret passageway.

Samuel turns around and tells Squinch to reach into his

backpack and remove the decorated oyster shell he found in Pearl Cave and kept as a keepsake.

"When you move the throne back in place, leave this on the seat," Samuel says.

"What is it?" asks Squinch, holding the sparkling oyster shell.

"It's a bread crumb," Samuel responds, winking at Squinch. "I promise, we will meet again. Be safe, my friend."

Squinch never heard anyone call him a friend before. It fills his heart with joy. After years of being bullied and treated as an inferior, he finally has met someone who appreciates him.

"And you be safe too…friend. Until we meet again." Squinch waves his tiny claw goodbye. He watches Samuel carry the princess gracefully in his arms through the passageway and disappear into the darkness.

Squinch pushes the throne back until it is in its original position, then he places the sparkling oyster shell on the throne's seat. As he hears Clatheron's thunderous steps approach, Squinch swiftly exits, waiting for him to discover the oyster and screech his name one more time at the top of his lungs.

The Element of Surprise

Thump…thump…thump thump. Samuel repeats the secret knock a second time, and the large boulder door at the council's secret hideout slides open.

With great anticipation, King Zedorious and a large crowd of Aquatanians flock around the entrance, bombarding Samuel, Lennox, Crawler and Princess Izadora with questions. They want to know what their heroes encountered on their journey and whether there is hope for the kingdom and its subjects.

"Please, everyone. Give them some space. There will be plenty of time for questions," commands King Zedorious who parts the sea of eager Aquatanians with his royal staff.

"Actually, King Zedorious…we don't have much time at all," warns Samuel. He hands the princess to one of the council members, having carried her most of the way back to the council chambers. Lennox and Crawler also took turns carrying the princess whenever Samuel's arms grew tired.

When the king sees his daughter, he freezes. A grave look appears on his face. He pushes back her jet-black hair from her weary face. Izadora is still quite weak from her ordeal.

Heartbroken, King Zedorious asks one of his followers to take Izadora to her sleeping quarters.

Samuel tries to soothe the king's anxiety. "Don't worry, Your Majesty. The princess is just exhausted from a long and difficult journey. The best thing she can do to regain her strength is to get some rest."

"I suppose you're right. It's probably just fatigue. Thank you for looking after her for me. I am forever grateful," King Zedorious replies as he places his webbed hand on Samuel's shoulder and squeezes gently.

Then the king notices that Figlo is absent. He cannot bear the thought of losing his oldest, dearest friend. "What happened to Figlo?" asks the king, clenching his teeth as he nervously awaits Samuel's response.

"Wait a minute," asks Lennox. "He isn't here with you?"

"No. Why would he be here with us? He was with you all this time." King Zedorious grips his staff tightly with both hands.

"We sort of got split up along the way," says Samuel. "It's kind of a long story, one that I'm sure he'd rather tell you himself once he returns." Samuel does not feel the need to share the details of Figlo's treachery and redemption. Fortunately, a lot of good came from Figlo's disloyalty; his duplicity led to many discoveries about Clatheron, his soldiers and their new friend and ally on the inside, Squinch.

"I'm sure he'll make his way here eventually. Figlo is a strong, intelligent creature. He can take care of himself," adds Samuel. "As for now, we have bigger things to worry about, such as making sure we're prepared."

"What do you speak of, Samuel? Prepared for what?" asks one of the council members.

Chapter Nineteen

"Prepared for the battle to come. The Battle of Pearl Cave."

The room erupts in loud voices, all expressing surprise and concern. Council members fire questions at Samuel from all directions, but there are too many questions to answer all at once.

King Zedorious slams his royal staff on the table. "Please everyone! Let the boy speak!"

Before he begins to explain, Samuel asks for some food for himself and his friends. He is exhausted and famished. His stomach growls, sounding like the roar that Clatheron made when Izadora escaped.

"Yes, of course, Samuel. You there!" Zedorious points to one of his fellow Aquatanians. "Make something special for our weary travelers. They've earned a hearty meal. Use the fresh kelp." King Zedorious looks at Crawler and then back at Samuel before adding, "No need for dessert. I see you brought your own."

"How dare you, sir. I am not food!" Crawler declares. Crawler is not only offended but a little scared for he is now aware that Aquatanians eat worms."

"Your Majesty," Samuel interjects. "This is Crawler, our friend, and if it weren't for him, we wouldn't be standing here right now." Samuel lifts his hand toward the worm, palm facing out, signaling him to remain calm. But Crawler squirms in his chair and keeps his guard up just in case someone is looking for a snack.

Samuel then shares the details of their recent excursion and finally reveals to the king that Izadora, Lennox and Crawler were captured by Clatheron's minions. "Toward the end of our journey, the princess was captured by some Malquars and placed next to your old throne in a cage," he says. Ooohs and ahhhs echo throughout the room. "Not to worry. As you can see, I was able to rescue her along with Lennox and Crawler, who were moments away from becoming a feast for Clatheron and his soldiers."

"Go on," King Zedorious says. He listens intently as Samuel explains how he sneaked into the castle by using the Aquacuff provided by the Oracle. He mentions Squinch, their new friend, and how he risked his life to help them escape through a secret passageway behind the throne. Samuel then interrupts his tale to ask the king if he will look out for Squinch's well-being if they ever cross paths.

"Anyone who puts the safety of another, especially my daughter, before their own is always welcome in the kingdom. I will not only look out for the creature known as Squinch, but I will formally thank him if we ever meet," replies the king.

Samuel thanks King Zedorious for his kindness and begins to describe Clatheron's weakness to the council. "I sort of realized something about Clatheron during the rescue." Samuel pauses to catch his breath. Everyone in the room is hanging on his every word.

"Don't keep us waiting. What did you realize, Samuel? Speak freely," urges King Zedorious.

"Let me ask everyone here something. What's the one thing we have that Clatheron doesn't have?" asks Samuel. Puzzled faces whisper to one another, kicking around possible answers.

"You, Samuel," one of the members shouts.

Chapter Nineteen

"Yes, that is true. You have me, but we have something even greater than me, something way more important, something we can use to our advantage in the battle to come." He pauses. "Anyone?" Samuel asks. He pauses again. "No one? Fine then. The reason I was able to save the princess and my friends was because Clatheron didn't expect it."

King Zedorious and the council members look baffled. They are not catching what Samuel is throwing.

"Don't you see," he continues. "The one thing we have that Clatheron and his Malquars don't have is the element of surprise." The room fills with ahas.

"Very true, my boy, but how can we use this to our advantage?" asks King Zedorious.

Samuel unveils his plan. He speaks about the oyster shell that he left behind on Clatheron's throne in hopes that he will assume that the Aquatanians' secret hideout is in the waters inside Pearl Cave. He is sure that Clatheron will take the bait and that Squinch will help by guiding him there.

Samuel then speaks of the fishing hooks in the room next to the council's chambers, where King Zedorious entrusted him with the Sword of Luminesence. He explains how they can turn the hooks into swords. He then mentions how little time they have to prepare for battle and how it is imperative that the resistance reach Pearl Cave before their enemies or else lose the element of surprise.

"So now you see," Samuel continues. "This is why we must move fast. Right now, as we speak, I assume that Clatheron is preparing his army at this moment for a gruesome battle at Pearl Cave."

The council, lingering Aquatanians, and most crucially, King Zedorious, are impressed with Samuel's plan of attack.

This is not the same insecure boy who left on the impossible journey. This is a man with wisdom and solid ideas on defeating Clatheron and his soldiers for once and for all. What impresses everyone the most, however, is that Samuel speaks with confidence and conviction. This certainly is not the timid soul they knew before.

Samuel's next words give everyone goosebumps. His powerful message fills them with the same courage that he gained during his journey. He ignites in them a flame that will light the Aquatanians' path to victory. Samuel scours his memory to combine elements of every great speech that Grandpa ever read to him throughout his youth. His jam-packed motivational speech inspires the inhabitants of Aquatania to fight the greatest battle ever known.

Samuel begins in a soft tone and slowly raises his voice to build momentum. "My friends, when I first arrived, you asked me to lead you. You asked me to free you from enslavement and return you to your rightful home. I survived the impossible journey and unlocked the possibilities within myself. I saved the princess and my friends from the very evil that we will soon face together."

Samuel stands up abruptly and slams his hands on the table. His audience jumps. "All I ask is that you swear your allegiance to our cause. Dig deep within yourselves to muster up the courage to face our greatest enemy. Together, we will stand in unity, fight our enemy on the battlefield and watch them inevitably fall one by one. Together we will write a new chapter in history and regain your former homes, your families, your friends and the lives that were stolen from you."

Samuel takes his seat at the stone table and, in a more

subdued tone of voice, continues. "When I was younger, every time my grandfather and I came to visit the lake, Grandpa used to read me books in our study. A book about one great leader, Winston Churchill, made the biggest impression on me. It was he who said, 'We shall defend our island, whatever the cost may be. We shall fight on the beaches. We shall fight in the fields and in the streets. We shall fight in the hills. We shall never surrender.' My friends, those are words to live by. Together we will not fail. We cannot fail! Together, we will fight as one, and together, we will be victorious!"

The room erupts with loud cheers and thunderous applause. All of the creatures in the chambers jump to their feet. Samuel has touched their hearts, inspiring them to go to war, to confront their mortal enemy. He wants to spend more time enjoying the applause but knows they have a lot of work to do. Time is running out. Clatheron will surely figure out the meaning of the clue that Samuel left behind and assemble his army for battle in Pearl Cave. The resistance has to be there first to gain the upper hand.

A young Aquatanian returns with the food ordered by King Zedorious. He places a plate of mixed kelp, algae and mashed worms in front of each of the three heroes while everyone continues to rejoice.

"Ahhh. What's this?" asks Crawler with a disgusted look on his face. "You must be kidding me!"

"Sorry about that, Crawler," apologizes the king. "Your attention, everyone. In honor of our friend Crawler, from this day forward, we will no longer eat worms to satisfy our hunger. From this day forward, we will follow a strict vegetarian diet." No one objects to the king's ruling. Everyone understands.

"Thank you, Your Majesty. Much appreciated," says Crawler, pushing his plate aside. He sheds a tear for the unfortunate worms who became part of his meal.

"My pleasure, Crawler. I'm sorry to have made you feel so uncomfortable." The king orders the plates removed and replaced with something greener.

"Any chance you have a steak back there?" asks Lennox.

Everyone laughs hysterically at Lennox's continual attempts to satisfy his hunger with a type of food that they never heard of before.

***

Time passes, and the Aquatanians begin their preparations for the battle. All is going according to Samuel's vision. While everyone works hard into the night making weapons and building traps, King Zedorious pulls Samuel aside for a chat.

Samuel and the king perch themselves on a set of rocks outside the secret hideout. They gaze upon the star-studded sky through the wavy waters above, enjoying a moment of inner piece together.

"Before I forget." Samuel tries to return the Sword of Luminescence to King Zedorious. The king refuses, pushing the sword back toward Samuel. "No. You keep it. You'll need it now more than ever."

"Thank you, Your Majesty. I don't know what to say."

"You don't have to say anything. Your actions tomorrow will speak louder than words." King Zedorious responds to Samuel's gratitude with a smile.

They gaze again at the sky for a few minutes until

King Zedorious breaks the silence. He stares at Samuel's face. "You've changed. You're not the same timid boy I met when you left with the others for the Hall of Mirrors."

Samuel grins. "I guess in times of disaster, you have to pull yourself together, stand up on both of your webbed feet and find a way to persevere," he answers, making a fist with his right hand for emphasis.

"See. Right there. Though you may not realize it you've changed from a boy to a man." King Zedorious pats Samuel on the back.

"Thank you. I sure hope you're right, King."

"Please. Call me Zedorious. No need to be so formal with me. You've certainly earned my trust and friendship."

"Thank you, Zedorious." Samuel feels a bit awkward saying his name without the prefix of King, Sire or Your Majesty.

They sit in silence for a moment to admire the sky. The blackened sky is breathtaking with sparkling stars lighting from above. Slight ripples in the water create a wavy effect that adds a subtle beauty to the stars' bright glow.

"Your grandfather would have been so proud!" says King Zedorious.

"Wait? You know Grandpa?"

"Why, of course I do. How do you think you found your way here so easily?"

"But how do you know him."

"Do you think you're the first human to stumble upon the magical glowing red pearl?" he asks rhetorically.

"What was he doing here?" asks Samuel.

"I'm afraid that's a long story, a story for another time. Just know he would be proud of who and what you have become."

"I miss him!" Samuel feels homesick. He has not seen Grandpa in what seems like ages.

"Don't worry. Soon enough, you'll see him again and be reunited." King Zedorious can sense Samuel's exhaustion. "Why don't you retire for the night? I'll oversee the others. You need your rest for tomorrow."

"I suppose you're right. I am kinda tired." Samuel excuses himself and heads toward the princess' sleeping quarters, which she is kind enough to share with him, Lennox and Crawler.

"And Samuel," says King Zedorious.

"Yes?" he replies, turning around to look at the king before he swims inside.

"Good work!"

"Thank you again Your Maj...I mean Zedorious."

The End of Days

Clatheron jumps out of bed as he wakes up from his afternoon nap. Blob is still out cold on the floor. "SQUUIIINCCHH!" yells the dark ruler.

He instinctively reaches for the string around his neck and notices that his precious key is missing. He is angrier than he has ever been before.

Clatheron storms out of his bedroom and heads straight for Capitol Hall, where for all he knows, the princess is still in the cage next to his throne. He bursts through the entrance, ready to pummel anything and anyone in his way.

"SQUUIIINCCHH!" he shrieks again. "Where is that good-for-nothing slave of mine? He's never around when I need him. NEVER!"

Angered by his servant's absence, Clatheron tears an antique wood-framed painting off the wall and throws it down violently on the floor. He stomps on it, puncturing thousands of little holes in it with the hard pointy tips of his spider-like feet until all that remains is shredded canvas and wood splinters.

Squinch hides outside another hall entrance. He knows it will take a pretty long time for Clatheron to calm down, but knowing that he is a vital part of the plan to lure his keeper to Pearl Cave, he decides to enter anyway at his own risk.

"Yes, master," Squinch replies softly from the doorway. He enters the hall slowly and cautiously. "I was tending to the vault and preparing your dinner when I heard you calling my name. What seems to be the problem?" he asks, pretending as if he does not know the answer to his own question.

"What seems to be the problem? What seems to be the problem?" Clatheron repeats, mimicking his slaves thin voice. He approaches Squinch, who now is wondering why he decided to enter the hall after all.

"The problem, Squinch, is that a certain key, my only copy that unlocks the princess' cage, has mysteriously GONE MISSING!" Clatheron towers over Squinch while he roars, casting a shadow over him. "You wouldn't happen to know what happened to my key now, would you?"

"Mu...mu...mee? Wh...wh...why would I know where yu...yu...your key is?" he replies, curling up in a ball of fear.

"Maybe because...you're supposed to know everything that goes on around here!" Clatheron hollers at the top of his lungs. He wraps a tentacle around Squinch's shoulder, freezing him with fear. "I don't know why I bothered taking you under my wing. Why am I so nice to you, treating you as if you were family?" He releases Squinch and paces back and forth with his arms crossed behind his back, the two tentacles sprouting from his rib cage gesturing to give his words emphasis.

"I clothe you. I feed you. I protect you and show you appreciation, and this is the love I get in return." Clatheron stops pacing and lifts Squinch by the neck. "This is nothing more than insubordination!" shouts Clatheron as he shakes Squinch wildly, turning his face pale green.

As he shakes Squinch, Clatheron looks around Capitol Hall. He notices that the cage where the princess has been locked up is empty.He stops shaking the tiny Malquar, who is dizzy by this time. "Um. Squinch," Clatheron asks softly, gently placing Squinch back on his two feet.

"Yes, sire," Squinch replies, wobbling and barely able to stand up.

"Look around this room and tell me if you notice anything out of place." Clatheron wraps his hand around Squinch's shoulder as Squinch begins to look around. He doesn't want to be too obvious, so he pretends he does not notice the empty cage. He shrugs his shoulders.

"No? Nothing at all?" Clatheron asks again, giving Squinch a chance to redeem himself. He calmly escorts Squinch to the cage. "How about now? Anything? Anything at all?"

"Um...the princess is ma...ma...missing," Squinch replies with a stutter.

"That's right. The princess is ma...ma...missing," Clatheron says, mocking his servant again. "And do you have any idea how that might have happened?" he asks, pinching Squinch's shoulder with his sharp fingernails.

Squinch shrugs again, appearing clueless. Clatheron's grip grows tighter, causing him to wince in pain.

"WHY IS IT THAT NO ONE AROUND HERE KNOWS WHY THE PRINCESS IS MISSING? AND WHERE IS MY KEY?" Clatheron screams with a roar that vibrates the water so forcefully that the black flags in the room wave as if they were flapping in a strong wind. He then throws Squinch to the floor.

Squinch covers both ears and curls up into a ball. Shivers course through his veins as Clatheron lifts the cage and throws it as hard as he can against the wall. In all of his years listening to Clatheron yell, Squinch has never heard his voice thunder so loudly before.

"What is this on my throne?" Clatheron asks scornfully, noticing the oyster shell that Samuel told Squinch to leave in plain sight. Out of curiosity, he picks up the shell with one of his tentacles to examine it more closely. "An oyster shell? Now how did an oyster shell get on the seat of my throne?"

Squinch knows he will be better off playing dumb. Still, he thinks he might be able to save his life if he helps Clatheron decipher the clue.

"May...may...maybe it was left behind by accident by whoever freed the princess. Maybe it's a clue that will help us find the thief."   Squinch does not divulge too much information lest he give away his complicity in the escape. "But what do I know, Your Majesty? I am but a humble servant," says Squinch, bowing his head.

"That's right. You know nothing," says Clatheron, clearly trying to play off the fact that he did not reach the same conclusion on his own. "An oyster shell? Hmm...I'm curious. Where in Lake Aqueous do you find oysters?"

Squinch hesitates to reply. He does not want to anger Clatheron by answering the question and making him feel inferior.

"WELL. ANSWER THE QUESTION, YOU FOOL!" Clatheron walks over to his throne and sits down, waiting for Squinch's response.

Chapter Twenty

Squinch kneels before his master and bows his head, making sure to avoid direct eye contact. "If I may, sire."

"You may," Clatheron grants.

"The only place in Lake Aqueous with oysters is Pearl Cave."

"Pearl Cave. Interesting." Clatheron rubs his chin.

"Do you think it's possible that maybe that is where the princess was taken?" asks Squinch.

"Why of course that's where she is, you dummy. And I would bet your life that Pearl Cave is also where the Aquatanians have their secret hideout. What else would this clue mean? Do I have to figure everything out by myself? Why must I always be the smart one around here? It's as if I were given a gift of intellect from the gods themselves that none of you could ever understand. None of you. Imbeciles."

"Absolutely, sire. None of us holds a candle to your intellect." Squinch continues his routine of praising Clatheron until he grows tired of the compliments.

"ENOUGH!" Clatheron shouts. "Here's what I want you to do."

"Yes, sire. Anything for you," Squinch says, cupping his claws as if in prayer.

"Gather up all of my troops," Clatheron orders, continuing to stroke his chin. "Have them meet me within the hour. I want them in formation and standing at attention so I can outline my plan to them and get them ready to do battle tomorrow morning."

"Yes, my king, as you command." Squinch speeds toward the exit to carry out Clatheron's order and gather up every Malquar in the kingdom.

"Oh, and Squinch?" Clatheron asks.

"Yes, sire. How else may I assist you?"

"Tell them...tell them I said to prepare for all-out war. Whoever dared to take my trophy won't know what hit him. No one steals from the all-mighty, all-powerful Clatheron." He laughs maniacally. "We will leave for Pearl Cave first thing in the morning. Tomorrow, we begin our search for the princess, and then, we will not rest until we round up Zedorious and all of his faithful followers. I want them all destroyed for once and for all. They'll never know what hit them."

Clatheron bellows with laughter as Squinch leaves Capitol Hall to gather the troops.

The Battle of Pearl Cave

The water is brisk on the morning of this fateful day. The Aquatanians and friends of the resistance worked diligently throughout the night to prepare Pearl Cave for a surprise attack against the enemy. They toiled in shifts, alternating rest and work, to carry out Samuel's instructions and meet the deadline before the Malquar army arrives.

By morning, not a sound can be heard in Pearl Cave. The current is steady but carries with it a chill to the body and soul, one that foreshadows the epic battle about to take place, a vicious battle beyond anything anyone has ever experienced. Blood will be shed. Loved ones will be lost. But all committed to the Aquatanian cause know the risks. Warriors in their quest for freedom are prepared for whatever comes their way. They are ready to fight. They are ready to die for their beloved kingdom.

Samuel equips everyone in the fight with the necessary weapons and motivation. He delivers another touching speech that inspires the people to launch a crusade that will go down in history as the greatest battle ever to take place in Lake Aqueous. Today is the day to leave all doubt behind.

The Battle of Pearl Cave

Today is the day to take up arms and accept nothing less than victory.

Scattered throughout Pearl Cave, hiding behind rocks and wedged into small dark corners, Aquatanians and their allies lie in wait.

Suddenly, oysters perched on rocks and ledges throughout the cave begin to rattle. Corked glass bottles that line the base of the walls, filled with nervous glowing fish, begin to vibrate. They sense the approaching Malquar army. Lennox and Crawler tense up as they stand next to Samuel, their anxiety worsening as the rattling intensifies.

Lennox has expressed his disapproval of their mission many times before, but he now understands the battle's importance. There is no way he will let Samuel fight without him by his side. He will do all that he can to protect his lifelong friend, even if it means taking a razor-sharp spear to the shell to protect Samuel.

Soon, the oysters stand up, lie down and stand up again in unison over and over. Up, down, up, down, up, down. The Malquars are getting closer.

Samuel looks around to see if he is the only one who feels uncertain about the outcome, but his comrades in arms seem less frightened. Their steely eyes display a laser-like focus on one objective: winning. Their jaws are tightly clenched, their brows furrowed, displaying a look of fierce determination. On a personal level, they are struggling to regain their homes, to live again without a care in the water. They have grown tired of running every time a Malquar patrol swims nearby, spending too many years in confinement. A momentous battle is the only way to escape a life of constant fear.

Chapter Twenty-One

King Zedorious glances at Samuel and sees fear in Samuel's eyes.

"It's okay to be frightened, Samuel. I'd be worried if you weren't a little bit scared," says King Zedorious.

Samuel nods, remaining silent as their enemies approach by the thousands. The oysters, once perched on rocks and ledges throughout the cave, come crashing down to the lake floor. The Malquar army has arrived.

"Prepare yourselves! This is it!" shouts Samuel. He reaches for the Sword of Luminescence, which he keeps safely tucked away in his leather belt.

The ground shakes furiously as thousands of Malquars pass underwater through the entrance to Pearl Cave, marching in rigidly straight rows, shaking the lake floor like a mighty elephant stampede. The tremors grow stronger with each step. Some of the soldiers take an "aerial" approach, swimming above the other Malquars with spears pointing forward and their undulating tree-trunk legs leaving behind furious trails of white bubbles. Clatheron's troops are extremely disciplined, the result of years of training, each focusing on one objective: to seek and destroy.

Samuel and the resistance position themselves below the spot where he was transformed from a young boy into his current form. Above them is the magical glowing blue pearl, which is still resting in its shell above the water's surface on a large bed of rocks. The magical pearl remains undisturbed, illuminated by a light that shines through the very same crack in the ceiling that led Samuel to find it.

The Malquar army will travel far into the cave to reach the dimly lit spot where the battle is destined to take place.

By now, the battalions of soldiers are almost there.

"Everyone, take your positions!" orders King Zedorious. "Stand your ground. Don't make a move until I give you the signal." The lionhearted king stands beside Samuel, ready to attack. His sword, once a fish hook, is fully drawn. He is not the slightest bit nervous. King Zedorious has been in battles before and is ready for anything that comes his way. Zedorious looks to Samuel and gives him a reassuring nod of support, but he can tell that Samuel is still nervous by the blank stare on his face.

Samuel is biting his lower lip, almost drawing blood. His eyes are wide open, pupils dilated, overwrought as he awaits his enemies' arrival.

"I hope we come out of this alive," says Lennox, who has taken up a position next to Samuel.

Samuel says nothing in response.

"Don't worry, son," says King Zedorious to Samuel. "It will all turn out okay. Remember to stick to your plan, and if that doesn't work, remember what you told us. *Together, we will fight as one. Together we will be victorious.*" The king is right. They are stronger this time around, they have a plan, and unlike the last time his people fought for the kingdom, they are prepared.

By repeating the last few words of Samuel's speech, the king reminds him that all those fighting by his side are committed warriors. Samuel lights up from within. He had forgotten how powerful his speech was and how true his words rang. He looks around once more, this time observing a sea of gallant warriors. This is his family, and together they will stand up and fight for their freedom. The last thing Samuel will ever do is let his family down, just like how Grandpa did not let him down after his parents' death. He is ready to boldly lead his newfound family to triumph.

Facing forward, Samuel keeps his eyes on the haze of mud and debris that the Malquar soldiers are kicking up as they approach. Clatheron and his army have almost reached Pearl Cave's innermost point, where the resistance is waiting.

Finally, the first rows of Malquars are in sight. Upon reaching the back of the cave, the army stops. The mud that their feet kicked up settles to the lake floor. They see their opponents' eyes peeking out from behind rocks and see silhouettes lurking in dark corners. Clouds of white foam dissipate as the aerial Malquars float in place. The ground stills, and the only sounds that can be heard are the bubbles emanating from the Aquatanians' ears and the heavy breathing of the fearsome Malquars.

Clatheron gazes upon his enemies. Fueled by hate, he has only one thing in mind: destroy every last Aquatanian in the cave. He will show no mercy. For him, this war is not about establishing power; he had already proven his might when he took over the kingdom after the Great Invasion. No. This war is about defiance and insolence: Clatheron will accept neither.

The opposing armies exchange no words. There will be no negotiations on this frigid day. Then Clatheron releases a mighty roar. It is so powerful that everyone can feel the thunderous vibrations as he releases an explosive bellow. He raises his hand high in the water. The Malquar soldiers begin beating their spears against their chests in unison. Thud. Thud. Thud. It continues for what seems like an eternity, slowly increasing in volume. THUD. THUD. THUD. Their light green slime-covered chests turn deep green from the forceful beatings.

"What are they doing?" asks Samuel.

"It's called intimidation," replies the king. "But you can't allow it to bother you. You must remain focused."

"It's definitely working," adds Crawler, who stands trembling by Lennox's side.

When Clatheron raises his other hand, all of the Malquars begin to scream the most fearsome war cry anyone ever heard. Samuel cannot help but feel slightly terrified.

"Would you like to do the honors?" asks King Zedorious, maintaining his composure.

"I suppose so," Samuel replies in a weak voice. He struggles to swallow. His throat feels like it is filled with stones without any saliva to help them slide down to the pit of his stomach. His head fills with horrific images of dying comrades, making it hard to comprehend King Zedorious' request. If Samuel could sweat underwater, he would be doing so profusely.

"I said...would you like to do the honors?" King Zedorious repeats.

Samuel snaps out of his trance. He looks around at his comrades to see everyone eagerly awaiting his command. He answers again, this time with confidence. "YES, I WOULD!" Samuel raises the Sword of Luminescence high in the water. "In the name of the kingdom!" he shouts.

Samuel takes one last look at Lennox and Crawler before he makes his move. They look worried but ready to do what is necessary.

"NOW!" he commands. With both hands securely holding the Sword of Luminescence, he thrusts it downward, slicing effortlessly through a piece of rope that lies in front of his feet. Other Aquatanians follow Samuel's lead, slicing through the ends of ropes that they have strategically hidden throughout Pearl Cave.

During the night, they lined the cave's ceiling with netting woven from thick vines. Upon slicing the ropes, the netting falls from the ceiling, weighed down by attached rocks, landing on the Malquars floating above the lake floor. The netting entangles their bodies, leaving them temporarily helpless.

Lennox cues other Aquatanians to push boulders attached to ropes off the rock ledges near where the oysters are perched. The ropes are threaded through pulleys hammered securely into the ceiling. The other end of each rope is attached to nets made from thick vines lining the cave floor and camouflaged by mud and underwater vegetation. Samuel and the resistance had created snares to trap as many Malquars as possible before engaging the remaining army in battle.

Caught completely off guard, hundreds of Malquars standing on the lake bed fly up into the water. They are left to dangle in nets just below the aerial Malquars entangled in their own nets. Using both sets of traps, the resistance hoped to gain the advantage at the start of the battle by using the element of surprise. Their plan worked.

The resistance cheers loudly.

Malquars who are not ensnared race to free their fellow soldiers, but the sides of their spears are not sharp enough to cut through the thick-vine netting from which their comrades struggle to escape. All they can do is stand by idly and watch their fellow soldiers hang upside down. This is what Samuel had hoped for, total and utter confusion. The Malquars are vulnerable – at least temporarily.

Though outnumbered and seemingly overwhelmed, the Aquatanians go on the attack.

"Charge!" shouts King Zedorious. Aquatanians lunge at Clatheron and his army from all directions. Up from the shadows and out from behind rocks, they attack by the hundreds. With fishhook swords in hand, they speed heroically toward the enemy without a second thought. The waters above stir angrily as if a monstrous storm were passing overhead.

As the Aquatanians attack, some cry, "In the name of the kingdom!" Others shout, "In the name of Her Majesty, Queen Mizbeth!" The shouts send chills down Samuel's spine. He joins the rebellion, racing toward his enemies with his sword drawn, ready to eliminate anyone who stands in his way.

Clatheron does not wait for his soldiers to move forward. He is the first to advance, ordering his army to follow. He lets out a fiery yell, triggering a full-blown attack. Thousands of Malquars begin bolting toward the oncoming Aquatanians, their spears drawn, thirsting for blood.

The two armies crash into each other like speeding trains. The savage battle is in full force. Fishhook swords and Malquar spears smash against one another. The sounds of clanging weapons echo throughout the cave. Spears fly through the water, striking some of the Aquatanian rebels. A few rebels pick up the spears that have fallen to the lake floor and launch them like rockets back at the Malquars, hitting those still hanging from the cave's ceiling. Shrieks of pain emanate from both sides. Two Aquatanians perish for every Malquar. There are just too many of them. The tide is turning against the Aquatanians.

Out of nowhere, more Malquars pour through the opening in the cave's ceiling, the same opening from which the light shines on the magical glowing blue pearl. This is one of Clatheron's tricks. He had this in mind the minute he decided to go to war. Malquars dive through the opening and splash into the water below by the hundreds, outflanking the Aquatanians and attacking from behind. The Aquatanians are no match for the Malquar army. They can barely hold their positions, giving up more and more ground as the fight progresses.

While the battle continues, Squinch finds a hiding spot in a dark corner. As he watches from the sidelines, he struggles to watch the second fall of the Aquatanian Empire unfold before his eyes. He doubts the Aquatanians will win. Squinch places his hands over his eyes. He cannot bear watching the pain and anguish, nor can he bear the loss of what would have been his freedom if the Aquatanian army had prevailed.

Clatheron drills through his enemy's line of defense, tossing Aquatanians left and right, when he notices an odd-looking creature that he had never seen before. Clatheron watches as the creature rips through his soldiers one by one with its sword. He believes the creature must be Samuel, the one that Figlo said was the boy with the power to take him down. He then realizes his soldiers must have made a mistake at the Hall of Mirrors. They had not captured Samuel after all.

"Worthless soldiers. They had no idea who they captured at the Hall of Mirrors. I should've known that the weak creature in the green shell and his pink friend could not possess the strength to take on Malquars. All they did was beg and plead for their lives in my torture chamber, weeping incessantly like tadpoles."

Clatheron targets Samuel as his next kill.

His breath grows heavy as he prepares to attack. "I'm coming for you, boy!" Clatheron shouts as if anyone could hear him over the clanging and clatter of weapons.

In the meantime, King Zedorious is fighting his own battles, taking on two or three Malquars at a time. Despite his age, he is quite a powerful warrior, ducking and dodging spears and rapidly striking his enemies' armor. King Zedorious is in complete control of his situation, anticipating each enemy soldier's next move.

In the middle of battle, Zedorious looks for Clatheron and sees him charging at Samuel at full speed. The king lowers his shoulder as a Malquar comes charging at him. As they make contact, King Zedorious lifts his shoulder and flips the Malquar into the cave wall. He swims as fast as he can toward Samuel, who is fighting off Malquars of his own. Clatheron raises his heavy hand preparing to deliver a powerful blow to the back of Samuel's head. King Zedorious reaches Samuel just in time, blocking Clatheron's hand.

"Do you really think you can save him, Zedorious?" asks Clatheron, laughing. He lifts his hand once more, providing King Zedorious a small window of opportunity. The king's sword pierces one of the brute's nine legs, which begins to bleed excessively. No matter. With a forceful blow, Clatheron punches Zedorious in the chest with a tentacle, causing him to fly across the cave and hit his head against a rock. King Zedorious is unconscious as aqua-blue blood seeps from his head and mixes with the surrounding water.

Samuel turns around just in time to witness the entire thing. "Noooo!" he cries. "You're going to pay for that, Clatheron!"

Samuel reaches back and swings around in a circle to build momentum, slicing through another one of Clatheron's spider legs with the Sword of Luminescence. He howls in pain but quickly returns to the one-on-one fight with Samuel, more enraged than ever.

"Why you little!" Clatheron screams as he tries to capture Samuel with both hands, nipping at his heels as Samuel swims around and around his body as fast as he can.

Samuel searches for an opening to stab Clatheron with his sword. He kicks his webbed feet furiously, swimming between the leviathan's legs, around his underbelly and up and around the top of his back, all the while looking for opportunities to strike. At the same time, Clatheron is doing everything he can to swat Samuel like a fly.

Samuel lands on his enemy's neck. The monstrous third eye, attached to the end of the tube sprouting from Clatheron's head, turns to look Samuel in the face. The savage grabs Samuel with one of his tentacles while Samuel is in mid strike, throwing him down on the lake floor. He lands on his back, stunned. Lennox and Crawler watch as Samuel hits the ground and try their best to come to his rescue. But there are too many Malquars in the way. They seem to be multiplying, creating an impenetrable wall.

Clatheron raises his hand once again, then drops it down forcefully toward Samuel's body. Samuel lifts his sword in time to halt the blow. Clatheron continues to push down hard as Samuel struggles to stop his powerful hand from crushing him. But Clatheron is too strong. Samuel knows he will not last much longer. Eventually his arms will give out. Samuel looks out of the corner of his eyes at Squinch, who is still hiding in a dark corner of Pearl Cave. He wants to help ever so badly but does not know how.

"Help me. Please…I can't hold him off much longer!" moans Samuel. His blade is the only thing blocking Clatheron's hand and preventing his death.

"Hang in there, Samuel. Hold out as long as you can!" shouts Squinch, struggling to find a way to come to his aid.

It does not take long for Clatheron to figure out who is speaking. "Squinch! You traitor! I'll deal with you later," Clatheron shouts as he pushes down harder on Samuel's sword.

Squinch looks around the lake floor for something, anything, to throw at Clatheron to distract him and give Samuel a chance to escape. He notices a glowing red pearl perched on the end of a stick, which is resting like a see-saw on a rock.

Clatheron's mouth is wide open, exposing his gritty yellow teeth, which he plans to use to tear Samuel apart, limb from limb. Squinch reacts instinctively by jumping on one end of the stick. The magical red glowing pearl launches from the other end of the stick like a shooting star, flying through the water toward Clatheron. He is just about to bite down on Samuel's head when the pearl flies into Clatheron's mouth, choking him as it travels down his esophagus and into his stomach.

Samuel pushes his adversary's hand away with his sword. A strong wind forms around Clatheron, lifting him off the ground. Samuel inches his way to safety, reaching Squinch, who left his dark corner to help drag Samuel out of harm's way.

The glowing red pearl gives off sparks as it did before for Samuel, only this time Clatheron's belly lights up like Fourth of July fireworks. A gust of wind grows as strong as a tornado, spinning Clatheron in circles. The pigment in his face turns a deep red to match the pearl's color. He starts to shrink to the size of a hermit crab as the spinning slows. Sparks continue to fly in every direction.

All of a sudden, Figlo rides valiantly into the battlefield on the back of the beast that lurked in the boat wreckage. Figlo managed to break the beast's will like a cowboy tames a wild stallion and gained complete control over it.

Figlo is accompanied by Princess Izadora and thousands of Aquatanians armed with whatever rocks and debris they can use as weapons. When Clatheron gathered up all of the Malquars to fight in the battle of Pearl Cave, he left the Coral Jail unguarded. With the help of Izadora, Figlo freed all the slaves and brought them to fight, including his sister Alaina and Queen Mizbeth.

The dynamic of the battle changes. The Malquar army seems less threatening. The cavalry has arrived, and the resistance is about to gain the upper hand.

With its mouth wide open, the beast tears through a line of Malquars, heading straight for Clatheron. The beast wraps its mouth around the tiny being, swallowing Clatheron along with the magical red glowing pearl. Within seconds, a tornado-like wind whips up, spinning the beast wildly in circles. Figlo is thrown off its back, as the leviathan shrinks to the size of a tiny fish.

The tornado abruptly ceases.

Samuel stands on his feet, badly hurt from his tussle with Clatheron. He looks around the cave to see that the resistance has gained control of the battlefield. Samuel is most impressed with Izadora's aggressive battle skills. He watches from afar as she effortessly uses her fishhook sword to defeat one Malquar after another. His brethren, who were once on the verge of defeat, have retaken the offensive. He raises his sword in the air, musters up every last bit of energy he can, and from deep within his diaphragm, he shouts the magic word, "LUMINOUS!"

The Sword of Luminescence begins to glow, emitting a gloriously bright light that, this time, does not falter.

"I did it," says Samuel with a wide smile. He proudly holds the sword as high as he can, covering his eyes with the fold of his arm because he is so close to the light.

The bright light blinds the Malquars, who are extremely sensitive to light. One by one, the opposing soldiers drop to their knees. As the Malquars cover their eyes in pain, the Aquatanians lunge forward. Lennox and Crawler climb out from piles of blinded Malquars who had jumped on top of them.

Along with other Aquatanians, Izadora, Lennox, Crawler and Figlo help round up all the Malquars who managed to survive the epic battle, forcing them to surrender. When it is safe to do so, Samuel repeats the magical mantra to extinguish the light.

"I hope I wasn't too late," says Figlo with a glowing smile. He holds two Malquars in his grip and pushes them into a line of prisoners.

Chapter Twenty-One

"Figlo...you couldn't have had better timing if you wanted to," replies Samuel. They break out into laughter as Samuel holds his rib cage. "Don't make me laugh. It hurts." It might hurt, but the joy that they share is worth the pain.

"The king!" exclaims Samuel, remembering Zedorious had been knocked out cold by Clatheron's mighty tentacle. "He was trying to protect me." Samuel swims toward the king, who has not yet regained consciousness. Izadora sees Samuel heading toward her father's lifeless body and rushes to his side.

Samuel slowly lifts King Zedorious in his arms and holds him gently.

"Is my father okay?" asks Izadora as she nervously looks over Samuel's shoulder. She cannot bare the thought of losing her father, especially after just having reunited with her mother.

"I'm not sure, princess." Samuel lightly shakes the king's body. "Are you okay, Zedorious? Can you hear me?" he asks.

King Zedorious turns his head toward Samuel and slowly lifts his fluttering eyelids. Samuel holds onto the king's wound to stop the blue blood from seeping from his cranium. The king wraps his free arm around Samuel's neck, pulling him in closely for a hug. He whispers in Samuel's ear. "Good job, my boy. Good Job!"

Samuel and Izadora smile in unison. They are glad the king is all right and would have been devastated if he had not survived the epic battle.

Samuel has accomplished everything he set out to do. He is proud of himself. He looks up toward the cave's ceiling, wondering if his parents saw what he accomplished. Then, he hears his grandfather's words ringing in his ears:

"When you're feeling sad, as if they're fading away, all you need to do is look to the sky and remember them in your heart. It's your heart that keeps their memory alive. They're a part of you, Samuel, and the beating of your heart gives strength to their memory, making it live on every passing day. Hold on tightly to their memory and don't let go. They love you and are with you always."

Samuel looks toward the cave's ceiling and presses his hand hard against his chest in order to feel his heartbeat.

"Look at me now, Grandpa. I faced the daylight," whispers Samuel.

"What's that, Samuel?" asks King Zedorious.

"Oh, nothing," he says with a satisfied grin.

Samuel lets out a celebratory cheer, and all of the rebels chime in while they round up the remaining Malquars.

Out of the Darkness

The kingdom again is an icon of freedom, loyalty and equality. Once more it is a magical place, a safe haven for all of the virtuous inhabitants of Lake Aqueous. And like before, their home is a place where all friendly creatures of the lake are welcome to share and exchange goods with one another in peace.

Within the kingdom's walls, the sunlight shines from the heavens above, piercing the dark clouds that formed during Clatheron's rule. As the light returns, so does a mood of harmony and joy among the inhabitants. The Aquatanians emerge from hiding to return to their true home with a deep appreciation for the kingdom's beauty and the many gifts that it will bestow again.

The first order of Aquatanian business is to imprison the Malquars captured during the Battle of Pearl Cave. This is the first time that the Aquatanians have ever used these facilities on anyone.

The second order of business is for every Aquatanian to chip in to help clean up the mess that Clatheron and his army made of their homeland. Aquatanians scrub off layers of filth, tear down Clatheron's black flags and knit new white ones that display the Aquatanian Crest of Unity, a blue circle with a golden heart in the middle. No one complains about the hard work because everyone is so happy to be home.

The restoration project instills a sense of pride in the community especially when they proudly watch their flags flap back and forth in the water's currents. The kingdom's emblem reminds everyone that peace has finally returned, that evil has been expunged and that citizens with good intentions and hearts of gold once again reside within the kingdom's walls.

To prevent an attack from ever happening again, King Zedorious stations two guards at the top of each watchtower instead of just one. And this time, King Zedorious will make sure that guards remain in the towers at all times, even during the next grand celebration. If the kingdom ever comes under attack again, the stationed guards will be able to sound the alarm in time for the royal troops to prepare for battle.

The third and last order of business is the grand victory celebration. Packed in tightly until Capitol Hall is at full capacity, Aquatanians and friends gather to celebrate their hard work, their love of their kingdom and most of all their glorious victory. High-spirited creatures from all over Lake Aqueous flood the hall: large inhabitants, small ones, tall inhabitants and short ones. All are friendly and in a cheerful mood. The hall echoes with laughter and joy. The citizens dance and sing to the sweet sounds of seashell horns and drums made from pots and pans salvaged from sunken ships. Legs and arms flail in all directions. Shouts of revelry can be heard from miles away. It reminds everyone of the good old days when life was perfect and peaceful.

Chapter Twenty-Two

King Zedorious has never been so delighted to sit on his throne inside the hall. He watches patiently with Queen Mizbeth by his side as he observes his subjects bask in sheer happiness. Then, in a dignified voice, he stands up and requests everyone's attention so that he can begin the royal victory speech. Lennox, Crawler, Figlo, Izadora, Samuel and even Squinch join the king and queen by the throne. They help King Zedorious and Queen Mizbeth welcome all of the Aquatanians and guests who fought by their side during the Battle of Pearl Cave.

The king clears his throat, and a hush suddenly falls over the crowd. "My fellow Aquatanians and distinguished guests, our world is very different now. We lived in the best of times and we survived the worst of times. We purged our kingdom of all forms of inequality. Once again we are all equal. We cleared our kingdom of all forms of slavery. We are now free like the very fish that swim among us in these waters. And we cleansed our kingdom of all forms of evil for we have triumphed over Clatheron and his army for once and for all!"

All of the royal subjects applaud enthusiastically and cheer thunderously. Those wearing hats fling them up high in the water.

"We dare not forget this day; instead, we shall embrace it. We shall forever celebrate our independence from Clatheron's rule on this day for every year to come." Cheers and applause again fill Capitol Hall.

King Zedorious waits for the cheers to die down before continuing. He bangs his royal staff against the base of his throne to regain everyone's attention.

"Let every unknown enemy know that we shall come

together, bear any burden, meet any hardship, support any friend and oppose any foe to assure the survival and the success of our freedom, loyalty and equality. Most importantly, let us not forget those who perished during this epic battle, those who gave their lives in the name of the kingdom."

"In the name of the kingdom!" shouts a member of the audience, echoing back King Zedorious' words.

"Yes. In the name of the kingdom, my friend!" repeats King Zedorious, laughing and smiling as everyone cheers and applauds. The king then lowers his webbed hands, signaling his subjects to bow their heads. The king bows his own head and joins his hands together in front of his waist.

"Now," King Zedorious says. "Let us fill the room with a moment of silence to pay our respects to those who gave their lives to uphold our way of life." Not a sound can be heard anywhere throughout the hall. All citizens remain motionless while they pay their respects. It sounds as if the hall is deserted.

"Thank you for your sacrifice," says the king, breaking the moment of silence and looking up at the heavens above. "We will remember you always." King Zedorious turns his attention toward his six guests. "Today is a proud day for all of us. We are here not only to remember the fallen; we are also here to celebrate our achievements and honor these special guests who stand before you. These six extraordinary beings deserve special recognition. If you'll please step forward, Lennox."

King Zedorious smiles as Lennox takes center stage. Samuel and his friends will be presented with the Medal of Aquatania as a symbol of their bravery and selflessness.

Receiving the Medal of Aquatania is considered the highest level of recognition that one can receive. Each medal is engraved with the Aquatanian Crest of Unity.

King Zedorious hands the medal to Queen Mizbeth to place around Lennox's neck. When she does place it gently around his neck, the queen lightly kisses him on the cheek. Lennox blushes. "Aw, gee," he responds, basking in the crowd's cheers.

Next up is Crawler, who is given a golden pot instead of the Medal of Aquatania because he lacks shoulders and a neck. The Aquatanian Crest of Unity is engraved on the pot, which is filled with the freshest topsoil gathered from the shores of Lake Aqueous in the world above. Crawler misses the fresh taste of a home-style meal and is overjoyed.

He opens the golden pot's cover and inhales the sweet aroma. "That's what I'm talking about!" he shouts. The hall fills with laughter. Crawler squirms back to his position in line as the crowd continues to cheer.

"Next, I'd like to call upon a very special guest, a new and welcome addition to our family, to whom we owe a tremendous amount of gratitude," King Zedorious says. "Without him, we would have never won this fight. As long as he wants, he will always be welcome among us, and among us he will be considered an equal. Squinch, please step forward."

Capitol Hall fills with thunderous applause as Squinch steps toward Queen Mizbeth. Squinch is overwhelmed by the king's words. His eyes swell with tears. He cannot believe that, after all these years of servitude, he has been accepted as an equal. He will no longer be considered a bottom-feeder or a worthless peon. No one will ever make fun of his shortcomings again. The queen drapes the Medal of Aquatania around his neck. The medal is so large and heavy in comparison to Squinch's height and weight that it hits the floor when the queen releases it from her webbed hands. Still, no one makes fun of Squinch. No one laughs. Instead, the audience cheers and applauds. Squinch returns to his place in line, taking a mental picture of his moment of fame so that he will remember forever what he considers the best day of his life.

"You all know Figlo," says King Zedorious, inviting Figlo to join him by his side. "What can I say about him? He has been loyal to our cause from the very beginning, especially when our days became troubled."

Figlo's heart floods with guilt. He interrupts the king. "That's not entirely true, my liege."

"Let me finish, Figlo. Now is not the time for that," Zedorious replies. "Every so often, we lose our way. The important thing to remember is how we find our way back, back to our home, our family and our friends. Figlo did just that, and for your faithful service, we would like to invite someone very special to present you with the Medal of Aquatania. Your sister, Alaina."

"You knew?" Figlo whispers to King Zedorious.

"A great king always remains one step ahead of everyone and everything around him," replies the king with a wink.

Figlo is at a loss for words. He never could have guessed that Zedorious would have somehow discovered the perfidious deal he made with Clatheron. No matter. The king understood Figlo's desperation and would have done the same for his daughter Izadora if he were in the same situation. The king forgives Figlo for his moment of weakness, entrusting him fully with his life as he did before.

Chapter Twenty-Two

King Zedorious hands Alaina the Medal of Aquatania. With tears of gratitude pouring from her eyes, Alaina places the medal around her brother's neck. Figlo gracefully accepts his award from his one and only sister.

"Thank you, brother. I am forever grateful for my freedom," says Alaina.

"You would have done the same for me, my dear sister." Figlo is overwhelmed with joy. He is grateful to have Alaina back in his life and looks forward to spending the rest of his days together as a family. He wraps his arms around her furry neck and squeezes her tightly. After many years apart, Filgo embraces his sister as if to make up for lost time. Alaina then rejoins the crowd, and Figlo returns to his spot in line next to Crawler.

"Our daughter," says the king as he shoots a smile toward the queen. "So intelligent, so determined, so...so stubborn like her father," he says. Everyone in the hall bursts into laughter.

When the laughter dies down, King Zedorious continues. "If it weren't for Izadora and her ability to put her people before her own needs, we would never have made it here today. I couldn't have asked for a braver, more giving, more loving daughter than the one I have. I'm so proud of you." Princess Izadora steps forward, and King Zedorious wraps his arms around her, squeezing tightly as if he never wants to let go.

"Izadora, please allow your mother the honor of presenting you the Medal of Aquatania, the highest of honors among our people," says King Zedorious as he steps aside.

"My sweet daughter," says Queen Mizbeth. "Oh how I wish I could have watched you grow from an infant into the strong woman that you've become. Luckily, your father was always by your side and did a great job of raising you on his own. But I am here now, Izadora. I am here to laugh with you, cry with you, support you in any way that I can." Queen Mizbeth pauses to hold back her tears. "Most important, I'm here to love you unconditionally."

"I've missed you so much, mother. You have no idea," says Izadora, so overwhelmed with emotion that she is not able to speak another word.

"I think I have a pretty good idea," replies the queen. She places her webbed hands on Izadora's face and tenderly kisses her forehead. King Zedorious hands the Medal of Aquatania to Queen Mizbeth, who places it around the princess' neck.

When the cheers and applause subside, King Zedorious asks Samuel to join him by his side. "And now for Samuel. We owe him our lives and will forever be in his debt." As Zedorious introduces Samuel, the crowd goes wild, screaming and chanting his name. Then, the crowd begins shouting a strange word in high-pitched voices.

"Coohaa! Coohaa!"

As the creatures in the crowd chant, they lift their webbed hands in the air, extend their thumbs and pinky fingers, and vigorously shake their hands from left to right. The ritual is called the Aquatanian Call of Appreciation, a traditional chant used to honor someone they deem extraordinary.

King Zedorious grabs Samuel's shoulders. "Samuel, I am so proud of the man you've become."

"Thank you, Your Majesty," replies Samuel.

"No, thank *you*," says King Zedorious.

"It wasn't that long ago that you came to me a timid, lost

boy without direction. You seemed unsure of yourself, lacking the confidence and motivation to take control of your life. But then, something inside you changed, and you embarked on a glorious transformation. You started believing in yourself. You started believing in the qualities that we all knew you had in you all along. You learned courage under fire. You learned the importance of being a brave leader. You learned to stand up to and outsmart your enemies, but most importantly, you learned what it means to be a man."

Samuel blushes.

"It is an honor and a privilege to present you personally with this small token of our appreciation, the Medal of Aquatania," says the king.

Samuel kneels down on one knee out of respect. Also, because he is taller than King Zedorious, Samuel wants to make it easier for the king to place the medal around his neck. The crowd cheers louder than before. Samuel waves at the audience, thanking them for their kind applause.

"In addition," continues King Zedorious, "this day will no longer be considered just another day. In honor of our newly gained independence, this day will now be known as Samuel Waters Day."

"Hey! Why does Samuel get an entire day named after him? It's not like he did this alone," Lennox blurts out.

"Hush!" shushes the princess, elbowing Lennox in his soft underbelly. He rubs his underside and remains silent. The crowd cheers and whistles. Many chant the Aquatanian Call of Appreciation, and others blow loudly on seashell horns and bang heavily on the drums.

"Why don't you say something on your behalf?" asks Queen Mizbeth.

"Oh, that's not really necessary," a bashful Samuel replies.

"You would deny the queen her request?" asks King Zedorious in a serious tone, leaving Samuel no choice but to deliver a speech.

"Okay...okay." Samuel turns to the crowd and begins to deliver a heartfelt speech. Not long before, Samuel would have been too shy to talk in front of an audience this large, but now he is full of courage. "My friends, I am very proud to be standing here as a guest in your home. It is a tremendous honor to have led the valiant warriors of Aquatania into battle, which we won together as a family."

"Coohaa! Coohaa!" shouts the audience members in unison with their thumbs and pinky fingers extended and their webbed hands shaking from left to right.

Samuel continues. "I would like to thank King Zedorious and all those who believed in me throughout this amazing adventure, this incredible journey of self-discovery. However, none of this would be possible without your help and without the sheer selflessness of the heroes standing next to me."

"Darn right," whispers Lennox. Once again, Izadora elbows Lennox in the underbelly.

"Thanks to all of you and these five heroes, I've learned so much about myself and about your wonderful species," Samuel says. "The lessons that I learned will stay with me for the rest of my life. I only wish I could share my stories with others to help them reach their full potential. None of you know my kind, but my people aren't used to worlds such as yours and would never believe the adventures that I encountered here or the challenges that I overcame. They couldn't possibly understand the reasons that I chose to help you in your crusade to lift the curse of Clatheron from these waters. Thanks to everyone here, I am a changed man. You have opened my eyes, and for as long as I can breathe, I will never close them again. I thank you all once more."

Samuel activates the Sword of Luminescence one last time before returning it to King Zedorious. He holds its shining light as high as his arm reaches and shouts, "Long live Aquatania!"

The crowd chimes in, all chanting his name in unison. "Samuel! Samuel! Samuel! Samuel!"

King Zedorious reaches inside a bag next to his throne and pulls out handfuls of sparkling kelp. He tosses the kelp high in the water as everyone watches the sword's light reflect off the vegetation, which sparkles as its floats through the water. Royal guards from around the room do the same, spreading glittery specks of kelp throughout Capitol Hall. Music plays again, and everyone dances as piles of food enter the hall for all to partake.

Lennox is the first to partake.

While everyone feasts and dances, Samuel pulls the princess aside to get away from the celebration. They duck into what used to be Clatheron's private quarters. Samuel asks her to sit in Clatheron's former throne.

"What's this all about?" she asks. "You're making me nervous."

Samuel struggles to make the words come out of his mouth. He wants to share his feelings and tell her how much he likes her. He wants her to know that without her, he would not be the man he is today. Still, the words do not come out.

"Izadora, you know how...er...okay, so there is you, and there is me...um...no, that's not it. So there comes a time when, you know," he continues, blurting out nothing but gibberish.

Princess Izadora grows tired of waiting for him to speak coherently. She grabs Samuel by the face and quickly pulls him in for a loving kiss. He falls silent as his lips touch her soft black ones. Mesmerized by her touch, he pulls her in closer, caressing her back and running his fingers through her soft black hair. Her tail wraps around his waist and gently entwines them both for what seems like an eternity.

"You were saying," she says, pulling away from his lips while continuing to enjoy his embrace.

"You know, I like you. I mean REALLY like you."

"I like you too, Samuel," she laughs. "I mean REALLY like you too." She giggles but sees that Samuel is not laughing with her. "Oh, I see," she says, lowering her head in sadness. "Is this about you leaving to return to the surface?" she asks, knowing he probably will go but hoping he will stay.

"So you know why I pulled you aside?" Samuel asks. If it were up to him, he would remain in the moment and avoid reality for the rest of his days.

"Of course I know why. I was hoping you wouldn't go, but I know that you had a life before this, one you will have to reclaim eventually," Izadora says.

Izadora tries to be supportive but struggles to hide her emotions. If only there were some way he could be in two places at once. She sees herself becoming queen and Samuel becoming king, having a life together.

"I do have a life above the water's surface, but more importantly, I have Grandpa. *He* is my life," says Samuel. "You would like him if you had the chance to meet him. He's just like your father. Imagine how Grandpa must be feeling in my absence. Besides, I still have a whole lot of growing up to do... topside."

Samuel puts his arm around Izadora. She rests her head on his shoulder, trying to hold back her tears, but resistance is futile. The last thing she wants to do is make this any harder than it has to be, but there is nothing easy about saying goodbye.

"Maybe, one day, I'll return," he says, pushing back a strand of hair from her face.

"Yeah...maybe one day," she replies in a hopeful tone followed by a lengthy sigh.

Though he is not sure whether it will be possible to return to the surface world, Samuel will never forget the princess. She will always have a place near and dear to his heart. Samuel will never forget his underwater adventures or the friends he made along the way.

Although he will feel a great loss when he returns to the world above, every time he gazes down upon the lake, he will gain peace of mind from knowing what he has done for the kingdom. Warmth will fill his heart in knowing that Izadora is safe and somewhere nearby staring back at him from below his wavy reflection.

"If you don't mind, maybe we can just sit here for a little while longer," he suggests.

"That sounds nice," she replies.

They sit in silence for some time, wrapped in each other's arms, enjoying the euphoric sounds emanating from Capitol Hall. Samuel and Izadora are together in the moment, savoring their time with each other to the very last second. This is their time alone to hold one another and to say their final goodbyes.

Depart a Boy, Return a Man

Samuel and Lennox swim toward Pearl Cave's entrance to find the glowing blue pearl. Samuel hopes the blue pearl will be as magical as the red one and transform him back into a human boy, but he is sad that he has to leave the princess behind. His sadness grows the farther he gets from the kingdom, and he begins to question whether returning home is the right thing to do. It is possible that one day they will get a chance to reunite, but life is unpredictable. Nothing is ever certain.

Lennox, on the other hand, is more than happy to return to a sedentary life of eating, sleeping and eating some more. He cannot wait for Samuel to feed him now that he knows his dietary preferences. As far as Lennox is concerned, he is about to go from poverty to riches, riding a meatloaf shaped like a surf board all the way to the penthouse suite.

They approach the cave's underwater entrance, and Samuel's doubts about leaving the princess fade like the wake that ebbs behind a passing boat. He now realizes that leaving is the right thing to do. King Zedorious, Queen Mizbeth, Figlo, Alaina, Izadora, Crawler, Squinch and all of the Aquatanians gave Lennox and Samuel an amazing send-off.

What more could Samuel ask for?

Samuel thinks back to when he and Izadora broke the news to the rest of his friends that he would be leaving. No one gave Samuel a hard time. Everyone knew that the choice was difficult and that making him feel guilty would not make it any easier. When Samuel found himself choking up, King Zedorious helped out by explaining to everyone that it was time for Samuel and Lennox to return home.

"Grandpa is probably worried sick. I have to go home," says Samuel to Lennox, trying to justify his decision. "There's a life waiting for me above this fantastic world. I'll miss everyone, especially Izadora, but it's time. It's time to live my life, a better life, the best life I can possibly live, on the surface."

"I couldn't agree more. Besides, Samuel, if I never eat another piece of kelp for the rest of my reptilian life, it'll be too soon," says Lennox, burping as he rubs his upset stomach.

Samuel speeds up, passing the Wall of Prophecies and reaching the battlefield. Samuel stops for a second to remember the comrades who perished during the Battle of Pearl Cave. He takes a moment to reflect upon what took place and all that he accomplished. From the impossible journey, to saving the princess and his friends, to gallantly leading his new family to victory, it all happened because Samuel learned to believe in himself. Because Samuel learned to be brave.

"Are you okay?" asks Lennox, wondering why he stopped.

"Yeah...I'm perfect. Couldn't be better," smiles Samuel as he nostalgically looks around.

"Then let's go home," replies Lennox, placing his hand on Samuel's shoulder.

"You're right. Let's go home, my friend," says Samuel, slowly nodding in agreement.

They approach the bottom of the rocky wall where Samuel was transformed into a being that could breathe underwater. Atop of the wall and above the water's surface, the magical glowing blue pearl is still resting undisturbed in its sparkling shell on a large bed of rocks. It is still illuminated by the light that shines through the very same crack in the ceiling that led Samuel to discover the pearl in the first place.

Samuel helps Lennox climb out of the water and onto the bed of rocks. "Push harder," shouts Lennox as Samuel struggles to push his friend's body and shell up the wall and onto the rocks. It seems that maybe Lennox overindulged during the grand celebration and put on a few unwanted pounds.

Samuel then climbs onto the rocks and stares directly at the glowing blue pearl. "Well, I guess this is it," he says, knowing that this will probably be the last time he will hear Lennox's voice.

"It's not like we're parting ways forever," responds Lennox.

"Yeah...I know. It's just...well, it'll be different from here on out. Nothing will ever be the same after all of this."

"Change is not a bad thing, Samuel. No matter what I've said in the past, this was all worth it." Lennox pats Samuel on the back a few times. Together they look at the magical glowing blue pearl. "It's time to go home," says Lennox, pushing Samuel with a tiny nudge toward the blue pearl.

"Home...," Samuel repeats, realizing how necessary it is to return to Grandpa and share his stories over a hot meal. If there is one person who will believe him, it is Grandpa.

"Don't forget," orders Lennox.

"Forget what?" asks Samuel.

"Don't forget to feed me steak, lots of steak," replies Lennox, his stomach growling loudly. He rubs his belly, eager to refill it the minute they arrive home with something other than pellets or kelp.

"You're relentless." Samuel smiles and places his arms around his best friend's neck one last time. He squeezes Lennox tightly, not wanting to let go, as if this is the end. Eventually, he releases him from his grasp. Lennox steps out of the way as Samuel approaches the magical glowing blue pearl. Samuel braces himself, reaching out and grabbing the gem with both hands. It is not much of a surprise to him when nothing happens right away.

He puts the glowing pearl back in its home when all of a sudden, a strong wind develops around him.

"Here we go again, Lennox!" Samuel shouts, trying to be heard over the powerful whirlwind. Lennox takes a few steps back so he does not get knocked down like before.

The magical glowing blue pearl begins to emit sparks, and the burst of wind grows stronger, forcing Samuel to drop to his knees. Turning into a tornado, the wind scoops Samuel off the ground and into the air. He spins around and around, his limbs flying in all directions as he spins. He starts to grow back to normal size. First his head, then his legs, then his feet, then his arms and finally his hands return to their normal dimensions. His flashlight, backpack, Medal of Aquatania, and even the clothes on his back grow along with his body. The only items missing are his sneakers.

The cyclone suddenly ceases, and his transformation is complete. Samuel sheds all of his underwater features, including his webbed feet and gills. He will surely miss his powers, but he knows that real power — the power of courage and to overcome any obstacle — comes from within.

Samuel opens his eyes. The first thing he sees is a small green object. It is Lennox, but not the same one he met underwater and could converse with. This Lennox is nothing more than a mute pet turtle that cannot spout wise-guy remarks. Still, Samuel feels he can talk to him whenever he needs and that Lennox will listen intently and understand his words.

Samuel gently picks Lennox up from the bed of rocks and places him in the front pocket of his blue hooded sweatshirt. He looks again at the water below and thinks he can see a pool of tiny creatures waving goodbye. Samuel waves back, just in case Izadora and his Aquatanian family have come to say goodbye one last time. A tear forms in the corner of his right eye.

It is comforting to know that thanks to his efforts, no more monsters threaten the kingdom. Samuel is safe now, and so are all the kind-hearted creatures that he is leaving behind.

Samuel finds Grandpa's rowboat just as he left it, securely fastened floating undisturbed on the water. Samuel unties the boat from a nearby rock. He tosses in his backpack and hops in, causing it to rock heavily back and forth. Samuel grabs the oars and stretches his arms out wide to regain his balance. When the rocking subsides, he sits down next to his backpack and settles in comfortably. He casts off and heads toward the entrance of Pearl Cave.

"Hello...hello...hello...anybody out there...there...there?"
Samuel's voice echoes back, but no one answers his call.

Chapter Twenty-Three

He lets out a giggle. What was once scary and unknown is now quite the opposite. Samuel no longer fears the unknown.

"VROOOOOMMM…," he says loudly as he begins to paddle swiftly through the entrance and across the lake, wildly splashing the oars against the water. He heads toward the horizon, eager to reach the lake house before dark. When Samuel arrives at the dock, he wonders if the Oracle is below, pleased with his efforts, happy that she, too, no longer has to live in hiding.

He recalls his grandfather's instructions for securing the boat to the dock and makes sure to leave everything as it was before he took the boat without Grandpa's knowledge. He is careful and meticulous in every move. He keeps one hand latched tightly to the side of the boat to keep it from floating away while making a figure-eight knot to tie the boat to the dock.

Samuel stops at the bottom of the hill and looks up at the house. As he draws in a deep breath, he fixes his eyes on the windows, searching for signs of Grandpa. Seeing it for the first time in what feels like months reminds Samuel of how much he loves his home and Grandpa. He races toward the front door, kicking it open with excitement.

"Grandpa!" he shouts, waiting patiently in the foyer for his grandfather's response.

Grandpa runs out from the kitchen, wearing the apron that says, "If you don't like my cooking, call 1-800-M-A-K-E-I-T-Y-O-U-R-S-E-L-F." To Samuel's surprise, he does not yell at him. Instead, he bends down on one knee and wraps his arms tightly around Samuel.

"Oh, thank God you're safe. I thought something might

have happened to you. When I woke up this morning, you were nowhere to be found." Even though the mystical world beneath the water had seen several sunsets and night skies, not even a day had passed in the surface world, yet Grandpa still showed signs of concern.

"Grandpa, I can't breathe," Samuel says, releasing a burst of air as he frees himself from the bear hug.

"You're not off the hook yet, young man. We're going to talk about this at some point."

Samuel is glad that Grandpa barely scolded him. He is not all that mad from what he can tell. The truth is, Grandpa is not angry at all because he has a good idea where Samuel has been all this time. Much like King Zedorious, Grandpa remains one step ahead of everyone and everything. He knows far too much about the mystical underwater world and the Kingdom of Aquatania from which Samuel just returned, maybe even more than he cares to remember from his own past experiences. Still, he worries about Samuel and is pleased by his safe return.

"Whatever you say, Grandpa. I'll tell you everything you want to know. I promise. But if it's alright with you, maybe we can finish this conversation some other time," Samuel says as he yawns. He is utterly exhausted. Grandpa can tell from the run-down look on Samuel's face that he went through one heck of an adventure, one that might have been crazier than his own.

"Of course we can. You're tired. Why don't we skip dinner, roast some marshmallows and put you to bed. We can talk about your adventure in the morning," Grandpa says, placing his arms around Samuel to give him another hug.

"Sounds good, Grandpa," Samuel replies, yawning again. "But let me sit down for a few minutes to relax."

Samuel lies motionless on the couch, paying little attention to the adventure book that he loosely holds in his hands. Reading a book is not quite the same after living a real-life adventure. His eyes are glassy as his mind drifts elsewhere, reminiscing about all the fun he had and about all of the new friends he made.

Lennox is perched on the table next to the couch, swimming in a bowl full of ground beef that Samuel asked Grandpa to prepare. Though Samuel cannot hear his voice, he knows that Lennox is content as he watches his pet turtle devour the bowl's contents. Lennox lets Samuel know he is happy by looking up at him every few bites with grateful eyes.

Grandpa sits back in his chair, smiling and watching Samuel daydream. He takes a deep breath through his wrinkled lips and exhales through his nose, happy that his one-and-only grandson returned safely.

Grandpa notices that Samuel seems different, as if something changed inside of him. He no longer sees his sweet helpless grandson, but a strong, confident individual. He shakes his head and sits back cozily in his chair, pushing his oversized black-rimmed glasses from the tip of his nose toward his eyes. He turns his attention to the newspaper that he has not yet read.

Samuel lifts his head from the couch and gazes at the lake through the living room window. He sits up and begins to wonder what Izadora is up to at that very moment. He dreams about the princess even when he and Grandpa roast marshmallows in the fireplace. Samuel so enjoys roasting them to a crisp and would have loved to share some with Izadora. Afterward, Grandpa helps Samuel upstairs, makes sure he brushes his teeth and gets into bed.

Grandpa tucks Samuel comfortably in bed, wrapping him snugly in a blanket as if he were a crepe.

Samuel swiftly untucks himself from underneath the blanket. "Grandpa!" he whines. "You don't have to tuck me in anymore. Can't you see? I'm too old for that now."

Grandpa releases a subtle laugh. "That you are, Samuel. That you are." He leans in to kiss Samuel goodnight on the forehead, but Samuel pushes him away as if he is too old for goodnight kisses.

Grandpa begins to leave the bedroom, but before he reaches the door, Samuel calls out his name.

"Grandpa?" asks Samuel before nodding off.

"Yes, Samuel?"

"There's been something I've been meaning to ask you."

"What's that?" Grandpa asks from the doorway.

"You knew where I was all this time? Right?" Samuel asks as he lets out another yawn.

"Let's just say I was always one step ahead of you," Grandpa replies with a wink.

"So it's true. If you were always one step ahead, then you must know King Zedorious?" asks Samuel. He can barely keep his eyes open at this point. It feels like bricks are weighing down his eyelids, growing heavier with every passing second.

"Why do you ask that?" Grandpa laughs, trying to avoid the question.

Samuel can tell that he is not going to get any information out of Grandpa, at least not tonight.

"Right. Well. He sends his regards," Samuel says, fighting unsuccessfully to stay awake.

"I'm sure he does," replies Grandpa as he turns the bedroom lights off. When he removes his wrinkly hands from the lightswitch, Samuel's eyes are closed shut.

"So you admit it. You do know him?" asks Samuel, barely able to complete the sentence.

The last thing he hears before he drifts off into a deep slumber is: "Samuel, my boy, that's a story for another time."

And just like that, Samuel Waters — now a hero — falls fast asleep.

About the Author

David Akseizer grew up in Mamaroneck, New York. There, he graduated Rye Neck High School in 1997. His favorite subject was English, taught by a man who helped him realize the importance of trusting his imagination and allowing his creativity to run wild.

After minoring in literature and majoring in interdisciplinary studies at American University, David worked in the creative field designing brochure layouts, web pages and catalogues for a small auction house in New York City. He later pursued a medical career, dedicating many years as a licensed radiation technologist before receiving a master's in Health Policy and Management from Columbia University. While proud of the hard work and assistance that he has provided for others, David's true passion is writing. By drawing from varied life experiences, he hopes to create entertaining novels with powerful messages that will inspire both children and adults.

David is surrounded by an incredible support team including his wife, family and wonderful friends. In addition to *The Legend of Pearl Cave*, David is determined to write several novels over the next few years.

www.ingramcontent.com/pod-product-compliance
Lightning Source LLC
Chambersburg PA
CBHW051248210726

48287CB00002B/393